The Body's Perfect

A Novel in Stories

by

Christopher Riebli

Illustrated by
Michael L. Loffredo

ISBN: 978-1477655795

Editors: Linda Hauser and Nathan Riebli

Book Design: Wordrunner Press
Petaluma, California

For Mom and Dad

"Everything is held together with stories. That is all that is holding us together, stories and compassion."

— *Barry Lopez*

Acknowledgments

Special thanks to Patrick Fanning, Daniel Coshnear, the Occidental Center for the Arts Writing Group, Mark Fuhri and Michael Loffredo for their invaluable assistance in getting this book to publication, and to Jo-Anne Rosen for all her help, input and creativity in seeing this project through. Also a shout-out to my son, Nate Riebli, who told me last year, "you need to finish those stories." To the various folks I shared story drafts with and who offered their feedback. And, of course, to family members, whose advice, influences and role modeling made writing these stories necessary.

Contents

First, a disclaimer. These stories are fictional. Yes, some of you may recognize actual names, places, events, so it's certainly an easy assumption to say they're autobiographical, even historical, based closely on my own family, relatives, friends, and the unfriendly. Well, they are and they aren't. It's never an easy task separating a writer's own experiences from those that are invented, and these stories are no exception. So, if you think you see yourself in any of the following narratives, you're both right and wrong. They aren't strictly history, nor psychological analysis, sociology, any of that. They aren't meant to canonize, or to hang anyone from a scaffold. They're simply twelve stories I made up. So, please, no lawsuits, no nasty letters. Let's remain friends.

Introduction

Some of these stories were started thirty years ago. Thirty years. It seems like a long time to finish twelve stories, doesn't it? Well, it is. In my defense, though, I wasn't visiting them much, and for long stretches of time, not visiting them at all. I was finding other, easier, sometimes more pressing things to do: mostly truck driving and teaching, helping to raise a son, handy work—"trying to make a livin' and doin' the best I can" as the Allman Brothers used to sing. When the story writing happened, it happened in small bursts—three, four weeks at a time, two, three hours a day—and then as quickly as it began, it ended. Several reasons can be proffered: the characters and myself grew tired of each other; I'd run out of time, and places to take the story; I'd questioned my own voice, and often convinced myself I had nothing much to say, and, if I did, was clueless how to say it. When there wasn't a good reason to be writing, I'd make one up. I got good at these excuses. The next thing you know, thirty years slip by, and there's still a roomful of people clamoring to be heard.

In my more desperate moments, I'd call on the Muse—an SOS, person-to-person, would somebody please pick up? But no answer. Off with some other guy, someone with more promise, more commitment, someone writing about the Congo, the mid-east, a European capital, where the intrigue was real, the narrative long and involved, more layered than a wedding cake. Not this "local color" stuff with some rube wandering around a hay field wondering how his dream had made a U-turn, and left him high and dry. This kind of material didn't seem to interest her. She rarely returned my calls, and when she did, she was always in the middle of something, and couldn't talk long. Her message was always the same: stay with it, and don't be discouraged. If it's meant to happen, it'll happen, but it won't happen by itself. I interpreted that as meaning: "Partner, you're on your own. Don't hold your breath waiting for that burning bush. Go out and light it yourself."

So, once again, expectation was dashed, the hope that some kind of divine inspiration would occur, some transcendent moment when a lightning bolt splits my skull and the story characters walk across each page, telling their stories as they go, my own involvement minimized. When you've given up on that kind of hope, you're left feeling desolate, left with the naked realization that it's you and you alone that will get this job done. Nothing too earthshaking here. It happens to all of us. The challenge, though, was how, out of this desolation, to muster the will, to find the routine to get things underway again. I'd waited long enough, exhausted all excuses.

Start with a simple declarative sentence, I read somewhere. Establish a routine. Impose a daily quota—a certain number of words or a certain amount of time you sit there and work on nothing but the writing at hand. Save the memoir, the letter to your congressman, the reasons why the bank shouldn't foreclose on your home, for another time. I had a certain advantage, too: some of the stories had already been started, and I was on a first-name basis with several of their characters. We were still talking to each other. They hadn't abandoned me for non-support. They hadn't forgotten who I was. Not yet, at least.

Mostly these thirty years speaks to the patience of my characters. Anyone else would have left me long ago, given up on that big ship pulling into their harbor, but not these folks. They hung in there. They killed time. Like soldiers awaiting their marching orders, they stood by, milking cows, listening to Sinatra, stealing a peep from the gypsy girl, drinking at the Parkside, picking up scrap metal, feeling a heart disintegrate, going off to war, and then returning and finding a piece of their soul in the soft loam of a summer garden. They wrestled and fought, drank and withdrew, and with a stubborn kind of resilience kept returning, waiting for me to get off the *schnide*. What else could they do? They remained ageless, locked into their tiny worlds, waiting for me to spring them, to cut them loose. If I didn't, they died, or, more accurately, they faded away, and disappeared. A door slams somewhere far-off, and the house these characters once inhabited is empty, or torn down, or never existed. And their voices? Just echoes of something you thought you heard. And how they looked? Now just long shadows cast from a tired sun.

Finally, last year, with more time on my hands than ever before, I'd run out of excuses not to finish the stories. These guys had waited long enough. And, I was tired of their carping, their complaining, the "you-never-let-us-do-anything" tact. Okay, fine. You want some action? You're going to get it. I sat down most mornings, working through the narratives I'd already started, but finding them lacking. Revision followed, the essence of all writing. The stories started reshaping themselves, and their characters shook off those long, lethargic years, and found renewed voices. Even during the lay-offs, they were always whispering something into my ears.

So, where did all these characters come from? Initially, they were drawn from people I'd known, family members, of course, and relatives, and friends, and the dozens and dozens of folks that crossed my path as I was growing up. But then the writer intruded—someone who wanted to put the house in order—and he crawled inside their heads, and ascribed motives to them that may have been quite different from any of their actual ones. Sometimes, for the sake of a good story, for the dramatics of a situation, we have to do this sort of thing. When you write fiction, you're allowed certain acts. Your characters might do things their original would have never considered. But you can't get too wild with them. They still have to obey certain laws, meet certain expectations that the story and characters dictate. When they don't, the red flags go up, and you've got a passel of unhappy readers.

Some of these characters grew out of the tales I'd heard as a young boy at Moach Luchessi's barber shop on Washington Street. My dad would take my brothers and me there on Saturday mornings whether we needed a haircut or not. It's where he and his cronies gathered, a place for a bit of comic-relief from their daily toils. It didn't hurt, either, that Moach's barber shop featured a convenient back-door that opened into Ghilardi's Tavern. Dad and his buddies—Frenchy, Ham, Johnny M., Lester Miller, Mickey Palucchi—to name a few—could shuttle back and forth between tavern and barbershop, down a quick draft, share gossip, swap both tall and short tales, and never be seen entering the tavern's front door. They were all natural storytellers and they'd take turns, each trying to out-do the other, each working his tiny audience for maximum effect. It was lively, raucous, and vital. For the hour, two hours we spent there, Dad could forget about the chattel mortgage, feed bills, sick cows, and be in his element.

And when I wasn't listening to their stories, I was reading comic books, stuffing my imagination with Marvel heroes and the Illustrated Classics, or running down to Elliott's Fountain with my brothers and ordering Green Rivers. When I did need a haircut, I sat in Moach's barber chair, a large mirror in front of me, and a large mirror behind me, staring at my image that receded further and further into the mirrors, each image smaller than the one before it, wondering if that image ever ended, wondering if it continued on and on, right up Washington Street, out Bodega, growing tinier than a grain of sand by the time it reached the coast.

Why write these stories? That's a good question, and my immediate response is that it was a way of capturing the remnants of a world disappearing quickly. In a way these stories are a eulogy to people long gone, to a life style and way of living whose underpinnings were already quaking while I was still a young boy. Years would elapse before its true impact hit home. Things are always changing, whether we like it or not, and I've struggled with these changes my entire life, saddened to see the small farms disappear, and with them that unique industry of the small man and the small woman, saddened at the inevitable growth, the loss of intimacy and vitality that I remember from my youth. There was another reason for writing them, as well. If I didn't write them, who would? Who else shared my unique perspective, saw things as I saw them? No one, perhaps not even my own fellow family members. It was my job, take it or leave it.

Moach's barbershop and the tavern are long gone. In their place a parking lot which doesn't seem nearly as lively, or raucous. You can walk around town and many of its buildings are the same as when my dad used to put a boot up on Moach's barber's chair, and talk about the "floosie" he brought to his aunt's anniversary, or the time he and Bib Ramaciotti turned two dozen rabbits loose in downtown. The buildings are the same, but they're just shells to earlier lives. You walk around and still hear those voices from the past. You think you see Fred Hopkins in his stained smock, glasses slid down to the end of his nose, repairing your dad's boots. You cross the bridge and head east out Washington Street, remembering the cool shade of Golden Eagle Milling that lasted a long block, maybe longer, before the lines of box cars and flat cars coupled-up alongside the train depot appeared. You pass the Tivoli and hear the dice cups slammed against the bar-top, smell the cooking noodles at the chop suey shack. At National Ice, a bit further, you find that same shade you'd lost a block earlier, and follow it up the railroad tracks to Hunt and Behrens. Beyond the creek, you stop at Pisenti Motors, and if it's Fall, you walk in and study the new Lincolns.

So, what's left? Is it just nostalgia? A longing for a past we often romanticize? A past that when scrutinized, was filled with as many disappointments as any present? What's left is story. Memory distilled. A bitter-sweet concoction. You lift your glass, take a long pull. Minutes, a lifetime later, you stare into the mirror, and there you are, one image folded inside the other, slipping on into infinity. You think if you keep looking, you're going to find that young girl, that young boy you once were. You're lost in thought. You order another round. Then someone comes up, slaps you on the back, and says, "Holy shit, it's been a long time. I didn't know you were still around."

You smile back. "Oh, yeah, I'm still around."

"Where you been?"

"Everywhere and no place—ain't ever left."

"What do you know?"

"Everything and nothing at all. But pull up a chair and I'll tell you about it."

May, 2012

The Body's Perfect

Big Shot

On a July morning in 1953, my dad and I rode out Washington Street past Golden Eagle Milling and Studdard's Meat Market, past the chop-suey shack, the Yosemite Hotel, the house on the corner where the Williams twins lived, out past the new houses being built east of State Route 101. I stared out the window at hay fields and Justman's Airstrip passing by, while he hummed *Your Cheatin' Heart,* toyed with the brim of his pork-pie hat, fidgeted with the radio knobs.

"Where we going, Dad?"

"You'll see."

"It's a secret?"

"Yeah, it's a secret."

"I do something wrong?"

He smiled. "No, you didn't do nothin' wrong."

We turned south on Adobe Road and two miles later pulled into the Good View Dairy. The dairy was vacant. Chest-high weeds grew everywhere—in the yard surrounding the white house, between the cracks in the cement corrals, along all the barns and outbuildings. We entered the house, our footsteps echoing in its emptiness. We walked from room to room. Dad ran his fingers along the wainscoting, turned the faucets on in the kitchen and bathroom, peered out the curved front window of the living room west toward town, toward open hay fields. The whole time he said nothing. We walked across the yard and into the coolness of the con-crete milking barn, its windows crusted with spider webs. He worked the stanchion levers, pulled open the thick door of the walk-in cooler. We wandered into the hay barn whose redwood siding had weathered to gray except on its north side where a patina of mold-green lichens spread across a thin layer of red paint. At the roof ridge of the hay barn was a sheet metal weather vane of a galloping horse riddled with bullet holes. It turned noisily in a faint breeze. Out past a grove of eucalyptus trees we climbed to the top of a hill that looked over the farm and west toward Petaluma. We both sat down. My dad pulled a blade of grass from near his boot and poked it into his mouth. He stared out across the hay fields, thought a while and then looked at me.

"Well, what do you think?" he asked.

"About what?" I said.

"About all of this?" He swept his arm in front of him. "About runnin' this dairy with me?"

"I don't know."

"You want to live in town all your life? End up workin' behind a desk?"

"I like living in town. It's where my friends are."

"And what are they doin'? Throwin' newspapers? Pullin' weeds? Deliverin' groceries for *Volpi's*?"

"Some of them, yeah."

"This'd be different. You and me, we'd be partners, building a business together. It's what you wanted, wasn't it? No one bossin' us around. Tellin' us, 'do this, do that.'"

"But there aren't even any cows here. There's nothing here."

"Oh, I can take care of that—it's all planned out."

We sat there on that hilltop while I tried to digest my dad's proposal. Partners. A business together.

"It'll be a lot of work, but this could be a gold mine," he said.

It all sounded good.

"And one other thing," he said. "No quittin.' If it gets tough, we gut it out. We stick to it, understand?"

A month later he left his job at Western Dairy, withdrew from the Teamsters, sold our house on Sixth Street, and bought sixty-five head of dairy cattle from his sister's brother-in-law, Vic Santoni. I quit the jobs I held in town—tossing the *Argus-Courier*, working as errand-boy at Volpi's—and told my friends we were heading east, toward real money, toward opportunity, toward being our own bosses, toward a gold mine. I was confident, eager to strike out for the country and start our new life. I believed in my dad, and I believed in his promises. I was twelve years old.

On a handshake and three hundred dollars in my Wells-Fargo savings account, my dad made me a partner. He signed a lease for the Good View Dairy and by summer's end we were in business with a 16 can contract at the co-operative creamery. We bought a 1953 Chevrolet flat-bed on time and two used tractors—a John Deere and a D-2 Caterpillar. We filled the hay barn with fifty ton of alfalfa. It felt good. I felt important, grown-up. Like my dad, like everyone, I wanted to be a somebody, to be recognized—a businessman, a success. I wanted to make money, and buy a jeep, and eventually a new Chevrolet from Price Motors, and then more cows, and one day own a ranch of our own with a sign that read Irv Miller and Sons Dairy Farms. I wanted to eat at the Green Mill Inn on Saturday nights where everyone knew our name, buy a new sweater at Mattei's. When I talked, I wanted people to lean in and listen. I wanted to buy rounds of drinks for my friends at The Little Hill and tell funny stories.

My dad got one thing right—dairy farming was a lot of work. He milked twice a day, rising at 3 AM every morning, working until noon, eating lunch, napping for an hour, before starting the afternoon milking. By 7 PM, he kicked his rubber boots off at the back porch steps, washed his hands in the laundry sink, and sat down at the dinner table, his body drained, his eyes hooded with fatigue. I did all the outside work—fed cows, the young stock, slopped our hogs, scraped manure from the corrals and wheel-barrowed it off to a pile just south of the hay barn, washed down the Grade A barn after each milking. My two younger brothers helped with clean-up. If there were any kinds of repairs—fences that needed mending, faulty wiring, busted plumbing—I worked alongside my dad, learning everything there was about keeping a dairy farm running. If a cow was calving, I'd stay with it. If it was sick with milk fever or mastitis, I'd inoculate it. If a tractor needed servicing, I crawled under it, working right alongside him. A layer of callus spread across both my hands hard as a cow's horn, and I often fell asleep during morning classes. For all my work, I pocketed forty dollars a month, with the promise of more once we found our feet.

But we never found them. We tried. We hoped 'next month' would be better, but it wasn't. The milk market was flat, our contract too small, and half the herd limped around, riddled with mastitis and old age. Still, we were out in the country, away from town. Our health was good. We were our own bosses.

"It'll turn around," Dad said. "It's the law of averages. You just can't keep losin'."

Dad tried to put a good face on things. I did, too. I told friends, classmates, I didn't miss town life—that I was a country boy now, a business partner, cutting my teeth, no time for sports. Nothing but work, and, yes, dairying was going through a rough spell, but we'd gut it out, see it through. We had to be patient. We had to keep our faith in the religion of effort. I repeated everything my father told me—used his phrases—"the good Lord this, the good Lord that," even borrowed his mannerisms—the way he'd look off as though waiting for an answer to inch its way over the horizon. Or how he'd run the back of his hand across his mouth, clearing the way for another great burst of hope. I'd become more and more like him. Words came out of me I could hardly believe, but I couldn't stop myself. I said things that ran counter to what I saw and felt everyday, and I didn't know why. I couldn't tell if it was just a stubborn faith or complete denial, some way of shoring up how I wanted to appear to others. I said things that made us look good, that shifted any blame to someone or something else. It was shameful how I went on. I promised myself that I'd change someday soon, that when I opened my mouth you'd only hear the truth.

Things soured between my folks, too. Month by month something vital between them drained away. You could feel the tension, at times arcing like two frayed wires. Around company, guests, they put on good faces, were polite to each other, but it masked what lurked below the forced smiles. They rarely agreed on anything. If Mom wanted to buy a household item, maybe even school clothes for my brothers, Dad objected. "But if it was for your goddamn cows, you'd buy it," she countered. Back and forth, back and forth it went. If Dad said something, Mom disputed it. Sometimes shouting matches broke out. But mostly it was a subtle kind of tension—the way she set his dinner plate down hard in front of him, glared, then looked away. And how he avoided that glare, grumbled under his breath, his patience exhausted. They were two sword fighters, jousting constantly. When they talked, it was rarely beyond business. You never saw them touch one another. Their most violent arguments they saved for the early morning when they thought my brothers and I were asleep. You could hear their voices through the closed doors, most of the words muffled, a cupboard door slammed. I'd wake up, walk out into the kitchen, and there on the table, spread out in rows like a game of Solitaire, were the unpaid bills.

Then my dad stopped paying me.

"What do you mean, 'you haven't got it?" I asked him.

"Just what I said."

"But this is a business, and everyone gets paid."

"That's right."

"Well?"

"Except there's nothing left to pay you with."

"Why not?"

"Arithmetic, son. Not enough money comin' in."

"This is bullshit," I said.

"I'm sorry, Junior."

"And my three hundred dollars? Where's that?"

My dad laughed. "Christ, that's long gone."

"I want it back."

"There's lots of things I want back," he said. "Besides, the three hundred was an investment. Investments got risks."

"You lied to me."

"I did not."

"You said this was a 'gold mine' out here."

"It still might be," he said. "We gotta ride it out, Junior. Remember what I said about being a quitter. You gotta have faith."

Quitter. The word stung me. And *faith?* There was plenty of doubt.

"When things change, we'll square up. You'll see how that three hundred'll work for you."

But nothing changed. There was no "squaring up." It only got worse. Vic Santoni dogged my father about past-due payments, sometimes following him around the ranch, waving a sheet of paper, threatening to foreclose on the note. I was fixing fence one day in the dry-stock pasture when Vic's youngest son, Marvin, stopped his pickup, and walked over to where I was working. Marvin was sixteen, and a brawler.

"Your old man's got a lotta balls," he said.

"About what?"

"Don't play fuckin'stupid on me."

"I'm not playing anything."

"Your old man's a bum. And a thief."

"He hasn't stolen anything."

"What he's doin' is just like stealin'"

"Is not."

"What do you fuckin' know anyway?" Marvin moved closer, staring right into my eyes. "You don't know shit. Nothing. Even less than your old man."

"He works hard and he's not a thief."

"Well, he ain't workin' hard enough."

"We're doing what we can."

Marvin spit near my boots.

"You got a big mouth, you know that? And nothin' to back it up with—just like your old man."

I tried to keep the exchange between Marvin and myself secret, but I couldn't. It welled up inside me, and I told Jimmy Olander, and before I knew it, word got out. This was a bad town for secrets. When it finally leaked back to Mom, she threw a pot down on the stove, ran out to the car, ready to drive up to Vic's ranch and confront Marvin. I begged her not to go, that it was my business and not hers. Mostly I was afraid what Marvin would say, that he'd accuse me of being a "momma's boy," and how he and his buddies would load up on me at school even more. I asked Dad to intervene.

"Give me the keys, Dorna. Goin' up there is just gonna kick the hornets' nest." He snatched the keys before she reached the car.

"I *hate* those people! I just *hate* them!"

"Goin' up there it's just gonna make things worse."

"Worse? How can they get any worse?"

"It can, believe me."

"This whole thing has been a mistake since day one," she said. "I warned you about them. About the kind of people they were, but no, you wouldn't listen. Not Irv Miller. Irv Miller has all the answers. Irv Miller thinks everybody's looking out for him. 'Sure, Irv, you want to go in the dairy business? We got it all set up for you.' The milk market? Yeah, it's down, but, hell, it'll come back.' Isn't that what they said? And the whole time they're up there laughing their asses off, thinking, 'here's another fat hog we stuck'."

"I'll go up and talk to Vic," Dad said.

"And while you're up there, ask him not to tell the whole goddamn town about our business either, will you? It's cash-only at Purity Market now, thanks to them."

Dad looked away, running the car keys through his fingers.

"Nothing seems to bother you, Irv. What's your secret, huh?"

"Don't worry, it bothers me plenty."

We couldn't talk to any of Irv's relatives, particularly Vic Santoni and his family, or anyone my folks considered Vic's friends. If we passed any of them in town, at school, in church, we looked away as if they weren't even there. When I overheard their names in conversations, or when Mom was on the phone, her tone of voice was always bitter, condemning. The lines were drawn, and we were forbidden to cross them. And the world that seemed so promising just months earlier? The world that would open up to me the harder I worked? A world as broad as the hayfields and hills around us? Well, it shrunk by the day.

I hated it. I hated the grudges and all the bad talk, and I prayed every night that it would change, that we'd make money and pay our bills, and that we could talk to folks and they would like us again. I hated being told who I could talk to, and who I couldn't. I hated not having a buck or two in my pocket. I hated not being around friends, and telling stories, and hearing them laugh. I hated not seeing my father happier, lighter. Hated not seeing him slapping his knee when something tickled him, his flushed face exploding into laughter. I hated all the lying I'd done, all the cover-up, the avoidance. Then late one Friday afternoon in early October, barely fifteen months into the dairy business, my mom took me aside.

"I'm going away," she said. "I'm taking Jackie and Angelo with me."

"Where you going?" I asked.

"We're going to my mother's. It's driving me crazy around here, Junior."

"How long you going for?"

"Until I feel better. All the worrying is wearing me down, making me sick." She looked at me and then over to the milking barn where Dad was still working. She ran a hand across her forehead. "I want you to know it's not your fault. I'd take you with me but I can't do that to your father. He needs your help."

"You're coming back, aren't you?"

"I will. Promise." Then she did something she hadn't done in a while—she hugged me. "None of this is your fault, do you understand?"

I nodded.

Rain had started to fall. Jackie and Angelo stood by the porch steps, staring back at Mom and myself.

"You got your suitcases out like I told you?" she asked.

"And you got 'em packed?"

"I didn't know what to put in it," Jackie said.

"Socks, tee-shirts. The corduroy pants your grandmother bought you." Mom walked back into the house, herding my two brothers in front of her. I walked to the hay barn, a hundred thoughts tumbling in my mind, dropped a dozen alfalfa bales onto the flat-bed, and drove the John Deere out to feed cows. A light, steady rain fell.

When I returned from feeding and parked the tractor back inside the barn, Dad and Mom were standing at the back of the Chevy, its trunk opened. My two brothers had trundled their suit cases out to the car, and Mom was arranging them inside the trunk.

"Get inside the car, boys, before you get too wet," she said.

They both sat in the front seat.

"Say goodbye to your brother," Mom said, leaning inside the car.

"Bye, Junior," they said together.

"Dad looked at me, then looked away.

"Where we goin' again?" Angelo asked.

"To Nana's. Where the sane people live."

"Sane people?" Dad repeated. "You call them 'sane'?"

"Compared to you they are." Mom looked at me. "I took some fish out of the freezer."

Dad said nothing.

"Call when you wake up from your dream world, Irv. You been in it long enough."

"Oh, get off your goddamn high horse," he finally said.

"I been telling you for months now, and you don't listen."

"I listen."

"To yourself, maybe."

"I've done what I can do," he said.

She opened the car door and slid in behind the steering

wheel. "Well, you'll have a lot more time now to listen to yourself. Then let me know if you hear anything that'll get us out of this mess."

The Chevrolet started up. Mom rolled the window down. Jackie and Angelo had all four hands up on the dashboard, looking at Dad and me through the windshield.

"Everyone told you this would happen. But no, you couldn't see it."

We stood in the yard and watched her back away from us, coast down the driveway, then point the Chevy south on Adobe Road, south to the city. Its red tail lights disappeared in the darkness. Rain dripped off the visor of my hat.

"Some gold mine," I mumbled.

My father stared off to where we'd last seen the car's tail lights.

"Maybe you shoulda gone with 'em," he said.

"I didn't want to go."

"Why not? You been inchin' up to it."

"I want to stay here."

"Stay here with the 'dreamer'? Isn't that what your mother calls me?"

"I'm not a quitter."

"That's good, Junior."

The rain fell all evening. Dad and I finished chores and walked back to the house. It was quiet inside, different-feeling. The fish had thawed, and Dad boiled two handfuls of red potatoes. He drained-off the potatoes and fried the fish filets in an inch of *Crisco*. We ate dinner while watching *The Friday Night Fights*. Carmen Basilio was fighting that night, one of Dad's favorite boxers. "They call him 'the Onion Farmer,'" dad said.

At the end of each round, Dad would look over at me in the television's glare, as if to see I was still there, that I hadn't gone anywhere, and he wasn't alone. The two boxers pummeled each other, Basilio taking a beating but always coming back, ducking, weaving, moving forward. When there was a good exchange, Dad moved to the edge of his easy chair and rammed a fist into his open hand. "Yeah, hit that bastard!"

When the fight ended ten rounds later, Basilio won a unanimous decision.

"What's the lesson here?" he asked.

"He didn't quit?"

"That's right! He didn't quit, goddamn it!"

Dad got up, stretched and yawned, and walked off to bed. I wanted to tell him I was sorry for what I'd said earlier, that I was in it for the long haul, and we'd see it through. That things would be different and that I wasn't a quitter. I'd make it all up to him, and he'd be proud of me. We'd work our way through any problem, and Mom would come back, and it would be just like starting over, but I couldn't find the words. I knew they were somewhere inside me, lining up, putting themselves together—all set to be heard. But just then, they'd scattered, deserted me. I switched the lights off and went to bed.

Gypsy Girl

The months of worrying had sickened my mom. Doc Murray called it 'nervous exhaustion.' She was talking to herself more and more, hardly starting a day without first reading her horoscopes. She hung rosary beads everywhere, made a little shrine to Saint Jude on her bedroom vanity that she'd kneel in front of and pray. Father Walsh came out and met with her, and they'd pray together, light candles, but nothing ever seemed to work. Out of options, she took my brothers, left the ranch, hoping to recuperate at her mother's place in San Francisco.

The morning after they left, I washed the milking barn down, scraped corrals, and fed all the livestock. With my brothers gone, I had to do their chores, and by ten o'clock I was back at the kitchen, ready for breakfast. Dad fried up a skillet full of bacon until it was crisp, forked it out and then dropped a half-dozen eggs into the hot grease. The eggs popped and crackled. When he set the plate in front of me, the eggs were brown and crinkled around the edges.

I toasted a stack of bread. He poured himself another cup of coffee, sat down, and spread yesterday's *Argus* to his right. He opened it to the sports page. It was game four of the World Series that afternoon.

"Giants'll finish the Indians off today," he said. "Liddle's pitching, and he's hell on 'em."

The world could be falling in around him, but there was always baseball, always sports.

"And they got Antonelli if Liddle gets in trouble," I said.

"And Mays hittin' the way he's been. This is a done-deal." He rubbed his chin, sipped loudly at his coffee. The clock ticked on the dining room mantel. He read while I stared at the eggs on my plate.

"What's gonna happen, dad?"

He said nothing.

"Mom'll come back, won't she?"

"She'll be back. She just needs to blow off some steam." He pushed his plate away from him. "The time away'll do her good. It'll do *all* of us good."

I spread butter on each slice of bread.

"We gonna lose the business?"

"Only if we quit."

"If we don't quit, we don't lose it?"

"That's right. You don't want us to lose it, do you?"

"No, I don't."

"So we won't. Don't quit, keep workin' and we won't lose it. It ain't that hard to figure out."

He folded the paper back together, and stared out the window. "Besides, the good Lord won't let it happen."

He said that a lot about the Lord. The Lord was some-one that played fair, that looked out for our interests. He did everything right, and knew exactly what to say. The Lord was smart, had no enemies, and the Lord never bullshitted anyone. He was a straight-shooter. Not only that, but the Lord was successful, and knew what was best. If the Lord had 65 cows, He'd know how to turn a profit.

After breakfast we loaded a spool of barbed wire and some hand tools onto the trailer, and rode out to the dry stock pasture. We strung fence wire until early afternoon. Every half hour or so, my dad took out his pocket watch. He worked quietly, absorbed in what he was doing. Dad escaped his daily concerns by working as hard and as long as his body could stand it. Others took vacations, took time off. Not my dad. Sometimes he'd hum the snatch of a song, or make that impatient, throaty sound when he missed a nail-head, or the wire didn't cut cleanly. He said nothing about Mom being gone. He just worked. When it was nearly one o'clock—and time for a quick lunch and nap before the second milking—we loaded the unused wire and the come-along winch onto the trailer and rode back to the yard. I lumped the remaining barbed wire and hand tools into the shop while dad walked off to the house.

After lunch, I sat outside on the back porch steps, chucking rocks across the yard at a pile of hay wire. With any luck, a plane would take off from Justman's, and I'd run out to the front yard and wave to the pilot as he banked his turn at the end of the airstrip. Petey, our dog, was sleeping in a circle of sunlight. The rain had stopped just after my mother left, as though she had taken it with them. In the orchard, the leaves on the fruit trees were yellow and falling. Unpicked apples still hung on the upper branches. In between throwing rocks, I just sat and listened and thought about all the things that had happened since yesterday. I wondered what it'd be like if we still lived in town and never sold our house, and I had a job that paid something. I wondered what I'd be doing this exact moment if I was someplace different, and my dad hadn't bought sixty-five head of dairy cattle. It was quiet enough that morning to hear the bulldozers working along 101 to the west, working in what had been McDowell's walnut orchards. Houses, whole neighborhoods of them—what dad called *crackerboxes*—flat-roofed, thin-walled affairs—sprang up where orchards used to be. I wondered what my two brothers were doing now. And I wondered about Mom, and when they'd return, and if things would be any different when they did. I wondered if we'd ever make any money. I wondered about praying, too, and if it did any good. I'd been praying a lot lately, and things only seemed to get worse.

In between all this thinking, I heard a car working its way up Casa Grande Road. It moved slowly, loud as a trac-tor—its muffler gone—disappearing behind the gum grove, before re-appearing again where Casa Grande Tee-d onto Adobe. The car lingered there, then turned north toward our ranch. Over the sound of its gutted muffler was another sound, a hissing, like a steam valve left open. Petey raised his head, straightened his ears. Whatever it was, it was loaded down, sunk low onto its springs, its front suspension riding high. When it reached our ranch, it slowed, then stopped. Petey raced toward it, barking, nipping at its tires. The sedan turned into our driveway, steam jetting straight up from its radiator, gravel crunching under its wheels..

It was a 1938 DeSoto, the kind I'd once seen the boxer Jack Dempsey posing in front of in an old car advertise-ment. Long and dust-covered, its roof was saddled with thin mattresses flopped over wooden fruit crates, and on top of the mattresses, a canvas tarp stretched from front to back, held down by a half dozen spare tires, all worn to their cords. Ropes ran back and forth through the tires like a spider's web. Gerry cans rode on its running boards, and behind the trunk were more wooden crates filled with metal grills and soot-covered pots and pans. Cast iron skillets were tied to the sides of the crates. The tops of the DeSoto's fenders were nearly eaten away with rust, and its windows so dirty you couldn't see into them. Dust and steam billowed behind the sedan. It rolled into our yard smelling like new rain.

The sedan stopped by our orange tree, its engine idling, steam still blowing up from its radiator. Petey circled it a dozen times, excited, lifting his leg on each of its tires. It sat there as though washed ashore, left there by a big wave. Nothing moved. Finally the front passenger window rolled down, and a big hand, stained green, fumbled with the outside door handle. The door swung open. I walked toward the sedan. A barrel-chested man shifted toward me in his seat. He dropped his feet onto the running board, and wiped the back of his neck with a rag. He looked like Bluto in the Popeye cartoons. A grin spread across his wide, dark face. The stump of a cigar was clenched between his back teeth.

"She get preeety hot, gacho boy." He looked over at the driver, motioned with his hand, and then turned back toward me. "Maybe water here, pleeeze?" he said.

I pointed toward the pump house where there was a faucet and length of hose. The DeSoto shuddered and rolled past me. One of its fruit crates was filled with walnuts. When the sedan stopped by the pump house, the barrel-chested man pushed open his door again, and swung his feet onto the gravel. He wore wool pants, rolled up at the cuffs, and suspenders whose straps disappeared into his fleshy shoulders. His leather shoes were worn at the toes, and he wore no socks.

"No!" he shouted to the driver, and motioned hard again with his hand.

With a groan and deep breath, he pushed himself out of the sedan, and stood up in front of me. He looked at his hands, and then offered the right one to me. "It's the walnuts the color. The tree they go," he said, pointing west toward town. "My name is Oso."

His big hand swallowed mine, its skin as hard and cracked as shoe leather.

"Pleeeeze." He walked in front of me, bent over and untied a strand of baling wire holding one side of the engine hood down. When he uncoiled the wire, he folded the hood over onto its other half. We both looked in. Steam and water blew from a split in the radiator hose. I walked over to the pump house and turned on the faucet while Oso covered the radiator cap with his rag. When he twisted it open, the cap and rag blew out of his hand, and a deep breathing sound—like the sound of a winded horse—gushed from the radiator. Oso jammed the hose into the opening. I walked back over to the sedan. Drops of water danced across the engine head and pooled in the spark plug sockets. The engine quieted, then shook and back-fired, sending the half dozen chickens scratching nearby, half-running, half-flying toward the hay barn.

Oso motioned for me to turn the water down until the flow from the faucet matched what was escaping from the cracked radiator hose. By now the back porch door opened, and Dad stood at the top step, holding a pair of rubber boots in his hand. He slipped into them and walked toward us.

"Your papa?" Oso asked.

I nodded my head.

Oso walked over to meet Dad, talked briefly, then shook hands. They walked to the DeSoto, and both of them looked into the engine compartment. I stepped back and stared inside to where the driver sat. A fedora was sunk low onto his head, nearly covering his eyes. Wisps of long, wiry hair sprouted from the tip of his chin. He looked straight ahead through the windshield. Dad walked back to the shop, opened its door, and disappeared inside. I circled the sedan, fascinated by all the things strapped to its roof, to its running boards.

"What do you do?" I asked Oso.

"Today we pick the walnuts," he said. "But the trees they go."

"And tomorrow? What will you do tomorrow?"

Oso shook his head and laughed. "Tomorrow is tomorrow, and far away."

Dad returned with a length of radiator hose, a screwdriver, and a knife. He laid the new section of hose along the old one, careful to avoid the fan blades, and scratched the length needed with his thumb nail onto the new hose. He placed the hose on top of the DeSoto's running board and cut where he had marked it.

"You can shut it off now," my father said to the driver.

Oso motioned back to the driver, and the motor stopped running. Water still gurgled inside the radiator. The sedan ticked and creaked while Dad loosened the ring clamps on each end of the old radiator hose, and worked the hose free. He handed the old hose to Oso who looked at it, turning the hose in his hands. "No good."

"No, it's shot," dad said.

The fat man looked around the yard. "Tis place look good," he said.

"Wish I could take its looks to the bank," Dad said.

Oso looked confused.

"We don't make money here," dad said.

"No?"

"No, not much."

"Maybe work here?" Oso asked.

Dad slipped the new hose back onto its fittings and retightened the ring clamps. When I looked up, the driver was out of the car, running his fingers along a row of abalone shells nailed to the pump house wall. His fedora—several several sizes too big for him—covered his ears. His hands, like Oso's, were stained green, the nails dirty and worn. He was slight, bony. An over-sized jacket hung on him that made his shoulders seem very square and broad. Both jacket's elbows were eaten through. He looked quickly away whenever our eyes met. Each time I saw him, he was in a different place, moving as quickly, as quietly as a school of fish.

"Maybe work?" Oso repeated.

Dad straightened up, and pointed out toward the road. "Can you hoe thistles?"

"Oh, yeah," Oso said. "Hoe *tistles*."

"You can have whatever fruit's left in the orchard, too."

"Tank you. Tank you." Oso shook my dad's hand again with both his hands. "And maybe a chicken? Yeah?"

"We can find you a chicken."

Oso pointed over to the other man. "Tat is Raymond. He my sons-in-law. No hear."

Raymond fingered the abalone shells.

"Junior, get them some hoes and a pitchfork."

From inside the shop I heard the sedan start up. It rolled past the open doorway. When I reached the orchard with hoes and pitchfork, the sedan was already parked under a large walnut tree, both its front doors opened. Dad and Oso were out between the road and orchard in a stand of waist-high thistles. Whenever Dad pointed, Oso shook his head. Sometimes he would pat my dad on the shoulder. And always, Oso laughed and stroked his big belly. Raymond had disappeared. I walked around the sedan, amazed at its cargo, amazed that so many things could be tied and strapped to it. Who were these strange folks that wandered onto our farm, so different from anyone around here? In the middle of these thoughts, a baby shrieked from inside the sedan. I stopped and moved closer, curious, trying to see inside the sedan's dark interior. One step. Two steps. Clothes and blankets were piled around its back windows. I set the hand tools against a tree. Then the rear passenger door swung open, and I was staring at a girl, or was it a young woman? I couldn't tell at first. Hair fell across most of her face, but when she glanced over at me, I looked into eyes as dark as burned oil. She cradled a baby

in her lap. She looked at me surprised, puzzled, scared—
I couldn't tell. "Shhhhh, gacho boy," she motioned me
toward her. The baby gurgled and fidgeted. She patted its
back. Her blouse was unbuttoned.

By now Raymond appeared from behind the gum trees,
buttoning up the front of his pants. I grabbed the hoes and
pitchforks and walked out to the road. I glanced quickly
back and saw Raymond leaning into the backseat of the
sedan, one foot up on the running board. Then I heard
him yell. When I turned around, he'd raised his arm as if to
hit the woman. He saw me, lowered his arm, and stepped
back.

I leaned the hand tools against the barb wire fence and
stared at Oso. Sweat already spread from his armpits, soak-
ing his shirt. He wiped at a face round as a melon's, and
covered with a short, thick beard that grew to the corners
of his eyes, down his neck, before losing itself in a tangle
of chest hair. Always, though, a force, something, drew
me back to their sedan, back to the young woman I'd just
seen. It quickened my pulse, raced my heart. Whatever it
was grew inside me. I knew it by another name, though,
and had been warned about it for years. It started out as
curiosity, that was the first sign, the nuns told us, and if we
didn't pray, didn't ask for guidance, it evolved into something much more powerful and beyond our control. It
claimed countless victims. And what countered it? Prayer.
Asking the Lord's help.

Seconds later, Raymond appeared behind me. He picked
up a hoe and walked out to the thistles where he joined
Oso and my dad.

It was three o'clock, and time for the afternoon milking.
Both the baby and its mother were asleep under the walnut
tree. Oso and Raymond hacked away at the thistles while
dad and I walked back to the house.

"Who are they?" I asked.

"Gypsies," Dad said. "Every year they come up here—like goddamn migratin' geese. Carl says they're from Antioch."

"What do they do?"

"Scavenge, mostly. Last year they were at Len Hartman's for a couple of days. Half his chickens went missin' and he run 'em off. It coulda been coons, but Len said it was the gypsies."

We walked on.

"They're gonna camp in the gum grove tonight," he said.

"Up the road there?"

"Yeah, where the old camp is."

"They're a little scary," I said.

"They don't bother no one. They pick whatever's left, work a little, then they're gone." Dad shook his head. "Why they wanna live like that beats the shit outta me."

"I don't know either," I said.

"Never knowin' where you'll be the next night—what you'll eat, *whethe*r you'll even eat or not. Whether you'll work. Livin' out of that old jalopy."

We stopped at the milking barn.

"Makes you realize how lucky we are, son—roof over our heads, steady work. A *place*, you know? *Roots.*"

I brought the cows in for milking. The whole time, though, thoughts of the gypsy girl swirled inside my head. They wouldn't leave me. I'd think of something else— Mom away in the city, my brothers with her, what they were doing, when they'd return—but always the gypsy girl forced her way back in. How young she seemed to have a baby, how very different from any of the girls I'd ever known. How mysterious she was. The wildness, the fear, like something caught in a cage, something both alluring and frightening that I saw in her eyes. And how the baby stared back at her. And Raymond, always appearing as though out of mid-air. And, of course, the unbuttoned blouse, her bare breasts. My prayers never lasted long.

After the cows were corralled, I paced back and forth in the hay barn, resisting that force that had now become more electric and powerful than ever—grabbing me, pulling me out to the orchard. I fell to my knees and prayed, "Please, Lord, let this temptation go away. Please." I looked around, but there was no sign that he'd heard me. "I know you're tempting me, testing me," I continued. "I know all about the devil and how he's a master of disguises."

You didn't go to Catholic school without learning about the devil. We saw pictures of him with that bird-like face, the clawed feet, always hovering, prodding, teasing, filling your head with all kinds of temptations and impure thoughts. Maybe *all* of them were the devil—Raymond and Oso, even the little baby. We learned that the devil showed up at moments just like this one, when you were weakest, when doubt surrounded you. We knew he waited for just that perfect time and perfect place. And in that inscrutable smile of the gypsy girl, her feral look, the breasts showing from the unbuttoned blouse, lie a perfect devil's hiding place. Despite the prayers, my heart thumped wildly when I thought of her, my breath choked off. A clatter grew in my brain, and if God was talking to me, I couldn't hear Him. Walk away from temptation, walk away was one voice. But another, louder, spoke to me. I walked back toward the orchard.

Raymond and Oso were still hoeing thistles. Tree by tree I moved closer to the orchard. I saw Oso stop and wipe the top of his head with a rag. Raymond's coat was draped over a fence post. Sitting upright on the blanket now, her back against a walnut tree, was the gypsy girl, the baby cradled in her lap. I moved from tree to tree, careful not to be noticed, careful not to step on any fallen branches. My heart hammered like a trapped bird's. Twenty yards from the gypsy girl, I stopped and peered around a gum tree until I could just see her. She looked off into the distance, vacant-eyed, her long hair falling to each side of her face, her shoulders bared. At one point she looked to where I stood, stared in my direction. I imagined she was think-ing of me, searching me out. The baby's head was inside her unbuttoned blouse. Its tiny right hand rose straight up in the air and then dropped onto the mother's blouse. It fingered at the buttons then pulled the young mother's blouse apart, exposing a breast, small and round, its pink nipple standing in the middle of a dark circle. I moved back behind the tree, excited, shamed. I stayed there, minutes, perhaps, trying to regain my breath.

"Gacho!" I heard her call.

I hugged the back of the tree. Oso was still out beyond the orchard, but now Raymond was nowhere in sight. I heard the one hoe chipping at the soil, the thistle stalks falling against each other.

"Sssshhhhh!" She motioned with her hand.

I turned and faced her.

She looked at me and then looked quickly behind her to the roadway, and off in each direction. I searched for Raymond. Maybe he'd moved further down the road, and out of my sight. Her head moved constantly. She hummed and cooed to her baby, and clapped its hands together. "Beauty-full boy," she said. She brushed at her mouth. Her fingernails were eaten away at the ends of her tiny fingers. I moved from behind the tree. She reached down and grabbed something—a rock, a dirt clod—held it in her fist, then looking back again toward the men, threw it at me. It landed near my feet and I bent down and picked up a piece of blue glass—the blue of a milk-of-magnesia bottle—worn smooth around its edges. I turned the glass around and around in my hand like a rosary bead.

Her face changed expression every few seconds—from a slight grin, to a broad smile, to a frown. Then it would relax, become expressionless. When she looked at me, her

eyes glowed with an animal brightness, a wildness, a curiosity I'd once seen in a coon's eyes trapped in our chicken coop
one night. Its newness, its mystery was unsettling. We stared
back and forth at each other. Something pulled, tightened,
within my chest. Should I walk over and talk to her? Or
should I just slip away?

Suddenly her eyes grew wide, her mouth dropped open.
She pointed. Something moved at the corner of my eye,
quick and cat-like. Then, before I could react, it was behind
me, breathing, waiting, close enough to smell the sweat
and kerosene worn into its clothes, the thistle dust, the walnut husks. When I turned, what I stared into first was a
dead eye, milky-white, hanging motionless in its socket like
a marble. The other eye—the good one—was fastened on
me as hard and unblinking as a snake's. My blood iced to
the tailbone. Raymond said nothing but just stared at me.

"Is okay," the gypsy girl said. "Is okay."

Raymond's one good eye stayed on me.

"Go, gacho boy," the woman said. She waved me off
with her hand.

I backed away step by step, keeping Raymond in my
sight. At the edge of the orchard I turned and retreated to
the barn yard.

Dad was milking. On his radio, above the vacuum pump
and the suction sounds from the milking cups, I could hear
the sportscaster's voice calling the Giants'/Indians' game.
Blood pounded in my head. A hundred images, a hundred
questions flashed before me. I wanted to tell somebody—I
needed to tell someone—what had just happened, but
nobody was around. My brothers were gone. No one except
Dad, and I couldn't tell him. It was like finding a five dollar
bill, and not knowing whether it was real or not until you
tried to spend it. Two hours remained until the milking
was finished, and my chores began. I grabbed my bicycle
and rode over to Casa Grande, and coasted downhill, well

past Bliss School and Lester Miller's, enroute to *Olga's Cafe* down on Lakeville Highway where Orlen Spoon washed dishes. Orlen Spoon, who would listen to me, who believed everything I said. I could tell him.

Orlen was sixteen, had dropped out of school two, maybe three years earlier. He was tall and skinny, with blonde hair that dropped over his forehead in a long, greasy coil. He talked in a drawl that sounded like ball-bearings moving in his mouth. My folks said his family was Oakies, and part of that world they wanted closed off to me. What folks around here didn't know about each other, they made up, particularly those who were different. And Orlen Spoon was different—his whole family was. Orlen's father worked at Cader Brothers Tallow shoveling carcasses all day. He wore a little welder's cap, a cigarette always dangling from the corner of his mouth, drank hard, but managed, somehow, to keep his job. Every other month you'd see Orlen's father in a worn coat and tie, hair plastered back, waving his bible at passers-by down on Lakeville Highway, shouting out repentance for all his sins. Dad said the father was feeble, and that all the kids were feeble, too, which was why Orlen wouldn't go to school. Others said Orlen's old man beat him up once on a bad drunk that scrambled his brains, and all he could do now was wash dishes.

We'd leased sixty acres along the Petaluma Creek to grow oat hay, and it was there where Orlen's family lived in a house built up on pilings, and it was there where I first met Orlen, picking the chocolate bars and cigarettes out of K-ration cans—the oldest of half a dozen brothers and sisters, all fair-skinned, pale like the mother, all of them shoeless and covered with mosquito bites. She kept a garden surrounded by chicken wire and in it she grew okra and beans, chard and mustard greens. The front steps to their house were missing, washed away by a flood-tide, but that didn't stop a pair of goats from sleeping there on a gutted couch. Cader Brothers Tallow owned the land. Some days when it was hot and the wind blew just right, the mix of smells—tidal mud and rotting carcasses, and the chicken shit heaped up at Elliot's closer to town—you had to swallow hard to keep everything down. Orlen said you get used to it, that if it happened enough you got used to everything.

I rode around to the back of the café, leaned my bicycle against a row of garbage cans, and walked up to the screen door.

"Orlen, you in there?" I called.

The screen door pushed open and Orlen Spoon stood in the doorway, shading his eyes from the afternoon sun. A rubber apron stretched down to his boot tops. The skin around his hands was bleached and wrinkled from dish water. He had long, wiry arms, and the start of a tattoo on one of his biceps. He unwound a pack of Lucky Strikes from his shirt sleeve and popped one out.

"Why you grinnin'?" he asked.

"Nothing."

"C'mon, Miller. Why you grinnin'?"

"Because of what I seen."

"What you seen?"

"Gotta give me a smoke first."

He shook another Lucky loose and offered it to me. I liked to wait, to keep Orlen hanging on what I'd tell him.

"What you seen, Miller?"

I paused a bit longer, surveyed the parking lot, took a pull from the Lucky and blew the smoke out in a straight hard stream.

"I seen a pair of melons that'd choke a horse."

Orlen looked at me.

"Bullshit."

"Don't believe it then."

"Who you seen?"

"Don't know her name," I said, "My old man told me they were gypsies. They were driving an old DeSoto—more shit tied to it than you could shake a stick at."

Orlen cocked his head as though he'd heard something.

"Folks like that stopped here earlier—radiator suckin' up water. I didn't see no woman, though."

"I didn't at first, either."

I told him the story about hearing the baby cry, and I took out the piece of blue glass and showed it to him. Orlen fingered it, and stared back at me.

"And she just peeled open her shirt?"

"Well, I had to ask her."

"What'd you say?"

"I gave her a nice smile first."

"You the cat's ass, Miller."

Orlen's mouth had dropped open, swallowing every word of mine as though it were a penny gumball. I wanted to tell him exactly what had happened, the way I tried to remember each event as I peddled down to Olga's, but once into the story, something took over inside me, the way it so often did, and everything changed. It was like some other person who looked and sounded just like me, got to tell the story, but it became *his* story, and not mine. Mine wasn't good enough.

"What was they like?" Orlen asked.

"Like what we seen in *Argosy*—only bigger."

"You one lucky bastard, Miller."

Orlen French-inhaled his cigarette. Every minute or so he'd walk over to the screen door and look inside to the kitchen.

"Remember that woman grabbin' me the way she done a coupla months back, and takin' me out to her car? Some hay truck driver's wife? You remember?"

"Of course I do."

"She have melons like that?"

"Yeah, only bigger."

"She rattled my socks a good one. But it was over 'fore I knew it."

Orlen was different all right—he was no valedictorian, and for as much as he worked, he was always broke, but there wasn't a more honest, direct, fearless person anywhere around. No bullshit about him. If he said he did something, he did it. I never doubted him for the moment. When he told me he fought Johnny Jensen, a bully who outweighed him by thirty pounds, and got knocked down three times, and got back up, that's what Orlen had done. He'd have the bruises and chipped tooth to prove it, too. If he'd gotten his ass kicked, he was the first to admit it. If he'd told you he was the one who'd set pigeons loose in the Cal Theatre, you could find the burlap sack used to sneak the birds in stowed away in Orlen's back porch.

"So—what you gonna do?" he asked.

"About what?"

"About the girl."

"Nothing, I suppose."

"But she's as much as invited you in."

I described Raymond to him—how he always just seemed to appear sudden-like. And then I told Orlen about Raymond's dead eye, and how Raymond never talked. Orlen shuddered.

"Still don't scare me like them nuns of yours do, though." Orlen said. "Them things around their heads. Them long black dresses." He shook his whole body. "Them's weird. Why they gotta dress like that?"

Orlen liked to poke fun at me for being Catholic. He never understood Catholics, never understood anything about religion or God, or how any of it could save you. He'd seen his own father thumping a worn bible, imploring the Lord and anyone else who would listen, and just days later be back drinking, roughing the mother up. I felt sorry for Orlen. I felt sorry that despite all his honesty, his good-heartedness, he'd never make it to heaven, that he'd always have to wash dishes, and put up with his father's drinking. I tried to explain it all to him one day, but his eyes got glassy, and it was clear nothing was sinking in. Before I could save his soul, Orlen looked at me and said, "Miller, why don't the two of us didn't just take some of the gold out of your church, buy an airplane, and look for heaven ourselves?" That was Orlen's dream— to fly an airplane. He wanted to step inside one, fly a long way off. He thought Tahiti sounded good.

"So, they gone now?" Orlen asked.

"My old man told me they'll camp at the gum grove tonight."

Orlen's eyes flashed. "Up the road here, Miller?" he pointed up Casa Grande. "You gonna lose your cherry?"

"Yeah, this might be it."

I said it as I'd said so many other things—without thinking, without a shred of regard for the truth. I talked to be talking, and that was it. If it was another lie, what did it matter? I'd confess it. But for right now I wanted to take it a bit further, stretch it out as far as I could take it. I wanted to string Orlen along, convince him that I could be as ballsy as he was, and see his reaction, see how my stories made him stutter with excitement. Then, when I'd taken it far enough, I'd break it off, say it was all bullshit. For as much as I pitied Orlen, I wanted to be just like him.

"You a fool if you don't go," Orlen said.

"She'll be disappointed, huh?"

"Let's go then—me and you—tonight."

"Sure. Tonight."

"Maybe she'll like both of us."

"Yeah, maybe."

"Nine o'clock at the bridge tonight? And don't bring the dog!"

"Nine o'clock. I'll be there."

After Orlen disappeared inside the kitchen, I rode my bike back up Casa Grande. My head was jangled up with thoughts that trailed everywhere. I wondered about Mom and my brothers, and what would happen between her and Dad. But then right in the middle of thinking about my folks, and what was going to happen with the ranch, the gypsy girl would elbow her way in, and there she'd stay. I re-played the gypsies showing up the way they did, and the girl tossing that piece of glass my way, and Raymond with his dead-eye. And then came my running-off at the mouth with Orlen, promising him things I knew I'd never do. I felt terrible. When I passed the gum grove, there, parked at its edge, was the gypsies' DeSoto. Everything was off its roof now, with boxes and cans all stacked around it. I could smell wood smoke drifting out between the trees. I wished for about the twentieth time that I'd never told Orlen anything. I wished I'd been honest, and not made up the things I did, and just told him only the things I knew for certain. But what did I know for certain? That we were losing money by the day. That I wanted a Jeep. That I wanted to be a big-shot. That things weren't turning out the way I'd envisioned? That I was going to heaven and Orlen wasn't? A half mile later I noticed the thistles were all gone along the roadway, heaped up in a big pile at the top of the orchard, ready for burning.

When I walked into the barn, Dad met me in the breezeway.

"The Giants beat 'em, seven to four," he said. "Antonelli closed 'em out." He was smiling, content, as if nothing had happened, as if Mom and my brothers had never left, as if we didn't owe a dime to anyone and everything was free and clear.

"I knew they would," I said.

After I left the milking barn, I backed the *John Deere* into the hay barn and dropped another dozen bales of alfalfa onto the trailer, then drove out to the hayracks. I broke the bales up and spread them along the racks, then fed the dry stock and all the young stock. Daylight was fading. I kept looking south toward the gum grove.

I kept thinking about the gypsy girl, and what she'd meant—if anything—by tossing the piece of glass my direction. I wondered what it'd be like doing it with a woman, if I'd even know what to do. And I remembered Raymond, his quick, little movements, and how he never looked at me except that once, and how that dead eye burned right through me. So many things I didn't understand in this world. Finally I stopped, and kneeled down, and prayed that it would never turn dark, that it would always stay daylight, and that today would actually be tomorrow, and that none of this had ever happened. I prayed that I would never lie again. That I'd be the person I was, and not try to be someone else. I prayed that I'd never have another impure thought, that I'd never lie, that I'd never be tempted, never be goaded by Orlen Spoon again.

By now Dad had finished milking, and the cows were following each other in a long line out to the hay racks. I could hear him banging the steel buckets in the washroom. After I parked the tractor, I hosed down the milking barn and scraped the manure off the cement corrals and wheelbarrowed it out to the manure pile. When we'd finished, he switched the lights off in the barn and walked back to the house. We took our boots off at the back porch steps.

"How about some lamb chops for dinner?" he asked.

"Sure," I said.

I was hungry, but I couldn't eat. I gnawed at one of the chops, but every bite stuck in my throat.

"Your mother'll be back," he said, "if that's what's eatin' at you."

"I know she will."

As soon as Dad went to bed, and his snoring started, I

shut Petey in the house, jumped on my bicycle and raced to the bridge. It was dark, but a big full moon was climbing up from behind the hills. I hid my bike in the tall licorice weed, and climbed down the creek bank. Orlen was sitting underneath the bridge, smoking a cigarette.

"Thought maybe you'd changed your mind," he said.

He gave me a cigarette, and I lit it off of his and took a drag.

"Orlen, everything I told you was bullshit."

"Bullshit?"

"That's right."

He pulled two RC Colas from his jacket, and opened them with his belt buckle.

"You mean there ain't no gypsy girl in the gum grove?"

"Oh, there's one up there, all right, but she didn't do the things I said she done."

"She didn't throw no glass?"

"She did."

"And you didn't see her jugs?"

"I did."

"Then what's the bullshit?"

"She didn't *show* them—

"You made that up?"

"Yeah—

I told him about the nursing baby.

"That's as good as showin' 'em to you."

"No, it's not."

We argued back and forth. Orlen's mind was made up.

"I'm not going up there. You can, but I'm not," I said.

"You scared?"

"I am." I hated to admit it, but it was the first honest thing I'd said in days, maybe months.

"We go up and have us a look—

"I'm not going." I toed at a rock in the creek. "I know you don't believe in Hell, but I do."

"What we doin's wrong, huh?"

"We're having impure thoughts."

"Impure thoughts." Orlen repeated the words. "What's them?"

"It's when we think about girls like we do." The more I tried to explain, the more impossible it seemed to convince Orlen.

"So, if I think about a woman, that's an impure thought?"

"If you think about her in a certain way, it is."

"If I think about my ma, that's a impure thought?"

"No, *that's* not."

"I don't know, Miller. It sounds all balled-up to me. Sounds like lotsa folks walkin' 'round with impure thoughts."

"Say we go up there," I began to explain, "and one of us died—we'd go straight to Hell. You know what that'd be like?"

"What?"

"You burn forever and ever," I said.

"Hmmm. I don't see us doin' nothin' wrong." Orlen lit another cigarette. "We grab us a looky-looky, and then we hoof it on out—ain't nothin' gonna happen. Ain't gonna burn forever."

"How do you know?"

"'Cause if something happened everytime a person'd done something, there'd be no one left. We'd all be burned up." Orlen paused. "It'd just be trees and shit. And possums walkin' round."

I forced it out. "I'm scared, Orlen."

"We got that rain last night—it'll make it all quiet. They won't even know we been there."

His face glowed each time he pulled on his cigarette.

"Orlen, I'll give you five bucks if you forget the whole thing."

"You ain't got five bucks."

"When I do, though, I'll give it you."

It was a stand-off. I smoked my way through another cigarette, hoping Orlen would change his mind. I admitted what a terrible liar I'd been, and that half the things I'd ever told him, I'd made up. I told him I didn't know why I'd done it. I blamed my dad, mostly. I blamed us losing money the way we did, and keeping up a good front. I told him that even smart people could do really stupid things. I blamed everyone but myself.

"We head straight across Morettis, and circle up behind the school. Then stop where that big gum falled out into the field." Orlen spoke slowly, each step laid out. The tip of his cigarette moved in front of him as he motioned with his hands. "We got us a moon 'cept it'll be dark once inside the trees."

I started up the creek bank, back where my bike was.

"Where you goin'?"

"You know where I'm going."

"Chicken shit. You goddamn Catholics and your Hell and all your burnin' up. Just hocus-pocus if you ask me."

Orlen snubbed out his cigarette, climbed up the opposite creek bank, and looked over at me. "What was they? 'Impure thoughts?'."

He walked over to the barbed wire fence, and threaded his way through its strands. Once in the field, he jogged away.

"You big dumb Oakie!" I yelled out.

But the sounds his boots made disappeared into the moonlight. I thought of just turning around then—grabbing my bicycle and peddling home. It would have been the simplest thing to do. It would have been the *right* thing to do. I wasn't Orlen Spoon. I wasn't ignorant, and I wasn't fearless the way he was. I didn't know anything, only that I was Junior Miller, whoever that was, and I wanted to carve out something for myself early on, and that I trusted my dad, and the Church, and most folks to show me how.

But all I ended up doing was talking big, talking right out my ass, and not having two dimes to rub together. I bent down, grabbed my bicycle, looked up at stars—where I'd been taught to look. I thought some more. Then I set the bicycle down. I walked over to the barbed wire fence, and eased through it. Then I ran. I ran across Morettis in the bright moonlight, and turned at *Bliss* School. I ran like I'd never run before. I felt so light, like I was made out of balsa wood and a big wind was scooping me up, howling in my ears.

My feet barely touched the ground. Then the voices started up—all kinds of voices—the devil's, my guardian angel's, the gypsy girl's, every nun and priest that had ever cautioned me about temptation—all of them clamouring, shouting, all trying to be heard. It was like they were bidding at an auction for my soul. Right then I remembered not caring who won, who claimed me. Not caring if there was a heaven or a hell, and who was right or where I ended up. None of it mattered at that moment. Only that Orlen was running across an open field, running toward something exciting, forbidden, and nothing else mattered to him. He was running toward Hell. I knew that. He was running toward Hell and right then I didn't care. I'd run to Hell with him.

Orlen was waiting by the fallen tree.

"I knew you wasn't no chicken-shit," he whispered.

My breath came in big gulps, the air mentholated by the eucalyptus. It felt chilled, aromatic, peeling open my lungs, reaching down almost to my crotch.

"You okay?" he asked.

I looked at the moon and saw Raymond's big dead eye.

From inside me, a voice leaked out, "I'm okay."

"Pretty soon we'll see your girlfriend."

It seemed pointless to argue with Orlen anymore.

Through the gum trees, maybe thirty, forty yards away, bits of orange light flickered from a campfire. Both Orlen and I knew the campsite where the gypsies were staying—an opening in the middle of towering eucalyptus trees that had fallen against one another over the years. In the center was a circle of rocks from the nearby creek and a half dozen eucaplyptus stumps that circled the campfire. Hobos had stayed here years earlier when they rode the trains north. A footpath that led through the campsite cut the grove in half. Orlen and I often met here and smoked cigarettes, and flipped through the pages of *Argosy* and *Man Magazine* to view women posing in two piece swim suits. He'd tell me about the places he wanted to fly away to—islands out in the middle of the ocean where the water was the color of stones in Indian jewelry. We'd fish cans and bottles out of the campfire ashes and shoot them with .22's

"We get coon-quiet from here on," Orlen whispered.

"And once you see her, we high-tail it, right?"

Orlen nodded.

"You swear?"

"Goddamn, Miller—you and your swearin' and all your crossin' your heart shit."

Long strips of tree bark lay everywhere. We stepped over and around them, each step landing soft as though walking through a grove of egg shells. Deeper into the trees, the moonlight disappeared, and it became just shadows and outlines against the darkness. We felt with our feet. Each time my shoe touched, I held my breath, my ears cocked for any sound my feet might make. Orlen's outline moved slowly, smoothly in front of me like a night animal's. The air was cool, the gum smell burnt at my lungs. It grew darker, more forbidding, with each step. But with each step, the firelight brightened through the trees, and now we could smell the smoke, and see wisps of it hanging in the branches. I heard the fire crackle.

We were ten, maybe twelve yards from the opening. Long, waving shadows shimmered against the upper branches.

Sparks spit and circled in the air. Everything seemed to beat and sway, as if powered by a gigantic heart—the trees, the moon, the stars, myself. Maybe it was my own heart moving everything—it felt that large. There were sounds every-where—a drum pounded in my head. The voices I'd heard earlier never left me. If I stepped or moved, those steps and movements seemed amplified, heard, surely, miles away. We inched closer and closer until we were just beyond the perim-eter of the camp. I saw the tops of the flames. Orlen turned to me and brought his fingers up to his mouth. Something moved into my throat—a wad of phlegm—a big wad of fear itself, tasting like barn tin. I tried swallowing. It wouldn't go down. It bobbed back up. I raised my head above a fallen limb and looked into the campsite.

Raymond and Oso sat on opposite sides of the fire. Oso leaned forward, his elbows resting on the tops of his knees, his rubbery mouth hanging open. His bottom lip flapped loose, his eyes looked tired, bloodshot, watery from the woodsmoke. A newspaper was spread by his right foot, and in the middle of the paper was a heap of chicken bones, all of them picked clean. By his other foot was a half a jug of wine. He wiped at his mouth after each swig, and then passed it across to Raymond, who sat on the ground, his back against a stump, both feet spread out in front of him, his toes nearly touching the fire. Raymond's hat was pushed back, his long, stringy hair tucked behind his ears. His forehead was high and bony and glistened as though it'd been smoothed with oil. Neither of them talked. They drank wine and stared into the fire. A tent was pitched at the edge of the opening. A circle of yellow kerosene light leaked through its canvas roof. Orlen turned back to me and pointed toward the tent, then moved away from the opening. I pulled at his arm but he shook it free.

Orlen stayed low, like a cat. Then he disappeared. I waited, hesitant to move any further. Flame shadows swayed against the trees like dancers, the fire hissed and popped. Voices and sounds within my head rumbled again—many of them recognizable, each of them shouting over the other. I remained there, frozen, unable to move. When one voice died down, another took its place. As much as I wanted to run, as much as I told myself, "You're here at the camp, and that's enough," another part of me resisted, another part of me wanted to see the girl again, and calm this craving, this odd, deep impulse that drew me toward her.

I felt one leg move, and then another, moving on their own with no signal from me. Moving as though under their own command. They weren't taking me away from the campsite, though. They were taking me into its belly, each footstep lighter than the one before it, each cushioned as though walking on crepe. I moved around tree trunks, ducked under low limbs, felt for the strips of long bark, with a deftness and agility as new and foreign to me as everything else happening this night. When I finally saw Orlen again, his nose flattened against the tent wall, his eye stuck in front of a four-bit sized hole in the canvas, I wanted to see what he was seeing. I *had* to see what he was seeing. Something had leaked into my blood by then, had taken me over. It was raw and primal. It swam through me like a powerful drug, exciting, powerful, mindless. It sang. It promised. It opened its soothing arms to me. I crawled over to the tent wall, squatted before a hole, welcomed Hell, and looked inside.

She sat with both legs under her, her back as straight as a hoe handle, her tiny shoulders thrown back, combing at the knots in her hair. Her arms cast long, elastic shadows against the canvas. She sang a little song to herself as the baby slept just a few feet from her on a pile of blankets. She leaned forward, her hair falling in front of her, before she would snap her head backwards, the hair lifting above her, flying as though it were a flag in the breeze before landing behind her shoulders. Hers was an inscrutable face, at once a child's and a woman's both, filled with wonder and pain, and a life I knew nothing about. She wore a different blouse now, again unbuttoned at the top, and each time she moved, I wanted to see more. I wanted to see the pale skin hidden under her clothes, the skin that swooped out to her breasts, a skin shades lighter than her arms and neck. Electricity crackled through me. When the blouse opened, there they were again-—not the ones I'd described to Orlen earlier in the evening, but the ones I'd really seen. Small, full ones. She turned one way, then the other. Always, her stare a blank, empty one. Her eyes bright and feral.

I heard Orlen moaning next to me, and then the moans became this little chant, "Yeah, yeah, yeah," just under his breath. I reached out to kick him, and he brushed my leg away with his fist. The girl stopped combing her hair, and didn't move. Oso called from the center of camp. She answered back. She stared in our direction. Neither Orlen or I moved. Seconds passed that seemed like minutes, hours. She resumed combing her hair. And again, Orlen began his moaning, "Ahhhh," but even louder this time. And again I went to kick him. But this time he yanked my foot hard, and pulled me off-balance. My upper body teetered, then fell into the corner of the tent. I reached out with my hands, but it was too late. A rope snapped by my ear, and before I could react, the tent corner had collapsed around me.

"Aaayyyy!" the young woman shrieked.

Oso shouted. Orlen howled, "Oooo shit!" and then raced past me. There was commotion, footsteps in every direction. Confusion and shadows. And fear. The young woman shrieked, her baby started crying. Folks were shouting. I thrashed at the canvas, and when I'd pushed it away, I sprang to my feet and turned. But no more than two steps later, a hand collared my neck and slammed me to the ground. I landed with a back-jarring thud. Raymond stood over me.

"Orlen! Orlen!" I called out. But Orlen was gone.

When I tried to get up, Raymond stepped on my chest.

"Let me up!" I pleaded. "I ain't done nothin'!"

Raymond grabbed my two legs and dragged me over to the fire. I looked up at Oso. Drunk, eyes crossed, he swayed back and forth.

"Let heem go!" Oso shouted.

Raymond shook his head and grunted. The woman was standing by Oso now, clutching her crying baby, her eyes wide and bright.

Raymond spun me over, and planted a knee into the middle of my back. When I opened my mouth, he ground my face into the campfire dirt. I spit and coughed. Raymond worked both my hands together, and tied them at the wrists with twine..

"Let heem go, goddamn it!" Oso shouted again. The big man stumbled forward. He pulled at Raymond. I felt Raymond's weight lift from my back, and then the two of them fought—shoving, tugging at each other, their breathing hard and forced. Oso tried to talk between breaths. I turned on my side, crabbed away from the fire.

"No, eees not good!" Oso's words came out in little bursts. Then Oso's body hit the ground like a felled tree, and didn't move. The young woman cried out, "Pa-pa!"

Oso moaned. Just as I got to my knees, Raymond grabbed me, and pulled me back to the campfire. And again I was face-down, with a knee planted in my back, my mouth filled with cold cinders. The baby was crying. I heard the young woman patting its back, trying to soothe it. She knelt near Oso, talking back and forth between her baby and the motionless man.

"No, no," she said.

Raymond lifted me to my feet, and pushed and bull-dogged me out the footpath to the DeSoto. His breath hard and sour, his grip like a vice.

"I'm sorry. I'm sorry," I kept repeating.

When we reached the sedan, he opened the door, shoved me into the backseat, and slammed the door shut. I landed face-down. The DeSoto started up, the whole car shook. It reeked of kerosene. My face was buried in loose apples and shoes, scattered wrenches, as the sedan pulled away. I'd pissed my pants. As the DeSoto accelerated, a worn drive-bearing underneath me began to howl. The faster the DeSoto moved, the louder the worn bearing growled. Warm exhaust fumes leaked up around me. I worked my way onto the seat, and tried again to reason with Raymond.

"We didn't hurt anybody—it was the Oakie's idea. Not mine."

His one good eye stared out to where the two headlights cut through the darkness, the other one bobbed in the bottom of its socket. I saw our ranch approaching, its yard light burning at the top of the driveway, and anticipated Raymond backing off the throttle, stopping, grunting— whatever he did—then letting me go. Maybe the DeSoto would wake the old man, and I'd have some explaining to do. Maybe my old man would throttle Raymond a good one for what he'd done. I didn't care. I just wanted out of the car. But Raymond said nothing, and the DeSoto howled past our ranch, right past our farm buildings, and the yard light, which seconds before burned as bright as a beacon. I watched it grow smaller behind me.

"What do you want, huh? What do you want?" I asked him.

Raymond kept both hands on the wheel.

"Are you deaf? Huh? Are you deaf? Say something, goddamn it!"

Raymond's one good eye looked out at the road in front of us.

"Let me out, goddamn it!"

I tried to work the twine loose, but with no luck. Each

time my wrists turned, the twine dug deeper, until both hands numbed. Frustrated, I kicked at the back of the seat and dust rose through the light thrown by the DeSoto's headlamps.

"They'll catch you and string you up—you don't know folks around here."

Still, Raymond said nothing.

I regretted for the hundredth time ever telling Orlen anything. Ever envying him for the things he'd done. I hated how easily I caved into temptation. How I couldn't keep what I'd seen to myself, that I had to tell somebody. That I always needed an audience. That I had to make things up, too. A big shot! That was me—wanting to be someone I wasn't. Then I began my confession—listing as many things I'd done wrong as I could. It was a long list, one thing after another. My rotten life, one incident, one lie at a time. "God, if you get me home safe, I'll never talk to Orlen Spoon again," I prayed.

The Desoto shimmied and whined down Adobe Road. Everything shook inside. What was stuffed into the back window—rags, baby clothes, musty-smelling shirts—rattled loose and fell on my head. Underneath me the DeSoto's exhaust barked, its worn bearings spinning like gravel in a colander. Exhaust fumes seeped up through the floorboards. In between tallying up my sins and wondering what Purgatory was like, in between saying my good-byes and assorted apologies, my stomach had twisted like a pretzel. I threw up the RC Cola Orlen had filched from Olga's earlier, and my head—which all evening pounded like a jackhammer—now felt as though it was finally breaking apart. I farted. I threw up. I'd already pissed my pants. We were a good two miles, maybe more, past our dairy, bound for some unknown place where they'd find my body the next morning. I was tied up, sprawled-out in a backseat, with a one-eyed gypsy at the wheel. Everything hurt. Everything seemed lost. And hopeless.

Somewhere south of Penngrove, Raymond let off the gas pedal, and the DeSoto slowed, back-fired, then banked hard into a right turn. It stopped me from thinking about my own funeral, and who the real mourners would be. I slid off the seat, and onto the floorboard again. The DeSoto started climbing, its engine working hard, its bearings howling against each another. Raymond shifted to a lower gear, and again, the interior filled up with fumes from the rotted muffler. We were going into the Sonoma Mountains.

"Let me out—we helped you today, don't you even remember that?" I pleaded. "My old man fixed your goddamn car! Are you stupid? Huh, are you stupid?"

Again Raymond stared out through the windshield, mute and impassive. The DeSoto snaked up Sonoma Mountain Road. I slid from side to side as it leaned into each turn. In a straight-stretch of road, Raymond shifted gears, and the sedan sped up. I managed to work myself onto the back-seat again. The headlights beamed up against oak trees and road-cuts, and the dark hulk of the hills above us.

I tried to remember my most serious sins: impure thoughts, lying, boasting. I said "Our Fathers" and "Hail Mary's" but with each turn in the road, each time the Desoto dipped or slowed down, I forgot about the prayers, and wondered, "Would this be it? Would this be the place?" When the sedan continued on, I began to pray again. I tried to imagine what death would be like. Would it be quiet? Would it be quick? Would it be like a long nap? Would everything just go blank like when they took my tonsils out? I wanted it to be fast, and I didn't want it to hurt. I wondered about Mom and my brothers. I wondered about my dad and how he'd take everything. I wondered about Orlen, and if I'd ever see him again, if we'd end up in Hell together, and what he'd think then. I was mad at him—but mostly mad at myself for making up the things I did, and then letting him talk me into all this. I was mad, too, that he just ran off the way he did.

Somewhere near the top of Sonoma Mountain Road, the DeSoto left the pavement, and I could hear dry grass brushing up against its undercarriage. It finally stopped, its motor still idling. I heard Raymond get out of the car. Then the rear door by my feet swung open. Raymond pulled me out until my ass was on the running board.

"They'll find you and string you up!" I said. "And I'll be glad when they do."

Raymond's dead-eye bobbed off toward the headlights. A knife blade glinted in his hands.

"It was the Oakie's idea, not mine." The words gushed out. "I wasn't gonna do anything. Honest—I told him about your wife, and the rest was his idea—I didn't want anything to do with it. You gotta believe me." My voice was shaking, tears puddled in the bottoms of my eyes. Then I began crying. Just bawling and sobbing and saying I was sorry again and again. "I made shit up, I did that." My words broke off. "But I never meant to hurt nobody."

The headlights beamed back. Raymond walked toward me, the knife at his hip, his one dead eye as still as the moon. We looked at each other, and I figured this was it. He spun me around. I waited for the knife to enter my back, wondered what that would feel like. I held my breath, and waited. I breathed again, choking back the tears and knots of phlegm in my throat. And I waited some more. Still no knife. Just the car idling and a half dozen stars framed through its side window. I waited—in between the breaths, the gasps, the sobs rattled my body—I waited.

Raymond's fingers fumbled at my wrists, and I felt the flat knife blade work itself between the twine and my skin, and then turn. Back and forth the blade sawed until the twine fell apart, and my wrists dangled free, numb and life-less. I turned and faced Raymond, and raised my hands in front of me like a pair of clubs. The knife was still in his hand. If he was going to stab me, he'd do it face-to-face.

We stared at each other. All the tactics I'd run through my mind in this situation—boot in the nuts, a big round-house across his jaw—all of them left me. I stood there stiff, power- less, unable to move. Unable to even run away. We looked at each other. My stare found his dead eye, but the eye had lobbed off toward the headlights. And when my stare met the good eye, the one that stayed with me, the one that had followed my every movement from early afternoon, some- thing seemed different about it now. Not as murderous. Not as bent on my destruction as before. And from a face as bar- ren as an executioner's, there was a movement, a turn at the corner of his mouth. Not a sneer. Not a twitch, but some- thing like the slightest of grins. He pushed me aside, closed the DeSoto's door, and walked around to the driver's side. He slid in behind the wheel, ground the transmission into re- verse, and backed the sedan out onto the road. Then he drove away, another pair of tail lights disappearing in front of me.

I looked around. It was all shapes washed in moonlight, and crickets chirping, and the smell of pepperwood trees. I rubbed my wrists, and felt blood flowing back into my fingers. My whole body continued to shake, but now it was in one big wave of relief. I looked up at the sky, and saw all the stars, and the moon. I wasn't crying anymore. I was alive. And I was grateful. I thanked God for sparing me the way he had, and vowed I'd never disappoint him again. In between vows, I heard the DeSoto back-fire down the mountain, and thought about what had just happened to me, if I'd imagined it or not. I sucked in the night air, and felt oddly cheated that death had breathed so hard and so close into my face and then just drove away.

I wondered what time it was. Was it midnight? Earlier? Later? I wondered if Dad had noticed me gone, and, if he did, what kind of story I was going to make up. I hoped he wouldn't throttle me, but if he did, I deserved it. I was going to work hard at the dairy again, and do what I could to make it a success, to make him proud, to make Mom never want to leave again. I'd go to confession. Avoid Orlen. Then I started walking home.

On the road above me, I heard a truck slowly working its way down the mountain, its loud air brakes puncturing the quiet, its headlights flashing across the hills with each big turn it made. When it appeared behind me, I turned and stared into its headlights, and raised my arm up. It slowed and then stopped. I walked up to its driver. It was a milk truck, a flatbed loaded down with cans of milk it had picked up at the dairies above.

"You lost?" the driver asked.

"No, but I could use a ride down the hill." I said.

I climbed in the other side, happy to be moving off the mountain. I sat there, at first, not wanting to say anything, still reciting little prayers of thanks to God and all my guardian angels—everyone that'd helped me out of that mess. But then the truck driver wanted to know how I'd ended up on Sonoma Mountain Road in the middle of the night, and my prayers abruptly ended.

I didn't know quite where to start, but right away mentioned the young woman, and wanted to recount exactly what had happened, but shortly into my story, there she was blowing kisses to me, and the jealous husband knocking me unconscious, and when I came to, I was in the backseat of a DeSoto up here on this mountain. And when the dead-eyed gypsy came after me, I kicked him hard—right in the teeth—probably knocked a half dozen of them out, I said. I was tied up or I would have finished him off. But I let him get away, and finally, against the jagged edge of a rock, I managed to cut through the twine.

"That was when you saw me," I said.

"Goddamn, you got yourself a story there," the driver said. "Maybe I oughta take you down to the police department and they can go after those guys."

"Hell, they're gone by now."

"You sure?" he asked.

"Oh, I'm sure."

The driver was headed toward the creamery in town. He dropped me off at the end of Washington, and I walked the last two miles. I walked past our ranch, careful not to make a sound that would alert Petey. The house was dark. Good. The old man was still asleep. I cut back across Moretti's field, the gum grove on my left, and hopped the fence into the creek. Orlen was waiting there.

"You all right?" he asked.

"No thanks to you."

He popped a Lucky out of his pack and gave it to me. He ran a match along the back of his thigh, cupped the flame, and brought it up to my cigarette.

"I got roughed-up pretty good," I said.

"What happened? C'mon, tell me."

I told him pretty much the same story I told the milk truck driver, but sweetened it with even more details. One lie led to another. I couldn't help it.

"He pulled a knife on you?"

"That's right. And when he turned me over, and was about to run me through, I kicked him square in the nuts."

"No shit?

"That cross-eyed gypsy went flying." I took a drag from the Lucky. "He probably ain't landed yet."

"How'd you get untied?"

"There was a file on the floorboard, and I worked it back to my wrists."

"Goddamn, Miller!"

"So when he swung that door open, I came after him— like a tiger let out of its cage."

"Why didn't you take the car then?"

"He got to it before I could. I ran up alongside it, though, and jumped on the running board, but he pushed me off and I tumbled ass-over-tea-kettle thirty yards. Maybe more."

"Shit!"

My mind raced between what I remembered and what I was making up.

"That was one scared sonofabitch."

Orlen's mouth hung open the way it did whenever he was biting on one of my stories. I couldn't stop talking. Words crowded against one another, and it didn't matter if they belonged together or not.

"He wanted to get outta there faster'n I did."

Orlen laughed.

"Sonofabitch, Miller."

Orlen wanted to know everything. About what happened after I fell into the tent, and he'd run off, howling like a coyote. I told him how Oso and Raymond had tussled, and that Oso hit the ground and didn't move. I told him how Raymond sucker-punched me, and the last thing I remembered was the girl begging him to stop, and after that everything went blank. When I woke up I was in the backseat of the Desoto, at the top of Sonoma Mountain. I told Orlen about the fight, trying to keep all the details straight in my mind about how I'd kicked Raymond, and he came back with some hard punches, and I fell, and then Raymond fell, and how the knife corkscrewed out of his hand. I couldn't stop talking. After I'd finished, Orlen wanted me to run through the whole account again. I told him I was tired, that I needed to go home, that if my old man caught me out, there'd be even more trouble.

"You don't wanna go back to their camp and finish business?" he asked.

"No, I don't."

"They had 'nough of you, right?"

"They sure did."

We pushed our bikes back onto the road.

"You sure you ain't goin' back for one more peek?" Orlen asked.

"No, I've seen enough."

And I had. I rode back home and left my bike by the backdoor. Petey whimpered, happy to see me. I clamped his mouth shut with my hand and tip-toed into the house. I undressed and got under the covers. I couldn't fall asleep for the longest time. The whole night kept playing back like a movie. In one scene I was the hero, unable to separate the imagined from the actual. Defiant to the end. The next scene I was the coward, shivering-scared, crawling toward where I thought God would be, repentant, sobbing, begging forgiveness. Before I fell asleep, though, I thanked God with yet another prayer. I thanked him for my faith, for sparing me this time. I told him the lesson was learned. I asked him to go easy on Orlen, too, because Orlen didn't know. Orlen meant well, but he just didn't know.

Birthday

Life wasn't all bad. Dorna learned again and again what she'd forgotten in her despairing moments—that there was a balance to things. Yes, the raccoons had killed ten of her Leghorns—she raised them all from chicks—but the remaining twenty-five had grown into excellent layers. She gathered their eggs each morning, carried them back to a corner in the granary where she sorted each egg by size, by the quality of its shell. She sanded away their blemishes with an emery board and saved the double-yolkers for Irv. Whatever eggs her family couldn't eat, she packed into one-dozen cartons and sold on a little table she kept alongside Adobe Road. She deposited all the proceeds in a cigar box high on an unused shelf behind her dinner china. She told no one about it. She vowed no matter how badly she needed money, the contents of the box would remain untouched. When quarters and fifty cent pieces filled the box, she slipped the coins into paper rolls and exchanged them at the bank for dollar bills. There were many things she wanted to buy—the gingham pedal pushers she saw in the window at Carither's, a swimsuit at Bee's Apparel, though the thought of ever entering the water in it frightened her silly, a set of encyclopedias for the boys. There were back-to-school clothes they needed, and, of course, the unpaid bills, so many of them they troubled her sleep. But her earnings remained untouched—nearly sixty dollars now—reserved for Irv's birthday gift, something she knew he'd consider foolish, unnecessary—but both compelling reasons in themselves. She'd bought Irv a 16 gauge Browning shotgun.

On Irv's birthday, a warm day in August, after she'd fed Irv and the boys breakfast, she washed the breakfast dishes, then drove into town. She parked the Chevy in front of Milner's Sporting Goods on Western Avenue, and on Milner's front counter, she counted out the sixty dollar balance—she'd left a twenty dollar deposit the month before—mostly in one and five dollar bills. Bud Milner brought the shotgun out to her, laid it on the counter, and at the last moment, tossed in a carrying case and a box of shotgun shells. Bud looked at Dorna, "Tell Irv 'Happy Birthday" for me."

She hid the shotgun in the back of their closet, and then baked a chocolate layer cake that she let cool in the kitchen window. That evening when Irv came in from the milking, she had Swiss steak with mashed potatoes and carrots—Irv's favorite—waiting for him on the kitchen table. After dinner, she brought the cake out with the number '42' traced in candles. She lit the candles and turned off the kitchen lights. Dorna and the boys sang 'Happy Birthday.'

"Make a wish," Dorna said.

Irv's eyes were bloodshot, and, at first, he slid the cake over to Irv Jr., but Dorna made him push it back in front of his father.

"It's *your* birthday, not Junior's."

Dorna and the boys clapped when he blew out the last of the stubborn candles. She served everyone cake and unplugged the percolator and poured Irv and herself cups of coffee. She filled the boys' glasses from the milk pitcher. After cake and coffee, Dorna said, "Let's go sit in the living room, and you can open your present."

Angelo, the youngest, lugged out the shotgun, and handed it to his father. Irv slid the shotgun out of its case, and held it at arm's length.

He didn't say anything at first.

"Well?" Dorna asked..

"It's a beauty," Irv said.

The boys all took turns holding it, always with the command from their mother to point its barrel toward the floor.

Dorna looked at Irv. "Let's load the boys in the back of the truck, and drive down to Gilardi's."

The shotgun straddled the seat between Irv and Dorna. The three boys sat behind them in the bed of the pickup, their backs against the cab of Irv's truck. They drove down Frates Road to Lakeville Highway. Dorna turned on the radio, and a half minute later Patti Page was singing *This Old House*. There was half an hour of daylight left.

"You didn't buy it on credit, did you?" Irv asked.

"C'mon, Irv, who's going to give us credit?"

They drove on. Dorna hummed along to the song.

"Don't worry, Irv. It's not gonna break us."

Irv scratched his chin and it made a rough sound like rubbing sand paper. He wore his pork-pie hat. Out of habit, he liked to run his fingers along its narrow brim.

"And you didn't take none of the boys' savings?"

"The boys' savings? We spent that."

He shook his head, and scratched his chin again.

"Irv, the money fell out of the sky, all right? It dropped right into my lap, with a bow around it, and a card that said, '*To Irv Miller, who deserves it.*' And you do."

"But I don't need it."

"An even better reason—it's the kind of *no-reason-at-all-gift*, other than you turned a year older. Besides, it's something like this that puts a burr up your sister's ass—that's the real reason I got it." Dorna laughed. "They think any extra change we find in the bottoms of our pockets is theirs."

Dorna looked out at the hay flats, now just brown stubble. She smelled the tarweed, the warm musky odors carried up from the tidelands. The sun was setting behind the western hills, and the breeze blew in through the open truck window. She didn't want to tell Irv that months earlier she would have never considered buying a gun, that the idea of another one around the house frightened her. She knew Irv wasn't that kind of person, but still, the thought of yet another one had troubled her. Temptation, she thought. Dorna knew there were parts of Irv—parts of everyone—that would always be a mystery to her.

At Gilardi's, Irv turned off the highway, downshifted, and steered his pickup past a cluster of river shacks and onto a narrow levee road that paralleled the water. The truck bucked and dipped for another half mile until they came to a bend in the river, to an area where the road widened, and Irv could pull off and park. The wind stiffened here, blowing up from the bay, rippling the water into white-caps, bending the cattails. As soon as the truck stopped, the boys climbed over its sides and ran toward the river bank. Irv unzipped the case and pulled the shotgun out. He slid three shells into its chamber.

"You watch out for the boys," she said.

Guns frightened Dorna. So many things frightened her, even this small town she'd found herself in, this small town so idyllic at first, a place where her life could begin again, where everyone seemed related, warm, as inviting as family. But once its novelty had worn off, she learned that gossip here was torrential, that there were no secrets unless you kept them to yourself, that folks around her were rough-edged, their concerns petty, and that family could turn on you with a hard vengeance. At times she missed the city where a block from where she lived she could be anonymous, walk down a crowded street and no one knew anything about you, your family, your past, what you owed or didn't owe, what your dreams were, if you even had dreams. You could be anyone. Or you could be no one.

Irv eased himself out of the pickup and walked over to the water. The boys were trying to skip rocks across the river's surface, but the rocks lost themselves in the whipped-up little waves and sunk quickly. Dorna sat in the pickup and through the windshield watched Irv and her boys. Wind gusts rocked the pickup gently from one side to the other.

Junior and Jackie both pointed upriver toward a pair of mud hens flying toward them, barely two feet from the surface of the water, their wings working frantically. Irv motioned the boys back, and stepped closer to the water. He shouldered the shotgun, its barrel following the flight of the birds, and when they passed in front of him, he touched-off three rapid shots. Each shot jerked his shoulder back. The boys clapped their ears. From inside the truck, the shots sounded like the popping of cheap party favors. The two birds flew by. All three rounds had missed.

Irv stared at the mudhens as they flew upriver. The wind flapped at his pants. Dorna watched as Irv raised the shotgun above his head with both arms, and began dancing around and around in tiny circles, dancing a kind of jig with his feet taking quick, little steps. He lowered the shotgun to his chest and then raised it above his head again, continuing to dance in around and around. Irv's smile soon broadened into a grin, and then the grin became a full-blown laugh.

Junior ran up to the truck and pounded on its window. "Ma! Ma!"

Dorna rolled the window down.

"What's wrong with dad?" Junior asked.

"Nothing," she said. "There's nothing at all wrong with your dad."

Neighbors

Dorna Miller cherished Monday mornings. After the boys were in school and Irv was off to the auction yards with drop calves, she often called her neighbor, Annalee Avila. Sometimes they talked on the telephone for just a few minutes—a brief time to check in with each other, to take the pulse of events surrounding them. Other times their Monday mornings stretched out almost to lunch. For the most private matters, they met in each other's kitchens over coffee and cigarettes. They loved to talk on the telephone but it was a party line they shared with neighbors, and both were convinced that Gladys Sorensen, the busy-body of Adobe Road, listened in. They talked until they heard the click of a receiver picking up. A silence would follow. When they didn't hear the receiver replaced, one of them would say, "She's listening in again. Coffee at my place?"

This one Monday morning, Dorna Miller's phone rang.

"It's serious this time." Annalee's voice trembled.

"Tell me."

"No, not on the phone."

"C'mon up. I'll put a fresh pot of coffee on."

Minutes later, Annalee's Pontiac lumbered up Miller's gravel driveway and scratched to a halt. Annalee stepped out, still wearing slippers, her hair in curlers, a coat slung over her house dress. Dorna watched her approach. The coffee had stopped percolating, and she'd placed two cups and saucers on the table, emptied the ash tray and set it between the cups. She moved her lighter and pack of Camels alongside the ash tray. The kitchen door opened, and Annalee stepped inside.

"You look terrible," Dorna said.

"Thanks, I love you, too."

Annalee's eyes were red and swollen. The two women hugged briefly, then separated. Dorna looked into Annalee's eyes before Annalee looked away.

"Mario left this mornin'—we had a big fight," Annalee declared in a flat tone.

"I'm sorry."

"Bastard!"

"What happened?"

"More of the same. Fight and argue, fight and argue." Annalee sat down. "It's not like I'm spoilin' for a fight, either. I'm not. I just wanna know what's goin' on. But we can hardly talk to each other now before somethin' sets him off."

"Let me pour you some coffee."

Annalee patted her coat pocket. "I left my cigarettes in the car." She walked back to the car, reached in and grabbed her purse. Dorna filled the two coffee cups.

Annalee returned, and sat once again at the table. Her hands trembled. "I asked if he'd be home for dinner, and he said, 'Maybe. What, I gotta fill out my schedule now?'" She removed her coat and sat down. "That's all I asked him. And I said 'What do you mean, "maybe," and he said, 'Just what "maybe" means.' And I said, 'How about a definite "yes" or "no."'" And he said, 'Okay then. No.' Then I asked him if he was going to see his girlfriend. That's when he blew up. Started swearing at me, knocked the breakfast dishes off the table. Then he grabbed my arm." Annalee pulled the sleeve of her dress back and twisted her left arm toward Dorna. "Look what he did!" A big purple bruise, the size of man's hand spread just above Annalee's elbow.

"Asshole!" Dorna leaned toward Annalee and put both arms around her. "I'm so sorry, sweetie—I'll get you some ice."

"You must think I'm some kind of idiot not to know what's going on, I told him. 'There ain't nothin' goin' on,' he says, and I said. 'Bullshit, there ain't nothin' going on. I wasn't born yesterday. I know when the phone rings and I answer and then whoever calls, hangs up.'"

Dorna had taken a tray of ice out of the freezer, broke the cubes out of the tray and spread them across a terry cloth towel. She brought the corners of the towel together and twisted them into a knot. She carried it back to the table. Annalee lit a cigarette, tilted her head toward the ceiling and blew out a stream of blue smoke.

"Here, put this on the bruise."

Annalee held the towel against her arm, but the towel opened, and several ice cubes fell onto to the table and onto the floor. "I'm fallin' apart, Dorna. And there's Mother's Club meeting this afternoon. I'm so embarrassed."

Dorna gathered up the loose cubes and put them back inside the towel. "Here, put the towel on the table and just lay your arm on top of it."

"You're a saint, Dorna, you really are."

Dorna lit a cigarette. She inhaled then placed it on the little holder on the ash tray. Both women sipped from their coffee cups.

"Is it Geraldine Souza you think he's seeing?"

"Oh, I *know* it's Geraldine Souza—that bitch!" Annalee sipped at her coffee. "I saw her in Antler's Pharmacy last

week. You know that guilty look people have on their faces?
Well, it was all over hers. She says 'Hello' and I said 'Hello'
back, but all the time wantin' to tear her eyes out. When I
walked out of the pharmacy I was shakin'—my whole body
shakin'. Couldn't catch my breath. Thought I was gonna fall
over right there on the sidewalk. I kept askin' myself, 'What's
goin on here, Annalee?' When I got back in the car I started
cryin.' Right there on Western Avenue, the middle of the day,
in front of God and everyone—just bawlin' my eyes out."

Dorna reached across and stroked the top of Annalee's
hand.

"I know I ain't no prize, but I never cheated on Mario.
As much as I wanted to, I never did."

"You're fine the way you are, Annalee. You're beautiful."

"Now don't go paintin' the sow bright red."

"You are."

"I got fat. Can't get into any of my old dresses. Don't
even try." Annalee pulled at the middle of her housecoat.

"Well Mario isn't exactly Jack Lalanne—besides, it
doesn't give him any right to treat you that way."

"It's different with men. They don't have to watch
themselves the way women do. Their guts can hang over
their belts, and who gives a shit? But if we put on a few
pounds, look out! It's like we're always on parade—like
cattle at the fair. Someone always judgin' us."

Annalee crushed out her cigarette, and finished the first
cup of coffee.

"How are you and Irv doin'?"

"Well, we're as broke as ever, if that's what you mean.
Same old story. I didn't like the idea of going into the dairy
business from the start—you know that. I told Irv it jinxed
us—that it's been bad luck ever since. Of course, Irv thinks
I'm beating him over the head because of it. Maybe I am.
But it's what he wanted to do—I guess he had to prove
something, too."

"What do you mean?"

"Irv's naive—a real dreamer—stuck back in thirties or something. I can't figure it out. The whole time, too, his in-laws and cousins are up there on the hill sweet-talkin' him into buying Kate's herd—a real opportunity, better jump at it—they kept telling him. What a laugh! Why he idolized those people, I'll never know." Dorna pointed to the hills behind the barn, and shook her head. She re-filled their coffee cups. "And all the time Irv's thinking they got his interests in mind, and all the time I'm telling him, 'Be careful, Irv, they're blood-suckers'—but you think he'd listen? I might as well be talking to that wall. All the little guys going belly-up, milk prices falling, and Irv's got our house in town sold as a down payment. Still, I told him we'd give it a go, and we have—so blame me, too. It's been hand-to-mouth ever since."

"Okay, that's business, but what about just the two of you—you know? How's that?"

"He doesn't have a girl friend—at least, I think he doesn't—and he's not leaving bruises on my arm."

Annalee's face lost all expression.

"I'm sorry, sweetie. That was a terrible thing to say." Dorna reached out and touched Annalee's hand again. "We fight like everyone else and half the time my stomach's so knotted up I can't eat. When I've had enough, I take the two youngest and go stay with my mother for the night, maybe two. Then it blows over. Nothing really gets settled but it blows over, and we're back to square one again."

"I go to my mother's and she can't wait for us to leave," Annalee said. "The kids drive her crazy. She's got all those knick-knacks everywhere and Joey can't keep his hand off of them. Everything's got to be in its place, and it's hell to pay when it's not. 'I done my child raisin' already,' she'll say. 'And no one ever helped me.'"

"Annalee, if it gets bad enough, you stay with us, okay? The kids can double-up—we'll make-do, and no one has to know. Okay?"

"You're a sweetheart, Dorna." Annalee sipped at her coffee, and lit another cigarette. "Does Irv ever talk about what he's feeling?"

"He's pretty tight-lipped—doesn't like it, either, when I press him about that stuff. He thinks it's all bullshit—thinks if we just stayed busy there wouldn't be all this worrying, and wondering who's feeling what, whose toes are getting stepped on. So what do I do? I button up, too—carry it around just like Irv does, but it's not healthy. It's like I'm pissed-off half the time. Irv's tried—a couple of times he's tried—he doesn't like me going around mad anymore than I like it, and he'll fumble around with an apology, buy me a box of nylons—a peace offering is what I call it. Truth is he just wants to be left alone—just him and his cows and his dog. He loves the kids, but he's happiest when no one's bothering him. He could go on like that forever—the whole world could be caving in but as long as there were cows to milk, shit to shovel, it wouldn't bother Irv. Work, work, work." Dorna lit another cigarette, and stared out the kitchen windows, remembering how Irv once courted her. "Sometimes I wondered why he even got married—if it was just to show his cousins he could—that he wasn't a 'momma's boy.' He used to be romantic. And quite a dancer, but all that's gone now. He'll talk to anyone he meets, and folks say, 'What a great guy your Irv is.' So talkative and funny, and I'll say, "Yeah, he sure is something, isn't he?'"

"Irv *is* a good guy."

"I know he is. But what people see and what you see aren't always the same."

"You want him to bring you flowers all the time? Is that it? Sweetheart, that might happen in the movies but it don't happen in real life—oh, maybe once or twice a year—if you're lucky, but something dries up inside of them. Inside all of us."

"Why is that, Annalee? What do you think happens?"

"That's the 64 dollar question, Dorna. They're *all* romantic when it's new, and they want something. Then it isn't new anymore. Or they don't want it as much. Or think someone else offers them a better deal—and it's not just men, either. If you're lucky, you keep findin' something new that sparks it. Or, you're okay with things just as they are. Mostly we get used to each other and stick it out—unless you're Mario Avila, who thinks it's always better on the other side of the fence."

"Maybe *I'm* the dreamer, then, and not Irv." Dorna stared at the kitchen wall. "I just don't want to be someone who slides the dinner plate in front of him every night, does the laundry, cleans the house. I want to be appreciated, thanked. I want to be told that. Is that asking so much?"

Annalee shook her head. "Maybe it is. But look who you're askin'."

They both lit up fresh cigarettes. Above the silence that filled the kitchen, an electric clock hummed on the wall.

"What time does Irv get back?"

"Noon, or just before. He used to eat lunch at the yard. Can't afford it now. You want some toast? A couple of eggs?"

"God, no! My stomach's in knots."

"What about just kicking Mario out of the house?"

"I can't do that."

"Why not? He's hardly spending anytime there anyway. Just tell him to hit the bricks."

"With the kids and all?"

"You'd rather they see you fight all the time? What do they think?"

"Well, Joey loves his father. Wants to be just like him. I took him to *Southwick's* to buy him shoes last week, but he didn't want shoes, he wanted cowboy boots just like his dad's. Had a shit-fit right in the store until I gave in." Annalee buried her face into her arms, then she looked up. "Mario—I oughta shoot the bastard!"

"No, Annalee, don't do that!"

"Sometimes I think I could—without blinkin.' "Pow!" Annalee had shaped her thumb and index finger into a pistol.

"You left him before. Leave him again."

"I know I did. And he swore he'd be different, and I went back—lyin' sack-of-shit! What could I do? After two days at my mother's house, she wanted us out. There's no place for me to go."

Dorna re-filled Annalee's coffee cup.

"And, besides I don't want people talkin'."

"To hell with what they say."

"Oh, yeah, easy for you to say."

Dorna shook her head. She didn't like people talking about herself and Irv, either. She knew the power, and the shame, of gossip.

"What sets Mario off?"

"Everything. Nothin'. I don't even want to open my mouth around him anymore. He's like a powder keg. It's like he just can't stand the sight of me—I think that's it. I finally asked him, 'Is all this because of your girlfriend, Mario? Is this what all the shit's about? You want me out of the picture? Huh? Does she mean that much? Is that it? Am I just in the way?' I want to know! He denied it. Laughed at me."

Annalee reached out and touched Dorna's hand again. She ached for her friend, wished for a magical power, a particular knowledge that could help her, that could make her happy again.

"You're so lucky. I grew up with Irv, and half the women in town were crazy about him."

"I know I am." Dorna looked into Annalee's eyes. "But I don't always feel that way."

"We're funny—you and me. We each got a little of what the other wants—Mario makes a good livin' and Irv don't beat you."

"He just never says anything to me anymore about how he feels. Fact is, I don't know how he feels—I just read his expressions, what his body does when he talks or listens."

"That's men—that'll *always* be men."

"I know it's men, but sometimes you want a little clue, a few words."

"Men and women," Annalee said. "I overheard Mario's cousin, Lester, runnin' at the mouth one day out by the loading chutes, and Lester says, "Mario, if it wasn't for that little split-tail of theirs, a man and a woman'd never talk to one another."

"What a terrible thing to say!"

"Lester's an asshole." Annalee flicked at her cigarette. "Worse around women than Mario is. And Lester's wife? Did God put a stupider, homelier woman on earth? She just lets Lester run away with that foul mouth of his, and doesn't say a word—wouldn't know what to say if she could. But what Lester said got me thinkin' maybe it's true. That's all we're good for."

"Now don't you go believing that, Annalee. And anytime you do, you come and talk with me. Promise?"

Annalee stared straight ahead.

"Promise?"

"Okay, I promise."

"You need a break from each other. Let Mario spend some time on his own, and maybe he'll see he's got his head up his ass."

"I ain't holdin' my breath on that one—besides what'll people think."

"Let them think what they want."

"Oh, sure, easy for you to say."

"Who has to know?"

"Dorna Miller, how long you lived in this town?"

"Not as long as you—"

"There's no secrets in this place, sweetheart—you of all people should know that."

Dorna nodded her head, then smiled.

"What's so funny?" Annalee asked.

"I was just thinking of Lester—with the pants down around his knees, and half his ass spilling out—and the worst breath you ever smelled—like something died inside his mouth. And him talking about women that way—

"He ain't no dreamboat, that's for sure."

"You know who is, though?" Dorna said.

"Who?"

"The Colonial Bread man—

"Ed—oh, God! He reminds me of Errol Flynn!"

"You know who he reminds me of?"

"Who?"

"Burt Parks from "Beat the Clock."

"You know him then?"

"Know him? I buy half of what's in his truck just so he'll stay longer. 'You wanna try our 'butter-crust bread—it's new?' Hell, yes, I'll try it! Can you stay longer, we'll eat the whole loaf together?"

Both women laughed.

"I've got a surprise for you." It was a welcomed change of mood. Dorna's face broke into a childish grin.

"A surprise?"

"Irv'll kill me for buyin' it, but I'm bookkeeping three days a week now at the hospital, and thought I deserved something—you know, a little treat. Something besides the box of nylons Irv always buys me for my birthday, for Christmas, for *anything*."

"All right, enough suspense. What is it?"

"C'mon in the living room. Take your coffee cup with you."

The two women walked into the living room. Dorna motioned Annalee to the couch, then stepped over to the record player. She switched the player on.

"Close your eyes."

"Oh, come on, Dorna."

"Never mind. Close your eyes."

Annalee closed her eyes.

"I bought it at Harmony Music on Friday, after I left work. It's still in the wrapper."

"Oooh, a record!"

"Not just any record."

Dorna dropped the record album through the player's spindle. Its arm moved out from where it had been resting, then dropped gently onto the record. Within seconds the gentle pop and scratch of the record sounded in the speakers. Then a voice emerged, an unmistakeable voice—it was Frank Sinatra's—and behind his voice the sad-sounding strings of violins.

"Oh, Dorna! It's heaven!"

Dorna joined Annalee on the couch. The two women listened quietly, hardly moving, tears beginning to well in both of them.

"*. . . you're like a child that cries and no one heeds the crying, you're like a falling star that dies and seems to go on dying.*"

"Oh, I knew it'd be him."

"Just listen, damnit," Dorna said.

"Lemme see the album cover."

Dorna walked over to the record player, retrieved the album cover and handed it to Annalee.

"Look how sad he looks!" Annalee said. "All by himself, and all those people around him. That's all made-up though, isn't it? Frank Sinatra's never alone. How could he be?"

"No, he's just alone because he wants to be."

Dorna started to sit down, but impulsively, perhaps even habitually, moved to the big, curved window and stared toward town instead, across the mowed hayfields, and the stacks of hay that resembled simple houses without their roofs. She knew this vista well, the thoughts and nameless longings that had become part of it and how Sinatra's voice added color, mood to what she was thinking, this same voice she'd been listening to since her teens. Here, from this window, she imagined such tender fantasies—the thrill of a gentle touch, the absolute wonderment of a stolen kiss. Every wish, every dream, every little pain seemed to wrap themselves inside the words he sang.

The first song ended, then a brief silence before the next one began.

"*. . . my heart is heavy as we gaze upon a cottage for sale. . .*"

"Oh, God! I love this song!" Annalee shouted. "So sad, but I love it just the same."

"They're *all* sad." Dorna turned away from the window.

There was something delicious, almost welcoming about the feelings—the pain, the longing that the music stirred up inside her. It was a sadness, to be sure, but his voice coated this sadness with something sweet, a bitter confection, making it bearable, even welcoming—giving it a dreamy elegance, dressed up in an evening gown that Dorna imagined herself wearing. Sometimes she imagined it was Irv staring across to her, his face beaming above the gimlet glass, beaming as it did before they were married, the candle light softening his hardest features. Other times—in frustration, pure curiosity—she imagined someone else. Maybe even Sinatra. The song soon ended.

"Dorna?"

"Sorry, dear, I was off somewhere."

"Me, too. What were you thinkin' of?"

"Oh, nothing, really."

"*. . . don't know why, there's no sun up in the sky, stormy weather. . .*"

That voice, just so clear. Like a horn whose sound reached

into her heart. For years now it held her in a spell, carried her away from a confusing, often empty present to a dreamy land of soft shadows, tender caresses—to a land of fantastic romance. Dorna shuddered, turned around and walked back toward the kitchen. She stopped and grabbed Annalee's cup from the table. "Coffee's ready."

Dorna set the two cups down next to the percolator, then re-considered, and carried them over to the sink and washed both cups out. She wanted a few more minutes alone, to look out the window, to counter this uncertain present, and lose herself—as she'd lost herself so many times before—in a maze of daydreams.

Violins introduced the next song, the strings rising and falling in pitch, so sad-sounding that she felt a tear at the corner of her eye, a shudder pass through her, before wiping the tear away. It was a foolish tear, an unexplainable tear. Maybe even selfish, vindictive, in a funny way. What had prompted it? What was it about the music, this man's voice she was listening to that reached so deep within her? And why was loss the frequent feeling it evoked? What had she lost? Was it love, intimacy, the dreams she once held as a young girl? She didn't know. But to have lost something, you had to have possessed it first, to have held it in your hands, your heart, before it fluttered away. She heard Sinatra's voice as if sounding from a long corridor, "*I need your love so bady, I loved you all so madly. . .*"

"Dorna?"

"I'll be right out."

She dried the cups, wiped her eyes again and carried the cups back over to the percolator where she re-filled them. Back in the living room, she set the cups down on the coffee table.

"You okay?" Annalee asked.

"Oh, I think so—I had one of those moments. Too much thinking." Steam rose up from the cups. "I was remembering when I was a little girl," Dorna said. "I do that a lot when I'm sad." Dorna sat down next to Annalee.

"I've made you sad, haven't I? Talkin' about all my problems."

"Of course not—I do it to myself," Dorna confessed.

"This time together means so much to me. I don't ever want it to change."

"It won't," Dorna said. Anyway, when I was a little girl, I remember being sad as many times as I remember being happy—sometimes more. It shouldn't be that way, should it?"

"I don't know. How should it be?"

"Oh, I don't either—doesn't it seem that being young should just be about happy memories?"

"Woman, who has just happy memories? Tell me—and you call Irv the dreamer?"

"Irv says I never know when I've had enough—that I never know how good I have it. Maybe he's right—that I'm one of those people who'll never be satisfied. Maybe I'm just spoiled."

"You're a lucky person, Dorna. You really are." Annalee ran a finger along the rim of her coffee cup. Between songs she looked over at Dorna. "You said you were thinkin' about when you were a little girl—

"I was."

"And?"

"I'd gone up to Agua Caliente to stay at Grandpa's hotel," Dorna said. "I was maybe seven or eight. We spent part of each summer there. Papa liked the mineral baths, liked to sit on the front porch of the hotel and drink wine with his brothers."

The music swirled about the two women. Its volume rattled the window panes, before Dorna reached over to the record player to turn it down. She'd stopped talking, not wanting to intrude upon the song. When the song ended, there was a church-like silence before the next one began. The couch springs creaked as Annalee shifted her weight. The quiet was soon followed by, "*. . .where is that worn-out wish, after it brought my love so near?*"

"Anyway, I was at Grandpa's," Dorna continued. She sat down again. "I loved it up there. It was early September—Labor Day weekend—because I'd just had a birthday and my mother had bought me this beautiful silk scarf. It was pink. I don't remember liking anything as much I liked that scarf. I'd try it on several times a day in front of the mirror, strike different poses with it. Each time I put it on, I loved it even more. Even in the heat, I'd wear it to dinner. Each time it made me seem like a different person—someone very glamorous and grown-up."

"*I'm a glum one, it's explainable, I met someone unattainable . . .*"

The two women looked at each other and shook their heads. Dorna's voice rose just above the music.

"It was warm—hot, in fact. Each morning I'd walk with my cousins down to Boyes Springs where we'd swim at the bath house. Then a fire broke out in the hills. We could smell it first, and then the valley started to fill up with white smoke. It was like fog, except very hot, and it burned your eyes and it burned your nose. Guests left Grandpa's hotel. The fire spread, and the following morning Grandpa had gathered all of us up in Johnny Lucia's truck, and when all my cousins had been accounted for, Johnny Lucia started to drive away."

Dorna stopped talking and looked across the living room and out its window. Now, instead of the hayfields, she saw a valley filling with a smoke, a white acrid smoke that burned her eyes, and she smelled the sharp, stinging odor of a spreading fire and heard the panicky voices emerging from the smoke. She heard her grandfather—barking commands, half in Italian, half in English—watched him herd her and her cousins toward Johnny Lucia's idling truck, his loose suspenders flopping behind him.

"*. . .think of what we've been, and not kiss again . . .*"

"I was thinking about these songs out in the kitchen," Dorna said.

"Yeah?"

"They're all about losing something, aren't they?"

Annalee looked at Dorna. "What happened to the scarf?"

"When Johnny's truck started to pull away, I remembered the scarf in its little box back in the room where I'd slept, and I jumped out the back of the truck. My cousins all shouted at me, but I didn't care. I ran back toward the hotel, and just as I reached the first step, someone just lifted me right off my feet and carried me back to the truck. It was Grandpa. I kicked and screamed for him to let me go."

"You never told me this story before," Annalee said.

"It's my clearest memory as a young girl, and one that keeps playing again and again. It's as though it'd just happened yesterday."

The two women sipped from their coffee cups.

"Silly, I know—a stupid little scarf."

Annalee lit another cigarette and sat back in the couch.

"Don't sound that silly to me."

"But Grandpa's hotel didn't burn down, and the scarf was there when I returned. But I still think that I lost the scarf forever, that it burned up, even though it didn't."

"That's weird, Dorna."

"I was just imagining what Irv would think if he walked in on us now, with the record player on, and me in tears. I'd be embarrassed. Maybe even feel a little foolish. He'd look at me and ask 'What's wrong?' and I wouldn't know how to answer."

"You can't be workin' every wakin' moment, can you?"

"I couldn't tell him what's wrong because I don't really know myself—I'm sad, I have these feelings—they're not Irv's fault even though I try to blame him."

"It's normal."

"Normal?"

"I think so. What's it to Irv, anyway, if you take an hour or two for yourself? What do you think he's doin' up at the auction yards right now?"

"I feel guilty that I'm not doing more—that I'm wishing the business would go under just to prove I'm right—it's terrible to feel this way."

"You work harder than anyone I know, Dorna."

"I don't feel I match up, that I don't want the same things Irv does, and God's punishing me because of it."

Dorna listened to the music. The words were about being "just friends."

"Irv says it isn't so bad if you don't think about it, and I ask him, 'How do you do that?' That's when Irv grins a bit—the way he does when he thinks he knows something you don't. 'Just work hard all the time,' he says, 'and the good Lord'll provide. Work hard because that's what we're put here to do. No mystery to it. The more you think about it,' he says, 'the more complicated it becomes.'"

"But who wants to work all the time?" Analee asked. "I sure don't. Besides, you can't just work all the time—it's impossible. Sooner or later, you gotta stop—or fall over dead. What do they say? Stop and smell the goddamn roses?"

"Whenever he catches me crying—and it's less and less now because I don't let him see it—he asks, 'what are you so unhappy about? Is life that bad?' And I can't tell him why. All the things I've ever thought of saying disappear, and I stand there like an idiot. Maybe I'm afraid to tell him. Or maybe the real reason is I just don't know—can't put my finger on any one thing."

"We're a pair, aren't we?" Dorna said.

"It's my fault," Annalee said.

"What is?

"You're feelin' this way. If I hadn't come up here and

told you what I told you, you wouldn't be sad."

"I don't think it's that simple, Annalee."

The song played to its end and then a new one began. *"I'll never smile again . . ."*

The two women looked at each other.

"So, what do we do—laugh or cry?" Dorna asked.

"To hell with it—let's just laugh!"

They sipped at their coffee as the song played to its end.

"I need to start a load of wash."

Dorna followed Annalee out to the kitchen door. They faced each other and embraced.

"You feel much softer, more relaxed than when you arrived," Dorna said.

"I do?"

"You do."

"If you leave Mario, you have a place to stay here, okay? That's a promise."

"You're the best."

"Promise you'll tell me if things get worse."

"I will."

"Cross your heart?"

"Cross my heart."

The two women embraced once again, and walked out into the yard, their arms around each other. Annalee opened the door to her Pontiac, and slid in behind the wheel. She gunned the motor after it started, slipped the transmission into reverse, and the car lurched backwards. They waved goodbye to each other.

Back inside, the house seemed quieter, emptier than Dorna could remember. She bussed the coffee cups back to the kitchen sink and wiped off the table. She emptied out the ash trays, and in the living room, she returned the Sinatra album back inside its jacket. She fluffed up the sofa cushions. Now it looked as if no one had sat there. She looked around the room one more time, and picked up the record album and walked over to the cabinet and slipped it amongst the other albums. Irv would be home soon, and he'd want his lunch.

Willie the Wire Man

i

It was a late April morning, the rains had come and gone, and the grass was already browning along the hilltops. The sun shone brightly, so brightly Angelo Miller formed a visor with his right hand as he looked out past the gum grove, looking for nothing in particular. Everything appeared clear and newly washed, as though he were viewing his surroundings through a giant lens for the first time. It was quiet, save for the lowing of a distant heifer, and the approaching *put-put* sound of the John Deere tractor Angelo's dad drove to the shop to add air to an under-inflated tire. Angelo's two older brothers, Junior and Jackie, had ridden to town with their mother, and he enjoyed this rare time alone, when he could daydream freely, slip further inside himself, follow whatever impulses wandered across his ten year old's mind. He'd opened the door of the shop, switched on the air compressor, and within seconds, its motor quickly shattered the morning stillness. He dragged the air hose out to where his dad had stopped the tractor.

Irv Miller stepped down, grabbed the hose from his son, loosened the stem cap, and began filling the tire. Angelo watched his dad work, saw how the soles and heels of his dad's boots had worn to their outsides, and watched as the flattened tire swelled with air. Dozens of thoughts, sensations, tripped across his mind as he stood there, mute, absorbed. Junior, his oldest brother, often mocked him by singing "Beautiful Dreamer" whenever Angelo's attention wandered, which was often. Minutes, perhaps centuries later, when Angelo looked up, a jerry-rigged GMC flatbed truck with boarded sides had appeared in front of the hay barn, as though dropped from a distant planet, and a lanky man with skin the color of a Hershey chocolate bar stood by a pile of used baling wire, toeing at the wire with an over-sized boot. Angelo tapped his dad on the shoulder and pointed toward the man. Irv Miller glanced over, then shouted back, "That's Willie, Willie the wire man!"

Irv Miller reached up and shut the tractor off, while Angelo reeled the air hose back inside the shop.

The black man joined Irv by the tractor. "Toppa the mornin' to you, Mistah Millah—and I'll take whatever's lef'." He lifted a pork pie hat briefly, then returned it to where it had rested before, on a pile of tight, black curls at the back of his head. Army-issue khaki pants were gathered at his waist, and a khaki shirt, its sleeves rolled up past a pair of bony ebows, hung on the man's frame. The outlines of removed patches showed on both sleeves and above the pockets. Along his jaw-line sprouted silvery whiskers that looked like metal filings. His eyes reminded Angelo of pooled oil—liquid and dark, their whites yellowed, and the young boy observed how the black man's mouth seemed like elastic, broadening quickly into a smile, then collapsing, as though suddenly remembering something he'd forgotten.

"What d'you know, Willie?" Irv asked.

"Same as always which ain't that much, 'cept it's slim pickins' this trip. Mus' be my competition gettin' the one-up on me."

"You need to set that alarm clock earlier," Irv said.

"This here a little Mistah Millah?" Willie placed a hand on the top of Angelo's head.

"That's my youngest, Angelo."

"Where'd you get that red hair?" Willie asked. "Yo' daddy not tell you somethin'?"

Angelo shrugged his shoulders.

"I'm gonna call you, Mistah Red—that okay?" O', like my mama use ta say, 'Call me anythin' but late fo' sup-pah.'" Willie's mouth widened.

"Sure," Angelo said. "Mister Red's fine."

"Got a job for you, Willie," Irv said. "Interested?"

"Mistah Irv, you look the backa my truck, and it ain't but half a load a metal, and Dellah ain't gonna like me comin' back like that. This man's gotta haul 'im back somethin'—-so, I am 'deed interesed."

"I need a water line dug from the hay barn out to the pig pen. I'll pay you fifteen bucks, and a couple packages of beef. Junior's been carrying water out there in milk cans, and come hot weather he ain't gonna keep up with 'em hogs."

"This here Willie can do that, Mistah Millah." Willie took out a blue handkerchief and wiped at his mouth. "Mistah Millah, can I ask you somethin' fuhst? Somethin' a little troublin' ta me?"

Irv looked at Willie.

"It happen earlier this mawnin' and it ain't set with me

good, an' I thought you was one I could tell." Willie wiped at his mouth, and looked around, as though careful not to be overheard. "You know there's folks ain't like you, Mistah Millah. Folks that look on me different. Lotsa folks—you know what I'm sayin'?"

"Something happen?"

"Yes, sir, Mistah Millah, and I'm gettin' to it. This mawnin' I go past here and turned up the road—Sonoma Mountain, they call it? I was thinkin' a othah' fahms I could fetch some metal with. Down a stretch, maybe two, three miles, and I pull into the first fahm there up that road on the lef'. There's a whole row of gum trees runnin' up its side, and everywhere there's cahs and tractahs, fahm tools all of 'em broken, stacked up, scattahed hell to breakfas'. Is like this junk man's dream."

"Sounds like Jenkin's place."

"Two big boys live there? Don't see no older folks, jus' 'em two."

"Leroy and Buster. They're brothers."

"Got mean eyes—'specially the little one. I feel it right away. Them boys fixin' to no good. I stay in the truck, and say, 'You got scrap metal I can take?' They look at one an-othah, and grin some—but it ain't no friendly grin, no sir, it's a connivin' grin. I mean everywhere there's scrap metal that ain't been used—piles of it jus' rustin' 'way."

"Yeah, we got some, the little one said. Why you wanna know?"

"Why I haul it 'way fo' you.

"It ain't fo' niggahs. That's what he say—jus' bold like that. Now I'm from Mississipppi, Mistah Millah, and that's the kinda words I grown up hearin' down there. I mean, it ain't like you don' hear it up here—you do—but you don' hear it open-said like these boy's usin' it. Right away it give me a bad feelin'. Then they says it's a private road I drive up, and I need special permission to pass, and I said I don' believe that's true. Don' say no private road. Ain't seen no signs. That a private road, Mistah Millah?"

"No, that ain't a private road."

"That's when the little one, he stop grinnin' and say 'You arguin' with us? You come up here to startin' a fight, is that it?' And I said, 'No, I ain't. No way. I'm just pickin' up metal like I done fo' yeahz. 'We been heah a long time, and if I say that road's a private one, then it's a private one.' And I said, 'No, sir, I come up for haulin' metal away, and nothin' else. Don' want no trouble. But that road out there don' say 'private' no where."

"The littler one, he don' let up. Come right to my truck, his face a changin' color, spittin' hate all ova 'im. 'You get yo black ass outta here,' he say, and don' come back. All of you's coons, he says. Go back where you come from 'cause we don't want you here, undahstand? Why you come up heah, huh? Makin' trouble, that's it. Why didn' you stay back where you was?' And I tell 'em, Mistah Kaisah sent fo' us to build them ships, and that's what we done. Now we finished, and it back to scrapin' by again. 'Mistah Kaisah, my ass,' the little one say. Y'all a bunch of fuckin' cotton pickahs!"

"Now I'm a peaceful man, Mistah Irv. Don't get no back up 'bout most peoples. Jus' as soon let things slide ovah me—Dellah been my teachah. The bible, too. I keep my mouth shut, mostly. Bear up and try to tuhn the othah cheek, just like the bible say, even though the blood inside it's a stirrin'. But I don' like bein' talk to like that. Ain't no man like it. That's when I put the Jimmy in geah and drive outta there, but the little one he walkin' aside my truck, and he's a pointin' his fingah at me sayin' 'Don' come back up that road out there again. That's *our* road!"

"You done the right thing, Willie," Irv said.

"And all them farms above 'em? Can I get to 'em without usin' that road?"

"You can't. That's the only road up and back."

"It got me riled, Mistah Irv. Scared, sho' but mad, too. This man's heart just a thumpin' hard—all roiled up the whole time."

"Willie, it's best just to avoid those two. Leroy ain't so bad, but that Buster—he's just mean, real mean. He caught Mikie Coleman fishing in their pond last year, and beat him bad—tore patches of hair right out of his head. I don't know why Buster ain't in prison—but their old man's been around here a long time—he's got friends, connections."

"Show me that ditch you want dug, Mistah Millah. Need to get my mind off 'em two."

Irv, Willie and Angelo walked out through the back corral and stopped at the corner of the haybarn. "The water line's here." Irv pointed down to a galvanized pipe stubbed out with Tee. "And the line needs to go out to those little sheds there." Irv motioned to two hog houses eighty feet away. Their metal roofs glistened in the morning sun. "Trouble is this was old creekbed at one time—rocks everywhere."

All three walked out past the corral. Angelo followed a step behind, noticing how Willie's arms and legs moved with an easy rhythm. Willie stopped every few steps and scraped at the soil with his boot. "I'll give her a go," Mistah Irv. Like I said, can't go home with jus' half a pocket."

"Angelo'll show you where the hand tools are—he can help you, too."

"You gonna help ol' Willie, Mistah Red?"

"Yes, sir," Angelo said.

"That's good. Fuhst thin' we scratch us a line where the hole go."

Angelo walked back to the hay barn, took a wheelbarrow and filled it with hand tools—a pick, a square-point shovel, a round-pointed one, and a steel pry bar. He tossed in a pair of leather work gloves. When he returned to the work site, his dad had run a string line out from the corner of the barn, across the corral and to the pig pen. Willie took the pick and began scratching a line alongside the string. Irv walked back to where Willie was working.

"You're on your own now." Irv handed Willie a tape measure and a pencil. "Make the ditch about eighteen inches deep—I usually mark the handle of the shovel so you'll know when you're deep enough . Don't have to be wide—just enough to drop a galvanized pipe down. You need anything else, just ask Angelo, and he'll get it for you."

"Yes, suh, Mistah Millah. Got me Mistah Red, heah, my helpah."

"Water's good right out of the tap," Irv said. "The missus fixed sandwiches for lunch. Should be enough for you, too. "

"That's mighty fine, Mistah Millah."

Willie swung the pick down, straddling the line he'd scratched in the soil, while humming, *Jesus, won't you help me, I'm fallin' again.* The first few inches of ground broke up easily, and Angelo followed behind shoveling the ditch clean. Within an hour Willie had dug a shallow trench the entire distance. But as Willie dug deeper, the pick clanged off buried rocks, and the digging became harder, slower. "Them's rattlahs, Mistah Red. Vibratin' me right down to my toes."

Willie would dig for ten, fifteen consecutive minutes, then stop, set the pick down, take out his blue handkerchief and wipe the sweat from his face. "How's by you, Mistah Red?" he'd ask.

"Good, I'm doing okay," Angelo said.

"Say—whach you? Irish? German?"

"My mom's Italian—

"Whach you do if someone say can't do somethin' 'cause you Eyetalian? O' poke fun 'cause you's a Daygo?"

"I don't know—I'm pretty tough. I knocked Ronnie Brock down last month," Angelo said.

"He call you somepin?"

"No, they were just being mean. It was after school and I was going to Elliott's for a *Green River* soda when they come up behind me, making fun of my school uniform, and saying things like, 'I wish it was Friday, 'cause I'd jam a fish down his throat.' Stuff like that. They're all public school kids. Then Ronnie Brock jumped on my back, and I threw him down. He hit the sidewalk hard."

"They don' be messin' with Mistah Red." Willie clapped his hands together.

"He got up up fast and swung at me and I ducked. Then I hit him just above the ear, and he went down and started crying. Not loud, but you could hear him sniffling."

"Where'd you learn to fight like that, Mistah Red?"

"From my brothers."

"You like to fight, Misah Red?"

"No I don't, but Ronnie Brock jumped me."

Willie rested his arm on the top of a shovel. "Don' know if it's the same, though, but maybe it is. Maybe don' mattah the reason—if you a black man o' you some religion someone else don' like. Some folks is jus' stupid—no more sense than that there pile of rock." Willie dropped his shovel and grabbed the pick. "Reckon don't do no good to think abou' it much. Take away from the ditch diggin', but it's teasin' inside my head jus' the same."

"You like working?" Angelo asked, "Doing what you do?"

"That's like askin' if I like breathin.' Sometimes I do and sometimes I don', but I ain't got no choice in the mattah. Besides, why you ask me that?

"Junior says you folks don't like to work."

"How Junior know what we like an' what we don'?"

"That's just what he says. And Junior's pretty smart."

Willie stopped and thought. "Sometimes I like it jus' fine—'specially when the Jimmy purrin' and I got a truckload of metal behind me. And Mistah Red, there ain't purtier country to be ridin' through than whach you got heah. Last month I come up that rise there by the mud buildin' and look out, and it's 'bout as purty a pickchah this man evah seen—jus' like them calendahs. Yo' daddy's cows out there eatin' grass, jus' so fat and happy. I think how could heaven be better'an this? Yes, suh, you one lucky fellah, Mistah Red, to be livin' where you do."

"You could move up here, too, couldn't you?" Angelo leaned against the shovel handle.

Willie laughed. "Oh, yeah, I guess I could. But you know there's gonna be folks that ain't gonna like that at all—I can think a two right now."

"Maybe you could stay here on the ranch. We got an old bunkhouse that my dad just stores stuff in now. "

"Well, thank you, Mistah Red, for considerin' that, but my Dellah, she settled in where she is now, and seem to like it fine. Besides we got us a passul a kids and cousins roun' the house—they'd drive yo' daddy crazy." Willie swung the pick. "I be talkin' too much, Mistah Red."

Willie had worked through the easier top soil and now had reached ground peppered with rocks the size of soft-balls. Willie picked and pried at them, scooped the smaller ones up in his shovel and tossed them to the side of the ditch. The larger ones he reached down and grabbed as though picking melons in a field. He'd stop every few minutes, wipe his brow, look at the trench deepening below him. Angelo followed behind and tossed out any of the stones Willie had missed.

"You an' me, we a team, Mistah Red."

"Maybe we'll finish before lunch," Angelo said.

"Now I ain't sayin' that 'cause we still got us a distance." Willie looked toward the pig pens. "If I could choose, though, I'd pick me easiah groun' to be diggin' and it'd all be in the shade with a little breeze a coolin' me, and when I was done, somebody'd be handin' me a mint juleep. But if I'm goin' that fah, I'd jus' wish me piles of ol' brass radiatahs and a new truck to haul 'em away in, and forget 'bout this diggin' all togethah. And if I go to wishin' even mo' I'd have me a junk yahd. And I'd have me hawgs. But what a man to do?" Willlie glanced back at Angelo. "Howz 'bout you?"

"I want a horse."

"Then get yo'self one! That seems easier wishin' than what I done."

"I'm saving. Got nearly ten dollars in the bank. Every Tuesday I give them something."

"That's good. Preparin' yo'self fo' what's ahead, 'cause unless you bohn with 'em silver spoons, we all be workin'. Thatz o' lot, 'specially you heah with all 'em cows. But you one-up on the Mistah Willie heah—you got yo'self some lan' and some cattle."

Willie walked back to the corner of the barn, stooped over and drank water from the faucet there. When he stood back up, he bent backwards, put both broad hands over his kidneys, and then turned from side to side. He pulled his handkerchief out of his pocket, soaked it under the tap, wrung it out, and ran it across his face.

"You like Elvis Prezzly?"

"Yeah, I do."

"Why don' you get yo'self a guitar and do what he does? Practice some when you ain' diggin' ditches. You get good 'nough you buy any horse you wan'."

"You think I can do that?"

"Shoh, you can do anythin'. He juz took what we'd been doin' and made it fo' white folks, you know that? Where you think he got to singin' about some houn' dog?"

"He just made it up?" Angelo said.

"It *all* made up—then get made-up again—I ain't be-grudgin' him nothin. Myself, I like Elvis—he from same part of Mississippi as I am—a section of Tupelo called

"Gum Pond." It blowed 'way in '36, and thatz how I end up in the country—Baldwyn, New Albany—my family movin' 'round like the birds, stoppin' anyplace at'll take us in. We both Mississippi stump jumpahs, Mistah Red, me an' Elvis Prezzly. You know that?"

"I could ride my horse and play guitar," Angelo said.

"You can sing them cowboy songs, Mistah Red—wear them duds them cowboys wear, and purty soon them cowgirls be fallin' ovah you, jus' like they fallin' ovah Elvis Prezzley. An' if you evah need a truck to be haulin' yo'self 'roun in, you think of Mistah Willie, heah, wonch you?"

Angelo smiled at the thought of Willie behind the wheel of a brand new GMC.

"If you like me—you need some time for philosphizin' too. You can' be workin' all the time. If I can do that while workin' that's good work. Like earliah, I'm thinkin' what if I jus' kep' diggin' deepah and deepah, then what? Down, down, diggin' deepah all the time. Whach you think gonna happen?"

"I don't know—maybe hit water?"

"You smaht, Mistah Red—you do one kind of philosophizin' and I do the othah. You know what I was thinkin'? If we keep diggin' we hit them China men with them funny hats—that's my kind of philosphizin'. Yo' kind probly make mo' sense."

Angelo turned to see his dad walking toward them.

"How's the diggin', Willie?" Irv Miller had one foot up on the corral fence.

"You was right 'bout the rocks, Mistah Millah—there's a pile of 'em."

"The missus made sandwiches before she left, and set a table under the palm trees. Let's go eat."

"My stomach, it's been a talkin' to me. My mind jus' a chatterin' too, Mistah Millah."

Willie put the hand tools in the wheelbarrow. Angelo,

Irv and Willie walked back toward the house where Dorna Miller had set a table beneath the palm tree closest to the house. All three washed their hands in the back porch laundry sink. In the refrigerator, Angelo found the platter of egg sandwiches covered with wax paper and carried them outside. Dorna had sliced pickles into long wedges, and stacked them on a smaller plate. Irv Miller carried those out along with a pitcher of lemonade and set them in the middle of the table. When all three were seated, Willie removed his hat, bowed his head, and muttered a prayer to himself. He waited for Irv and Angelo to bite into their sandwiches first.

"Ain't nothin' wrong with this." Willie ate two sandwiches after some coaxing by Irv. After he'd finshed the sandwiches, he drank the last of his lemonade, set the glass down and stared off across the yard. "I wanna buy me a gun, Mistah Millah."

"What kind of gun you wanna buy, Willie?"

"Somethin' I can hunt with."

"What do you wanna hunt?"

"Rabbits—I was thinkin' rabbits."

"You're not thinkin' about those Jenkins boys, are you?"

"Oh, no, Mistah Millah. I was thinkin' mostly 'bout rabbits."

"A .22's probably your best bet then. A smaller gauge shot gun'd work, too, but these rabbits ain't gonna let you get close enough, so you're better off with a rifle."

"Thank you, Mistah Millah."

After lunch, Irv Miller excused himself, said it was time for his nap before beginning the afternoon milking. Willie and Angelo returned to their ditch work.

"That lunch was jus' right, Mistah Red. You eat any mo' you get lazy and jus' wanna lay down, say good-bye to workin'."

Willie picked and pried, and by 3 o'clock had finished the ditch. He'd marked a stick at eighteen inches, and walked the entire length, checking its depth every couple of feet. When he walked back and forth a couple of times, he looked over at Angelo. "Think yo' daddy gonna like it?"

"It looks good, Willie."

"You know, the devil, he been talkin' to me since mawnin'. Just chatterin', chatterin'."

"About what?"

"Mos'ly 'bout them Jenks boys. Paht a me wanna give 'em their come-uppance, you know what I'm sayin'?"

"You wanna punch them in the nose?"

"Yeah, somethin' like that. Hurt 'em bad. But anothah paht sayin' Mistah Willie, you jus' gotta turn the othah cheek."

"They don't even know you."

"Thas' right. An' maybe they'd feel the same way if they did—thas' what bother me mos'—that ol' Willie don't cut it no mo'. That ol' Willie bad, and them boys know it. You think they thinkin' that?"

"They called you names."

"Thas' right."

"And it made you mad."

"And it's a corrodin' me inside." Willie looked up and down the ditch. "It's jus' names, right? Don' mean nothin', ain't tha' what they say? No sense to think 'bout it. We haul them tools back?"

Angelo loaded the hand tools back into the wheelbarrow. His dad was bringing the cows in for the afternoon milking, and a long line of them walked past Willie and Angelo, down a wide lane that led in from the upper pasture and funneled the cows down one side of the hay barn.

"Them look like happy cows," Willie said.

"Dad's got names for most of them."

"He do? What kind of names?"

"That one there he calls 'Topsy.'" Angelo pointed to a little Jersey. "And the brindle one right behind her he calls

'Fatty Arbuckle.' And the big Holstein—that's Junior's—she's 'Laddie Arlene.' She's registered."

"Yo' daddy 'member all them names?"

"Everyone of them."

"You one lucky child, Mistah Red."

Angelo wheeled the tools back to the shop. As he crossed the yard, he noticed their Chevy was back in its garage. His mom and two brothers had returned from town. Junior, who was sixteen, met him at the shop.

"What's that truck doing here?" Junior asked.

"That's Willie's truck."

"Where's he at?"

"I suppose over talking with dad. He and I dug the ditch out to the hog pens."

"I was gonna do that—

"Willie needed the work, and dad hired him."

"Yeah, but dad promised me that job. How much he pay him?"

"I don't know. Fifteen dollars, maybe."

"Shit!" Junior looked at Angelo, and then at Willie's truck, before walking across the farm yard toward where Angelo and Willie had dug the ditch. Angelo followed behind him. The cows were all bunched into the holding corral, waiting now to be milked. Irv had closed the gate behind the last of them, and was talking with Willie. They both walked over and looked at the ditch again. Satisfied with the work, Irv reached into his hip pocket, pulled out his wallet, and counted out three five dollar bills. He handed the bills to Willie, and the two men shook hands.

"Thank you, Mistah Millah."

"Junior, Angelo—one of you—get Willie a couple a packages of stew meat out of the freezer, would you?" Irv put his wallet back into his pocket. "You like lamb chops, Willie?"

"Yes, suh, I do!"

"Get Willie a package of lamb chops, too."

"I'll get 'em," Angelo said. As he walked away, he heard Junior say, "You promised me that job." Angelo stopped and listened.

"I've been houndin' you to do it," Irv said, "And you're always busy with something else."

"You promised!"

"Willy here needed some work."

"You go back on your word? How else am I gonna buy that Jeep?"

"I don' want no hard feelins' Mistah Millah—I give the money back to you."

"Hell, no, you earned it."

"There's other jobs you can do, son," Irv said.

"Oh, yeah, that's what you always say—"

"C'mon, Junior—"

"You promised—"

"All right, I promised—"

"That's what you do—anytime I can make a little money, you give the job to someone else. You promise and then you break your promise. It pisses me off!" Junior turned and walked past Angelo. "You knew I was countin' on that job—you knew!"

"Mistah Millah, I didn' mean to go startin' somethin'"

"It's all right, Willie."

When Angelo had returned with the packages of meat, Willie had forked the pile of baling wire into the back of his truck, and tossed in a broken disc blade Irv had set aside. Willie circled his truck, kicking each of its tires, pushing against the side-boards, and glancing at the undercarriage. "Look all right," he said. He opened the driver's door and as he climbed up behind the wheel, he glanced at himself in the side-view mirror. "This man look tired." He dangled one foot out the door, and a big grin broadened his face when Angelo handed him the packages of meat. "Yo' bro-thah ain't too happy."

"He wants to buy a Jeep."

"If I knowed that I wouldn'a dug the ditch."

"He'd started to dig it a couple of times, but then he saw how hard the digging was."

"Dellah gonna be happy 'bout somethin', at least. Hey, Mistah Red, why don' you an' me, we can staht a ditch diggin' business? Whach you think?"

"And maybe dig where there aren't so many rocks?"

Willie laughed. "You a smaht boy, Mistah Red."

The truck started up. It shook and rattled. Willie slammed the door shut. Angelo climbed up on the running board as the truck started to roll forward. "See you next time, Willie."

"Yes, suh, you will."

Angelo watched Willie drive away. He walked back to the hay barn where Junior was dropping bales of alfalfa onto a trailer the John Deere pulled.

"Dad said he'd pay me to dig that ditch—he knows I'm trying to save money," Junior said.

"Willie needed work."

"So do I. And what's he go and do—hire a goddamn ni—"

"Dad said he'd find you more work."

"And pay me with what? Says he don't have it, but he's got if for others." Junior stabbed at a hay bale and threw it down on the trailer. It hit hard, and the bale split apart. "It's bull shit, that's what it is!"

"You want some help, Junior?"

"No, I don't need your help—I can do it myself."

ii

Three weeks later Willie appeared once again at Irv Miller's dairy. It was just before the afternoon milking. The hills were brown now. He parked his truck where he'd parked it before. Another pile of baling wire had grown up, and next to it was an old radiator Irv had found at the back of the shop and a fruit lug filled with rusted chunks of steel, bolts with stripped threads, a half dozen broken leaf springs—Irv Miller's offering to the metal scavenger. Irv and Angelo walked over to greet him. Willie stepped out of his truck, and shook hands with the two. Willie was smiling.

"Got somethin' to show you, Mistah Millah." Willie reached under the truck seat and pulled out a .22 rifle. He handed it to Irv. It was a pump-action. The rifle's stock had been taped and wired together right behind the trigger. "Bought it from a pawn shop on Telegraph Avnew fo' five dollahs and a radio I ain't been usin'. Whach you think?"

Irv worked the action back and forth. "It'll get you rabbits, okay.

"You supposin' I can try my luck today? Ain't nothin' like bringin' some fresh rabbit back home. Oh, and Dellah like that stew meat you give me, too. She says "God bless you.' And those lamb chops? I suck on them bones for half a hour."

Irv laughed. "Angelo, why don't you take Willie up above the hay racks? All along that dry creek bed, where the rabbits dug it all out. You'll find 'em in there. Let me get the cows in first."

"You good to me, Mistah Millah." Wille reached back inside the truck cab again and pulled out a green army-issue belt with a canteen attached to it, and a leather pouch tied to one side. He dropped a couple of apples into the pouch, and box of .22 shells. He lifted the belt onto his waist and slid the buckles together. "What you think?"

"I'd say you're ready to hunt rabbits." Irv Miller smiled.

Willie grinned, adjusted the belt around his waist, and pulled it down until it rested at the tops of his hips. Satisfied with the fit, he slipped it off, and placed it back on the truck seat. "Lemme load this wiah fuhst, and tha' give yo' daddy time to bring them cows in."

After removing a rear panel, Willy loaded the wire and the radiator onto the back of the truck, then hoisted the fruit lug up and pushed it forward. He climbed up and re-arranged the load. Half the truck bed was already loaded with baling wire. Stacked on each side were gutted water heaters, and a pair of long rusted steel I-beams.

"Got me a bettah load today than las', Mistah Red."

When all the cows were in, Irv whistled to Angelo and Willie. Willie grabbed the belt from inside the truck cab and snapped it back on, and took the rifle from off the top of the seat. He and Angelo walked to the top of the yard, opened the gate alongside the hay barn, and continued out toward the upper pasture. Petey, the dog, walked a half dozen steps in front of them.

"He ain't gonna run off them rabbits, is he?

"No, you just tell him to stay, and he'll stay."

"Tha's a smart dog you got there, Mistah Red."

Willie and Angelo walked out past the barns. "How that ditch doin'?"

"It's all covered up. Got a water line out to the hogs now," Angelo said

"And your brothah? He still mad at Willie?"

"He wants a Jeep bad."

Beyond the hay racks the pasture swelled into gentle hills shaped like rolling ocean swells. The soil was cratered where the cows' hooves had sunk in when it was muddy, and now, after the soil had dried, it was like walking across a giant honeycomb. The first rabbit popped up from the hay racks, a long stalk of alfalfa jutting from the corner of its mouth, its tall ears turning to each sound. Willie didn't waste any time. He shouldered his .22 and touched off a quick round that dropped the rabbit in its tracks. Angelo and Willie walked up to it, and the rabbit was lying on its side, its back feet still twitching. Willie grabbed the rabbit by its neck and give it a quick twist. "This rifle shoot good, Mistah Red!" Boils had pushed up through the fur on the rabbit's back. Angelo stuffed the rabbit into a gunny sack, and they walked toward the creek bed. The next rabbit sprang up from a dry wash, and Willie knocked the rabbit down with a hind shot, and finished it off with a clean one to its heart. Angelo stuffed that rabbit in the sack, as well. By now rabbits were zig-zagging across the field like pin-balls, disappearing down into the dry wash, before springing up again, stopping suddenly, still as statues, their long ears cocked, scanning every direction for sounds before bolting off in long graceful leaps. Petey whimpered and shook, and Angelo ran a hand along the dog's back, talking to it in a quiet voice.

"Look like I still got me an eye for shootin'. How they say in the army? A shawp shootah?"

They reached the top of the hill, but by then most of the rabbits had scattered after hearing the rifle shots.

"I need to sit a spell, Mistah Red." They sat down on the side of the hill, and Willie wiped his forehead with a big blue bandanna. "Ol' knees ain't used to walkin' up and down like this. I got me city knees now—jus'used to walkin' flat. They talkin' to me right now, askin' what the hell you doin' Mistah Willie?"

They sat down on the side of the hill. Angelo opened the sack and looked inside at the dead rabbits.

"Yes, sir, this a pretty spot all right." Willie slid the leather pouch around to his front, and pulled out an apple. "Any of my folks live up here?"

"Your folks?"

"Yeah, cullud folks."

Angelo thought. "Henry the Shoeshine lives in town. He lost his legs in a railroad accident, and pushes himself around on a mechanic's creeper. He's got a stand in front of Western Avenue Barbers. He's the only one I can think of."

"So, ain't a lotta us?"

Willie shifted, reached into his pocket and pulled out a knife. He cut a slice of apple off and handed it to Angelo, the apple section resting on top of the blade. Then he cut a section for himself. "Them's still a little bittah, and green, ain't they? Picked 'em off Mistah Biondah's place. He don' mind, says they early, but you help yo'self.'"

Angelo pulled up blades of dry grass by his boots.

"I miss the country, Mistsh Red. You know that? Everytime I come up here, I ask myself, why ain't I livin' in a place like this? Why am I livin' where the houses all stuck together, where they ain't no room to spread out— no room to grow things? It all run counter to my likin'"

"Why don't you move to the country then?"

Willie laughed. "Ain't all that easy once you got roots set. And, you know, it gonna rile some folks, too, us movin' up heah." Willie cut another wedge of apple, and handed it to the boy.

"You know if I lived up here, the first thing I'd do?"

"No, what would you do?"

"I'd buy me a hawg—a little piglet—and I'd feed that little pig everyday—stale bread, sour milk, greens everythin' folks toss away them pigs jus' lov. Nothin' goin' to waste. They slop it down like a buttahscotch shake. It plump 'im up, get 'im fat and round and then I'd slaugthah' 'im—don't like doin' it, don't like harmin' nothin' really but what you gonna do with a pig you been feedin' for ten months? Same with these rabbits. Ain't like you gonna keep 'im 'round the house, take him fo' walks, right? No, we all got purpose in this world—like the bible say somewhere, and it's the pig's bad luck his purpose is to get eaten. And what a rabbit for, but eatin'? Ain't that right, Mistah Red?"

"Yeah, hogs are unlucky all right. I don't know what else to do with a pig, either, besides eat it. We had little goats once, and they followed us around like dogs. Then we heard my cousins were coming to take them away, and we tried hiding them, but my cousins found them. I cried when they hauled those goats off."

"Well, with the hawg, you know what I do?"

"What?"

"Folks they all clamo' 'bout big roasts and such—now I ain't takin' nothin' away from roasts—a pawk roast done right with 'tateahs and greens with some biscuits and gravy on the side—it's bettah than—Mistah Red, I can't tell what it's bettah than—you too young—but if it was me, that pig'd be groun' up into sausages—fresh sausages—Lawd sakes, Mistah Red, if I had my way, the whole pig'd be sausages. You can eat sausages from one pig for days and days, weeks if you stretch it out with greens and gravy. But how long you gonna eat with pawk roasts? The dinin' gonna be rich fo' a coupla days, and that's it. Then it's gone, and you lookin' at a pile of bones, and wishin' there was mo'. Wishin' you done somethin' to stretch it out longah. You ain't gonna have but a coupla days with pork roasts—if you have that. But with sausages, you gonna have a month of eatin'." Willie stopped talking. A silence lingered between the two of them. "How them rabbits doin' in there, Mistah Red?"

"They're dead, Mister Willie."

"A couple more oughta make for 'nough eatin' to-night—I got some hungry boys, and Della ain't shy at the table herself." Willie looked off to the west.

"You know them Jenkins fellahs, Mistah Red?"

"I've always heard about them."

"What you heard?"

"Pretty much what my dad said. Buster's always picking fights, beating up folks. It's what they do."

"Them nasty boys, all right. What they said still ain't settlin' right with me, though, Mistah Red. I pray and pray, and think everythin' settled, but then them feelin's come boilin' up again. And them voices—they start in a chatterin' all ovah. It's the devil talkin' to me—I know."

"Dad says you best forget about it. That you leave them alone."

"I know all common sense point that way—and I'm a tryin' but it's stickin' in my craw. I pray on Sunday, askin' the Lawd to make me forgive 'em, but he ain't so free with it." Willie dropped a slice of apple into his mouth. "You look 'round here—'specially like I done the last time I was here, after it'd rained, and I come up over that hill there and what I seen make this man nearly cry. Mistah Red, it jus' seem so puhfeck. I know it ain't but I like to think it jus' the same. It couldn't be. Ain't no Promised Land. No way. Only heaven's puhfeck. If it my choice, I'd live right here—and I wouldn't care about heaven. That's the truth. Everythin' jus' look so perfeck. But I know it ain't perfeck. Perfeck's when the folks come out and wrap their ahms 'round you, and say, "Mistah Willie, you home now. You jus' like us. You free to slop that hawg, cut you some greens, put yo'chillun' on a bus that take 'em to school. But I know it ain't so. I know there's folks like them Jenkins boys out there—maybe more'an I evah suspeck."

"There's a house at Moretti's that's vacant. Maybe you could move there?"

Willie laughed. "I wish it was that easy."

"Hold out yo hand there, Mistah Red—go on, hold it out."

Angelo held his hand out, and Willie held his out right alongside Angelo's.

"Whach you see?"

"Two hands?"

"You look at 'em this way, they seem so different, don't they? Yo's is white and mine's black. Day and night, right? But flip that hand ovah. Go on. Now look at 'em. They look the same to you as they do to me?"

Angelo nodded his head.

"They the same. I wish mo' folks could see that, Mistah Red. I do." Willie stood up and stretched out his legs. "Time to get movin'. Headlights flickerin' on the

Jimmy—got it a shawt somewhere—so don't wanna be drivin' after dark. And still gotta skin them rabbits."

On their way back to the yard, Petey scared up another rabbit that zig-zagged back and forth, then headed straight toward Willie. He shot it from twenty yards, and shot one more lurking by the corner of the pig pen. Angelo lugged the sack with four rabbits back into the yard.

"You got us a place to skin and dress 'em, Mistah Red?"

"There's a sink in the tank house."

"That soun' good. Don't suppose you got a bucket for the innawds?"

"We got plenty of buckets."

"I'll get me my skinnin' knife and stone out the truck. Got a little coolah-box, too, I carry with me."

Angelo opened the door to the tank house. Inside was a laundry sink with a drain board to one side, and a window just above it that looked into the back yard. Willie followed Angelo inside, took the four rabbits out of the sack and laid them out on a counter next to the sink. He brought out his sharpening stone and ran it along each side side of the knife blade, then felt the blade with the pad of his thumb. "That's shawp now, Mistah Red." He picked the first rabbit up, laid it down on its back and cut around the front and back legs. He pulled at the cuts on the hind legs, and began peeling the fur forward evenly, up past the rabbit's thighs, peeling it all in one piece toward the front legs. "It jus' like takin' them long johns off," Willie said. When he reached the front legs, he re-cut around the top of each foot, then pulled the entire pelt up over the rabbit's head until slipped away from the body with a little slap. The rabbit's flesh was blue and ulcered along its back where the boils had blistered its pelt. Willie ran the skinning knife down the middle of the rabbit's under-side, opening the body cavity up. He reached in and pulled out its heart and lungs and a big clump of clotted blood where Willie had broken its neck. The rest of the guts Willie dropped into the bucket by his feet. Willie felt where the boils had blistered the skin, and cut around the base of each one, removing it as though it were a pit stuck in the middle of a peach. Junior walked in as Willie dressed the last rabbit. He looked at the rabbits laid out on the drain board.

"What's that all over their skin?' Junior asked.

"Them's boils," Willie said.

"You going to eat those rabbits?"

"Sho am."

"With all those boils?" Junior shook his head, turned and walked back to the house.

"Don't think he like me, Mistah Red."

When Willie finished dressing the last rabbit, he wrapped them in wet burlap and placed all four into his cooler-box. He washed his knife and dried it on the side of his pants. Then he washed his hands one more time.

"We got dinnah' tonight, Mistah Red—a most fine dinner."

Angelo followed Willie out to his truck. After Willie put the cooler box on the floorboard, he walked over to the milking barn. Irv Miller was in the breeze way, dumping milk into the hopper.

"Look like I'm all set, Mistah Millah."

"You got some rabbits?"

"Four of 'em—all skinned and dressed. You was right 'bout where to find 'em all right. They jus' a jumpin' up everywhere—that some dog you got there, too. He a real rabbit dog. And Mistah Red, heah, he was my guide." Irv and Willie shook hands. "Be goin' now—lights is actin' up on the truck."

Willie walked once around his truck, checking the tension on the ropes that kept the sideboards was splaying outwards. "She's ready," he said. "Gonna see you nex' time?"

"I'll be here," Angelo said.

"You save the metal fo' me, Mistah Millah?"

"Whatever I can find."

"Oh, tha's good, Mistah Millah—tha's real good."

Little billows of dust trailed Willie's truck down the driveway. Angelo followed behind, scooping his hand up through the tiny clouds. He walked out to the shoulder of Adobe Road, and watched the Jimmy crest the little hill before it disappeared.

iii

Angelo and Jackie were playing catch. Angelo had just thrown an inside fast ball, his best that late June morning. Mickey Mantle swung wildly at it and missed, nearly twisting out of his shoes. Angelo heard the phone ring. The musk of baled oat hay, the silence of fifty thousand Yankees fans hung in the air. Jackie returned the baseball in a slow, triumphant arc when their mother appeared at the back porch. "Get your father! Someone's been shot at Jenkins and they think it's Willie!"

Angelo dropped his glove, raced around the corner of the hay barn and found his dad replacing barn siding their bull had crashed through just a day earlier. Irv had just fitted a 1" x12" piece of redwood into the opening. Two 16 penny galvanized nails hung from the corner of his mouth. "Somebody shot Willy!"

Irv looked up. "Jesus Christ! When did it happen?"

"I don't know—c'mon, dad! Let's go!" Angelo pulled at his father's shirt. Irv quickly nailed off the board. Angelo, panicky, turned, dashed ten yards and turned back again. "C'mon, dad!"

Angelo sprinted back to the house, and into the kitchen. His mother was on the phone. "What'd they tell you, Ma?" She looked at Angelo, then stared down at the floor as she listened. "He's handcuffed? Oh, no! Did he die?"

"Ma! What's happening?" the boy demanded.

"Jenkin's place? Okay—Irv'll be right over."

"What happened? Tell me! They shoot Willie?"

"Someone's been shot—but I don't know who. That was Alice Baxter—she heard gunfire up at Jenkins' place, and called the sheriff. She said she saw Willie's truck stopped there."

Irv appeared at the kitchen door, still wearing his nail apron. Jackie stood behind his dad.

"Someone's been shot at Jenkins'," Dorna said. "You better go out there. Alice Baxter said it looked like Willie's truck—

"Goddamn it!" Irv shouted. "When'd it happen?"

"Twenty minutes ago."

"Where's the car?" Irv asked.

"Junior drove it down to Altenbacher's—you'll have to take the truck."

"Let's go!" Tears filled Angelo's eyes. He ran out the door to his dad's truck, started the motor, and then slid over to the passenger's side and waited. The back porch door slammed behind Irv and Jackie.

"Maybe you kids better stay here."

"No, I'm going! Willie's my friend!" Angelo grabbed the truck seat with both hands.

Irv climbed into his truck. Jackie slid in from the other side. "Hurry up, dad! Please!" Time slowed to a crawl for the boy. Irv's truck rolled slowly north on Adobe Road, mired-down, it seemed to Angelo, as though plowing the pavement behind it. The boy kept looking at the truck's speedometer, willing it to go faster. Angelo's hands remained on the dash board, his nose just inches from the windshield. His body trembled. "They shot him, didn't they?" Angelo said. "Those bastards shot him!"

"Shot who?" Jackie asked.

"The Jenkins brothers," Angelo said. "They didn't like

Willie 'cause he was black—"

"Did he die?" Jackie asked.

"Look, we don't know who shot who," Irv said. "Or if anyone died—nothin'. We don't know nothin' yet. So, just take it easy."

"What'd Willie do?" Jackie looked at his dad, then back at his brother.

"Willie didn't do anything," Angelo said. "I *know* him."

"He musta done something," Jackie said.

"He said they told him not to go up Sonoma Mountain Road."

"And he went up there?" Jackie asked.

"I don't know what happened—your mother got ten different versions from Alice Baxter," Irv said. "Alice can't remember her own name at times."

"Maybe Willie shot somebody," Jackie said.

"No—he doesn't even have a—" Irv stopped in mid-sentence.

"He's got the .22," Angelo said.

"Son-of-a-bitch," Irv said.

As they neared East Mountain Road, Angelo spied Willie's truck a half mile away. Irv backed off the accelerator, then braked hard as his pickup leaned around the corner. He shifted to a lower gear. Up ahead was Willie's truck, growing larger by the second in Irv's windshield. It faced downhill, angled off to the side of the road. Under its front axle was the back-end of a utility trailer still attached to an orange Farm-all tractor lying on its side in the ditch, the nose of the tractor buried in softened adobe. Angelo tried to sort out the scene. Two sheriffs' cars were parked on opposite sides of the road. Their radios blared through the open windows. At the entrance to Jenkin's ranch, two sheriffs and Leroy Jenkins knelt over a man, lying flat on his back, his feet splayed out. They weren't Willie's old army-issue boots that Angelo first saw.

Angelo sprung from his dad's truck before it even stopped rolling, and ran toward the men. It was Buster Jenkins on his back, staring straight up to the sky, his mouth open, a blank, dazed look on his face. Leroy, his brother, knelt next to him, repeating again and again, "You gonna be all right, Buster." Buster's shirt, soaked with blood, was torn open. One of the deputies was pressing down hard on Buster's collar bone, trying to stop the bleeding. Willie's rifle lie on the ground next to the deputy's feet.

Angelo looked everywhere for Willie.

"Buster, you all right?" Leroy Jenkins asked. It was the first time Angelo had ever seen the brothers up close. He'd always heard about them, had seen them from a distance—the big, hulking figure of Leroy, the cocky strut of his younger brother, Butch. Now, when Angelo looked at them, they seemed ordinary, not nearly as threatening as they'd become in his mind. Leroy's face and arms were sun-burnt, flushed, scarred deep from acne. He had big, work-roughened hands, and his work-shirt was cut off at the shoulders. "Buster, you gonna be all right," was all he said.

Buster winced, tried to raise his head.

"You just stay down there, Buster!" Leroy looked over at the deputy pressing down on Buster's wound. "I told him just let it go. Don't be stirrin' nothin' up. But he's got him a temper."

There was still no sign of Willie anywhere. Irv and Jackie Miller had now joined Angelo, Leroy and the two deputies. At first they stood just behind Angelo, before both leaned in for a closer look. Then Angelo slipped away and walked back to the road. Willie's truck had rolled over the rear of the utility trailer, and the GMC's radiator was leaking water. The whole truck smelled of over-heated brakes. Its left-front fender was caved in, the glass from a broken headlight lodged on top of the bumper. The trailer was completely flipped over, half of it wedged under the

GMC, its muddy undercarriage exposed. The tractor was on its side down in the ditch, tufts of tall weeds and adobe driven into its grill. The boy walked around Willie's truck, climbed up its back, and looked over its sideboards. The truck bed was full—as full as Angelo'd ever seen it— heaped up with baling wire, and underneath the wire were old steam radiators, tractor parts, truck rims, leaf springs, disc blades, plow bottoms, lengths of twisted steel, rolls of frayed electrical wire. Angelo climbed down from the truck and walked around to the driver's side. There by the running board he spotted Willie's cap, and picked it up. He walked toward the sheriffs' cars. He found Willie sitting in the backseat, slumped low, handcuffed to a ring at the car's center-post.

"Mistah Red." Willie turned to look at the boy, his left eye was nearly swollen shut. Blood had dried at the corner of his mouth, and flecks of dry grass and gravel were lodged in his hair. "You come see Mistah Willie?"

"They said you were shot."

"No, it ain't me who been shot."

"What happened?"

"That boy's waitin' fo' me when I come off the hill— he block the road so sudden ain't no time for stoppin'— mostly 'cause of the load. It send the tractah off flyin' with one a them boys—the little one—still on it. Don' hurt 'im none, jus' a tumble o' two, but he come up maddah 'n a wet hen. I say like I say befo' don' want no trouble, but what he hearin'? Hearin' nothin,' that what."

Willie's voice was a low montone. He stared down at his handcuffs, and then straight ahead, his eyes hardly blinking. "My truck hit the trailah and roll ovah it and stuck the wheels. Then I hear watah hissin' and figger it bus' the radiatah, so can' go nowhere, and here comes tha' Jenkin boy with 'no good' on his face. Ain't no reasonin' with 'im. He swing open the do' tryin' to pull me out, an' I kick hard at 'im. Then come the othah and he pullin' at his bro-thah while the little one he jus' wrestlin' and punchin' me. When I free up, I run 'round the truck, one chasin' me, the big one chasin' the little one—all like frothin' dogs, and thas' when I grab the gun. The big one, he stop, and the little one, he stop too. An' I say, 'you jus' star' walkin' backward from where you come, and I won' have ta shoot nobody.' They's was doin' that—the whole time the little one jus' runnin' bad at the mouth—niggah this, niggah that—nothin' I ain't heard befo'—and the big one sayin' 'shut yo' mouth, Bustah, can't you see he got a gun?' And then the little one he run at me. Tha's when I squeeze one off—ain't tryin' to kill 'im, just take a step o two away. I aim fo' the ahm, but hits 'im closer in. The big one tend to 'im while the little one kickin' at the duht, jus' a shoutin' he dyin'. We lookin' each othah' what seem like half a day, then come the sheriff. They tell me drop the gun, and I do and they cuff me up righ' away. Then they ten' to the little one."

Irv and Jackie had now joined Angelo. An ambulance's siren sounded from Adobe Road, turned and it soon braked to a hard stop where the men had gathered. Right behind the ambulance, another sheriff's car followed.

"You got your ass in a sling now, Willie," Irv said.

"I'm suspeckin' that, Mistah Millah."

"Buster's over there, saying you started the whole thing."

"Ain't no Jenkins Road—thas' what you said. Ain't no road jus' fo' certain folks—it's a road fo' all folks."

"It's different around here—I know it shouldn't be, but it is," Irv said.

"That always been doggin' me, Mistah Millah."

"I know it has—don't blame you, but then when I seen the rifle—well, Willie—

"It got me some rabbits—

"It got you more than just rabbits."

Angelo looked up to see the family Chevy approaching with Junior behind the wheel. He brought it to a hard stop, and leaped out. He ran toward his dad. "Ma said Willie got shot!"

Irv looked up from talking with Willie. "No, it wasn't Willie—it was was Buster Jenkins." Junior pushed in next to his dad.

"I was up early this mon'in, too, feelin' this my lucky day, thinkin' why not try them fahms up 'bove?" Willie rubbed his chin against his shoulder. "Ain' nobody go there, and I'm suspeckin' pickins' was good—you seen the back a the jimmy? I like to cry fo' joy loadin' all tha' metal and the folks they was happy to see it go, and I come down from the mountain jus' feelin' so good, but all the time, too, my stomach a knottin' up, hopin' I can slip by them Jenkins. You know, Mistah Millah, they ain't no takin's that's evah easy. Then I see the tractah pullin' ou' the road like I tell Mistah Red 'fore you come, and the jimmy's brake pedal's to the flo' but it ain' stoppin' in time. Then come the crash and splintah up tha' trailah jus' like kindlin'."

A deputy sheriff walked up to where Irv, Angelo and Jackie were standing. "All right, I'd like you to step back from the car, please." He opened the rear door. "You got identification, sir? "

"It's in the truck," Willie said. "Inside my belt."

"I'll get it," Angelo said.

Angelo grabbed Willie's army belt, opened its first pouch, and found Willie's worn leather wallet, bulging with cards and pieces of paper. He grabbed the wallet and returned to the sheriff's car. Angelo was now standing next to their dad.

"Pretty serious what you done here," the deputy said to Willie.

"What can I do? Let 'em thump me bad? No, sir, you ain't thumpin me no free-han'. No' withou' a fight you ain't."

"Officer, I know this fellah—been comin' by our dairy for a long time. He told me what these Jenkins boys said to him," Irv said.

"What'd he tell you?" the deputy asked.

"That they'd threatened him, called him 'nigger'."

"And what'd you say?"

"I told him to avoid them."

"Doesn't look like he followed your advice."

"This ain't Jenkins' road," Willie said.

"Maybe not," the deputy said, "but it seems like you walked right into where you knew there'd be trouble."

"Willie didn't start it," Angelo said. "He just wanted a load of metal to take back home so Dellah'd be happy."

"Are you the judge, too?" Irv asked the deputy.

"No, I'm not the judge but I seen plenty of trouble that could have been avoided if folks just used common sense."

"Common sense," Willie repeated the words. "I think I know what you sayin' heah."

Buster Jenkins was standing up by now, and the ambulance attendant and Leroy Jenkin helped Buster inside the ambulance. Leroy climbed in after his brother, and the attendant closed the doors behind him. Then the ambulance drove off. The other deputy carried Willie's .22 over to his patrol car, and placed the rifle in the car's trunk. He joined Irv and Irv's son.

"You filin' a report?" Junior asked the deputy that was with Willie.

"Yes, sir. I'm getting the details now." The deputy's cap was soaked with sweat.

"Sir, I'm Sheriff Reese," he said looking into Willie. "Deputy Bradford needs to ask you some questions."

"Yes, suh."

Irv motioned Sheriff Reese to one side. "What's gonna happen here?"

"Depends if Jenkins presses charges."

"For what?

"Assault."

"I know Willie—"

"Willie told me how it happened," Angelo said. "They blocked the road, and pulled him out of the truck—they were beating him, like they beat everyone else."

"We'll have to take him in, finger-print and book him," Sheriff Reese said. "That's the procedure. If he's deemed not to be a threat, he can post bail, and probably be released tomorrow. Can't say, for sure, but that's usually what happens. His family will need to be notified."

Angelo walked back to the sheriff's car. "You got to spend the night in jail, Willie. That's what the sheriff said."

"Dellah ain't gonna like that."

"Is there someway you can contact her?" the deputy asked.

"Oh, you can call our neighbah, and they'll pass it 'long."

"You have that information?"

"Yes, suh," Willie said. "And what they gonna do with my truck?"

"It'll have to be towed," the deputy said.

"We can tow it back to our place," Irv said. "We'll patch it up there."

"Mistah Millah—you mos' kind."

"Here's your hat, Willie. I found it by your truck."

"You gonna have ta put it on Willie yo'self."

Angelo set it on top of Willie's head.

"Thank you, Mistah Red. I suspeck I'll be seein' you soon, huh?"

"I hope so," Angelo said.

"Think they'll trea' me kind heah?"

"We'll put a good word in for you, Willie," Irv said.

"Okay, folks—that should do it for now," Sheriff Reese said. "You want me to call for a tow truck?"

"No, I'll bring the tractor down here and tow it back myself," Irv said.

"Don't let nobody mess with it, Mistah Millah." Willie glanced up through the open window.

Irv followed the sheriff around to the other side of his patrol car. "He ain't like what you hear," Irv said.

Sheriff Reese nodded his head, climbed into his car. He put a clipboard against the steering wheel and thumbed to a clear page in his tablet. After he'd written several lines, he picked up the radio receiver and spoke into it.

"So maybe it wasn't about huntin' rabbits at all," Junior said.

"What do you mean?" Irv looked at his oldest son.

"The rifle—he got it just for the Jenkins—to settle things up—even after he'd been warned about going up this road." Junior watched as the deputy turned the patrol car around.

"Willie didn't start no fight," Angelo said.

"What do you know?" Junior glared at his younger brother.

"I know 'cause Willie told me."

Junior laughed.

"You don't know Willie. You don't know nothing!"

"All right you two, knock it off!" Irv said.

"All's he cares about is his damn jeep—that's all!" Angelo stood between Junior and his dad.

"Bull shit!" Junior stared down at Angelo.

"It's true."

"He came over here to settle a score, that's what he done," Junior said. Wouldn't been no trouble if Willie stayed away."

"Did not!"

Irv pulled Angelo away from Junior.

"He's a trouble-maker—they all are!" Junior said.

"He never liked him—you know that, Dad."

"That's enough, son."

Angelo freed himself from his dad's grip and walked toward the patrol car. He waved to Willie, and Willie raised both hands as far as the cuffs allowed him. He smiled back at the boy. "I'll see you, Willie! You come back and we'll hunt more rabbits! Okay?" Willie nodded his head.

Angelo trotted alongside the sheriff's car before it gathered speed and pulled away. It stopped at the bottom of Sonoma Mountain and waited there for several minutes. Angelo could still see the outline of Willie's head through its back window. Then the car turned onto Adobe Road, and headed south toward town. A red light flashed from its roof before it disappeared.

The Body's Perfect

We liked to call it our little window—Irv and me—a snatch of time, two weeks, maybe, when it seemed we'd finally turned the corner, and things might work out. Looking back though, I could see it was just wishing on a star, no real reason to feel any different, except I was tired of feeling the same old way. We were losing money faster than we could find it, but still holding out hope that my father would loan us more. Irv thought buying up another milk contract would keep everything afloat, and the only way we could do that was borrow more money. So, while hopes were still high, we bought a new Chevrolet—a 1957 Bel Air hard-top, fire-engine red with spinners on the hub-caps. We took the savings we'd scratched together, the savings we'd set aside for the worst emergency, and the dealer gave us another four hundred for the old turtle-back. The rest was all installment plan. We bought it from DeLong's in San Rafael. Price Motors, the local dealer, wouldn't sell to us. Bad credit.

Irv loved that car. He kept it garaged, and spread a blanket over it so the sparrows and barn swallows wouldn't crap on its paint. He washed it on Saturday afternoons, and run a chamois cloth across it until the shine would hurt your eyes. He'd get the boys to help him. On Saturday evenings he'd gather everyone up, and we'd drive into town and order burgers and shakes at the Foster's Freeze. Afterwards we drove up and down Main Street with all the windows down, the radio playing, Irv waving to folks we'd pass like he was mayor in the Egg Parade. Irv would follow our reflection in the store fronts, then point and say, "Lookee there, Dorna. Who's that good lookin' family in the window?"

People find a refuge in hard times. Irv's mother found it in daily Mass, lighting candles, saying the rosary. Me? I'm still looking. But Irv found it inside his Chevy. He didn't even have to drive it, either. Sometimes he'd just sit in it, listening to the ball game, the news, whatever he could find on the radio. Other times he'd be staring straight ahead, lost in whatever world he was living in at the time. More than once I heard him singing along with the car radio. He didn't have much of a singing voice, and if you told me that was Irv singing, I wouldn't have believed it. One time he sang "Waterloo" and slapped his knees and kicked the floorboards along with the beat. Other times he hummed the tunes to music we used to dance to. Once I heard him say, "Sally, why don't we go out where the stars are a little brighter? Would you like that?"

People just don't wash up onshore without any life before you meet them. Irv and me both had our lives. He'd had girlfriends, that was no secret. He'd told me a little about his time in Santa Cruz. All innocent stuff, he said. I had a boyfriend or two. What normal person hasn't? All *before* we were married, of course. Still, he'd never mentioned Sally before, or any woman by name, so it stopped me short that day. I tried not to think about it. There are too many other things to worry about besides past girlfriends, past lives. And it wasn't as though Irv had the time or the money to be chasing girlfriends around town. If he did, it would have been news to me. Anyway, those things have a way of working themselves out.

My father never loaned us the money. No surprise there. He backed out at the last minute, and for the next couple of days Irv walked around like he'd lost his best friend.

"What are we going to do, Irv?" I asked him.

"About what?"

"Take your pick—the business? The bills? *Everything!* Now we got a new car out in the garage there that we can't even afford to drive."

"We ain't sellin' it, if that's what you mean."

"Fine. Maybe we all could just live in it—just like you do sometimes."

Irv makes this face when he doesn't want to hear what you're saying—the eyes look off, sad and wondering, and avoiding yours. The lips pout, screw themselves into different shapes. His fingers tap the table. It's like you're taking up his time with facts, with reality. The stuff Irv has a hard time swallowing.

Two months later, the bills kept multiplying. Finally I cornered Irv one morning and said, "Either the car goes, or I do."

"If it'll make you happy—

"It's not about making me happy."

He wasn't convinced.

"It's not my fault, Irv. It's no one's fault," I said. "We'll sell it and buy something used."

You'd think Irv was losing an arm, or one of our boys, the way he acted. It didn't make any sense to me how you could get that attached to a car, to anything. I'd learned that long ago—get attached to something and then you lose it, and your whole world caves in. But with a lot of things, you just keep re-learning them. We forget. Irv was level-headed about most things—it was a quality of his I liked—but when it came to that Chevy, the practical side of Irv went right out the window.

"It's just a goddamn car, Irv."

"*You* sell it, then," he said.

I tried to.

I drove it up to Santa Rosa, and spent the better part of an afternoon going from one used car lot to the next—from one end of the Santa Rosa Avenue to the other—but they all gave me the same song-and-dance.

"Eleven hundred's top, ma'am," they'd say.

"But that Chevy's practically brand new," I said, "You shoulda seen how my husband babied it. How he polished it, and covered it at night." It didn't matter. Eleven hundred was top offer.

When I drove back home, Irv was surprised to see the car again. I think a little relieved, too. He parked it back in its garage, and the next morning, after his breakfast of bacon and eggs, and before the rest of his chores, there was Irv, sitting in the front seat again, talking to himself.

Just over the radio I heard, "How about a drive out to Rio Nido, Josephine? We can do a little hoofin' to the Sam Dexter Band."

Irv wasn't a cheater. The ladies liked him, though, and I knew it. You'd have to be blind at times not to notice. Irv hardly seemed to care. Their attention toward Irv made me jealous, though—I hate to admit it. At his mother's birthday party once, Earlene Jensen had an arm draped over him and a feeling came up inside me like I just wanted to scratch one of her eyes out. But too much else was going on to think about being jealous. Sometimes I thought all the worry might be causing Irv to lose his marbles, that it was finally getting to him. Christ knows it was getting to me. Most nights I tossed and turned, and in the morning there were bags under my eyes the size of tea cups. My stomach was in knots, and I couldn't eat. And as much as I loved going into town, I was afraid of running into somebody we owed money to. It bothered Irv, too—it *had* to—but he kept it all inside him. How everything just didn't blow apart, I don't know. You're around people—sometimes for years and years—and they'll still surprise you with the things they do. I guess Irv was that way—still surprising me.

Annalee, my neighbor down the road, suggested just putting a *For Sale* sign in the Chevy's window, but I told her the truth. I told her I didn't want other people in town knowing the kind of trouble we were in, that we were so broke, we couldn't even keep our family car. She just laughed. "They can stick it where the sun don't shine," she said. I used to think I didn't care what other people thought, and I've done plenty of things that bear that out, but this time it was different. I cared. I worried. If I could have packed up the boys and moved a thousand miles away and started all over, I'd have gone in a flash. But with Irv, it was like he had to prove something, that he could make a go out of milking eight-five head of dairy cattle, pay rent, and still raise a family when no one else around us could. It was like all his cousins and in-laws were watching him—and they were—and wondering how long it would take before he tossed it all in. Irv thought they all wanted him to make it, but there were things Irv was blind to, and that was one of them. He thought I just said these things because I didn't like his family. All right, I didn't like most of them, and you want to know why? Because I could see through them. I could see things Irv couldn't. They *wanted* Irv to fail, so they could sit on their fat asses and laugh about it. That's the kind of family Irv grew up around.

More bills arrived in the mail. I said, to hell with it, and placed an ad in the *Argus.* Two days later, the phone rings, and it's some guy inquiring about the car, asking all sorts of questions. The voice sounded familiar, but I couldn't place it. I told him the same thing I told all the salespeople in Santa Rosa, that if the car could fit in our bedroom, my husband would keep it there. This guy says he's looking to buy a car for his oldest daughter who just got her driver's license. He's interested, he's definitely interested, and wants to know where he can see the car. I gave him our address, and he said his wife would be out in the afternoon.

A couple of hours later, a Cadillac pulled into our yard, and out stepped Lorraine Castanzio, the wife of Jerry Castanzio. People liked to bill themselves as 'kings of this' and 'kings of that' around here, and Jerry was no exception. He was the "Sausage King" which, I guess, made Lorraine, the "Sausage Queen." Jerry's father owned a slaughterhouse north of town, and to Jerry's credit, he'd worked hard and expanded the business. He bought a fleet of trucks and distributed sausages and other cuts of meat all over the bay area. He sponsored a Little League team, his business logo was on the center-field fence panel, he advertised everywhere, donated heavily to the church. The main room in the parish hall was named after his family. When you needed a fat donation, you contacted Jerry Castanzio.

Jerry and Lorraine lived in style. Their house sat on a hill that looked right into town. I'd see Jerry at Mass, and afterwards he'd always come over and talk to me. Lorraine would be off talking to someone else, usually Father Walsh. Irv didn't care for Jerry. Irv thought he talked too much and rode on his old man's coat tails. Jerry was a good looking man with thinning jet-black hair, and a face and neck that were already starting to thicken up and spill over the collar of his shirt. When he talked to me, he often moved in so close I could smell his cologne, even the flower in his lapel. I'd met Jerry shortly after meeting Irv, and he'd told me once if only we'd met a week earlier. I always thought that was the booze talking. Jerry was a natural-born salesman, so you had to sift through half of what he said. He wasn't a liar, and he wasn't dishonest. Jerry was smooth. Maybe it was his confidence, his cockiness that got to you. He had that certain look in his eye, too—a little gleam—that I ignored. At Father Kelly's 80th birthday party at the parish hall, Jerry'd been drinking, and near the end of the evening I'd wandered down one of the hallways looking at all the re-modeling that had been done, and when I turned around, there was Jerry Castanzio. His arm reached out to me, and I stepped back, took his hand. He kept trying to move closer, and I would step back each time. I never told Irv about it. Just something I kept to myself.

Lorraine stepped out of the Cadillac and straightened her skirt. Every strand of hair was in its place—like the *Clairol* lady in the magazine ads. She glanced around the yard and wrinkled her nose. Then she noticed me.

"Oh, it's you, Dorna," she said. "What a surprise!"

I smiled. Lorraine had never done anything to make me dislike her. She was always polite and well-spoken—the perfect wife, I thought, for Jerry Castanzio.

"So that was your husband on the phone earlier? I didn't recognize his voice."

"Yeah, our oldest is driving now, and we wanted to get her a good used car. Make it a surprise, though. " Lorraine looked at the Chevy. "It sure is a bright color."

"Irv picked it out."

She walked around the back of the car.

"You kept it so nice."

"That was Irv's baby."

"Why you selling it then?"

"Even babies gotta grow up," I said.

Lorraine looked puzzled by my remark.

"May I sit in it?" she asked.

"Go right ahead."

I looked around for Irv, thinking he'd be showing up anytime. I wondered what his reaction would be if he saw Lorraine Castanzio sitting in his car. She turned the wheel to the left and then to the right, and adjusted the rear view mirror.

"Dorna," she said through the open window, "I don't know a thing about cars."

"It's a good car, Lorraine," I assured her.

Lorraine got out, and looked the Chevy over once more, and then walked over to where I was standing.

"I think Tina'll like it," she said. "Twelve hundred, right?"

"That's what Irv wanted."

Lorraine asked if I could drive the car into town the next day, and she'd have a check for me, and then drive me back home. She wrote her address in a tablet with her husband's company logo at the top—Castanzio Meats—and handed the paper to me.

"We live near—

"I know where you live, Lorraine."

"It was so good to see you again."

"That'd be fine," I told her. "I need to get all the paperwork together, anyway."

Lorraine got back in her Cadillac, and flipped her hand goodbye as she disappeared down the driveway.

That evening at dinner, I told Irv we'd sold the car. He just grunted, and asked me to pass him the mashed potatoes.

"You didn't lower the price, did you?"

"No. She liked the car, and never said anything about the price."

"She?"

"Lorraine Castanzio."

Irv ran his fork across the plate, scooping up the last of the potatoes.

"They don't have enough cars already?"

"It's for their daughter, Tina."

"If I'd known it was them, I'd have asked two thousand."

"C'mon, Irv."

"They can afford it."

The next morning I gathered all the papers together for the car, and put them in a big envelope. I walked to the garage, started the Chevy up, backed it out, and while it idled, I emptied everything in its glove box into a paper bag and opened all its doors, and checked under the seats. I whisked off the carpets and opened the trunk, too, and pulled out the blanket Irv had used as a cover and hung the blanket on a nail inside the garage. Irv was working over in the corral, and he'd look over to me every few minutes. I felt bad, like we were giving up someone in the family. Irv and me had hashed it over enough times. There wasn't anything left to do. I reminded him again and again that it was just a car, and we'd get another one that we could afford, and if we couldn't afford a car, then we'd all ride in the truck. When I drove past Irv slow, he looked at me— not long—then looked away. I pulled past the corral and stopped. Irv looked up and I waved at him, but he didn't wave back. It was just before noon.

A sweeping drive lead to the Castanzio house at the top of a hill, and when I finally located it, I pulled the Chevy into their driveway, set the parking brake, and shut the motor off. I walked to the door, rang the bell, and waited.

When the door opened, Jerry Castanzio was standing in front of me.

"Dorna, so good to see you."

He stepped toward me, as if to embrace me, and I stepped back and shook his hand.

"Hi, Jerry," I said. "I didn't expect to see you."

"Well—I live here, too," and laughed out loud. "C'mon in."

The carpets caved under my feet. Just inside the entry way, three steps led down into a long living room. Through a wall of plate-glass windows the entire town spread out below me. I looked straight down to the steeples of Saint Vincent's Church, and beyond, to downtown and the Poultry Producers Building on the other side of the creek. If you looked closely enough you saw cars moving along the streets and the tiny figures of people on the sidewalks. And not a sound. Like watching a silent movie.

"What a beautiful view!" I said.

"You like it?"

"Of course. Who wouldn't?"

"Can I get you a drink?"

"No thanks, Jerry."

"Nothing?"

"All right, maybe a glass of water."

"Sit down. Relax."

Jerry disappeared into the kitchen. I heard him breaking ice cubes out of a tray and then the loud clunk the cubes made when they hit the bottom of the glasses. I looked around. It was the kind of house you'd see in the fancy magazines, the kind of house a movie star might live in—carpets thick and soft as lamb's wool, overstuffed chairs and couches, cabinets filled with colored glassware, expensive china—everything so neat and polished. There were pictures on the walls, too. Pictures of Jerry as a young boy with his dad. And photos of Castanzio's first slaughterhouse, a wooden building with one cattle chute and a Model-A truck with Jerry's dad standing beside it, his arms folded across his chest.

"You sure you don't want a drink?" Jerry called from the kitchen.

"I'm sure. I drink too early in the day, it makes me sleepy."

Jerry walked back into the living room holding two glasses. He slid a pair of coasters onto the coffee table in front of me, and set the drinks down. Then he sat down on the couch.

"Lorraine has a fit if there's marks on that table. I tell her I don't know why you care, it's not like she does the housework around here."

"Where is Lorraine?" I asked.

"Getting her hair done. Up at the club—I don't know."

We both drank from our glasses.

"I think I'm gonna stiffen this one up a little." He walked over to a corner bar with a big mirror behind it, and unscrewed the cap on a bottle of scotch. He poured scotch near the brim of the glass and then walked back to where I was sitting. I kept the envelope filled with car papers between us. He sat down and sipped from his drink.

"Ahh, much better."

I was nervous, and any little silence had me fumbling for words.

"So, Tina's driving already?" I said. "She's your oldest, right?"

"Same age as Irv, Jr."

"Just about. Junior drives the flat-bed around now—he's had a 'Farm permit.' At first, Irv wouldn't let him drive the Chevy. They'd argue back and forth about that, and Irv gave in. What Junior really wants is a jeep. That's all he ever talks about."

"How you doin' out there? I heard you're havin' a tough-go of it."

"Who'd you hear that from?" I asked. The question seemed a bit direct. Any other day I would have told him to mind his own business.

Jerry fidgeted, and stared out the window.

"Oh, you know in my business, you hear a lot of things." Jerry was trying to back up a little, I could tell. "Besides, it's no secret these are tough times for dairy farmers."

"It hasn't been easy. We'll figure out something, though."

Jerry drank down half his drink. He set the glass down and stared out the window.

"Did you ever think about how your life could've been different?" he asked.

"We all do that, don't we?"

"How some decision you make changes everything?"

"I suppose—I can't tell you how many times I'd wished Irv had never bought those damn cows—but it was what he wanted to do. He's stubborn—he gets something in his head, and it won't shake loose."

"I think of things I done. And what I'd do different."

"C'mon, Jerry—how could you do better than this?"

I pointed around the room, and out the window.

"I mean, look at this—a nice family, a beautiful house, a successful business."

"It's not everything."

"Well," I said, "After you've been scratching around for a few years, it's *mostly* everything."

The thought of Jerry Castanzio ever having to make a decision about what he'd do in his life seemed like a joke. It was all laid out in front of him, packaged up and delivered with a big red bow. He just had to step into it.

"I got a different outlook—Irv does, too," I said. "That happens when you've been hanging by threads as long as we have."

Jerry walked over and poured himself another scotch. I picked up the envelope, removed the papers inside and spread them out across the coffee table.

"Me and Irv known each other a long time," Jerry said from behind the bar. "I think he's known Lorraine even longer. She's always liked Irv."

"Can we take care of this now?" I asked.

"Relax, Dorna—just relax."

"I got things to do yet."

Jerry walked back and set his drink down again on the coaster.

"You sure there's nothing else I can get you?" he asked.

"Just the check, Jerry."

"And the amount on that?"

"Irv wanted twelve hundred."

"It's in the den."

"Could you call a cab while you're at it?"

"I can drive you home."

"No, thank you, but downtown's fine, thank you—to the bank. And I'll take a cab from there."

Jerry returned with a check, and I put it in my purse. I signed over the title, just above where Irv had signed his name the night before.

"That should do it," I said.

Jerry shook my hand, and as I pulled it away, his grip tightened.

"Please, Jerry."

Our eyes locked onto one another's.

"Please, Jerry."

We walked out to the Chevy, and Jerry opened the door for me. He got in behind the wheel, slid the seat back, and started the car up. We wound back down the hill and drove onto Western Avenue. It felt odd that Jerry Castanzio was driving our car, and I was sitting in the front seat next to him. Jerry Castanzio behind the wheel of something that Irv loved so much. Maybe this is what Jerry meant by decisions we made. I asked him to let me out at Kentucky Street, and he pulled over to the curb.

"I hope Tina enjoys the car," I said. "She won't find one that's been taken better care of."

"Dorna—

"Thank you, Jerry."

I walked into the bank, and approached the teller. I took out the check and endorsed it. "Deposit that please," I said.

"The entire fourteen hundred?"

"I looked at the check, and realized it was made out for two hundred more than Irv wanted.

"Deposit it all?" the teller asked again.

I thought for a couple of seconds. "Twelve hundred, please. I'd like to keep two hundred back. And an envelope, please."

I walked out of the bank, intent on mailing the two hundred back to Jerry Castanzio. I didn't like people thinking we were charity cases. At Antler's Pharmacy I was about to call a cab, but decided to cross the street to Carither's Department Store instead. I walked from one window display to the other, to the corner of Kentucky Street and around to Western Avenue, until I finally went inside. I thought about the two hundred dollars in my purse. At the Boys section I picked out three pair of corduroy pants and three matching shirts. In the Mens section, I found a sweater the same color as Irv's eyes, and I bought him a new belt. I bought a dress, too, the one I'd seen in the window and walked by several times, the one I thought I could never afford. And I couldn't. But today felt different. Today was another one of those little windows, I suppose. The dress was pleated at the waist, a spring-time dress, and when I tried it on, turning in the mirror quickly, its skirt spun out almost like a parasol. Spring wasn't far away. I could feel it inside. I paid for the purchase with the cash from the envelope, tucked the packages under my arm, and I walked outside. I called a cab, something I hadn't done since I was a young woman still living in the city.

While I waited for the cab to arrive, Gladys Sorensen, my eaves-dropping neighbor, walked by. Her eyes fastened on the shopping bags I was holding.

"Good morning, Gladys," I said. Her smile seemed forced, but I didn't care.

And not two minutes later, who walks by but Evelyn Borda. She tried to look the other way, as if I wasn't there, as if, secretly, Evelyn had heard that I was standing on a downtown sidewalk—me, Dorna Miller, without a nickel to my name—standing there with an armful of packages.

"Been shoppin,' Dorna?" she asked.

"Yes, I have. And spent a fortune."

"Waitin' for Irv?"

"No, I'm actually waiting for a cab."

She paraded past me.

The cab finally arrived, and the driver put my packages in the trunk. Once inside the cab, he asked, "Where to?"

"Adobe Road," I said.

"That's a good six miles away, ma'am."

"Your car doesn't go that far?" I asked. "I could have just sold you one that did."

"Oh, it'll go as far as you want it to," he said.

I sat there, and watched the town spill by as the cab headed east out Washington Street. I felt different than I'd been feeling—lighter, pounds lighter. The way you feel when you've finally done something you put off for a long time, and now that you've done it, you wonder why it took so long.

"Been doing some shopping?" The driver glanced at me in his rear-view mirror.

"A little bit of buying, a little bit of selling," I said.

"Good for you."

Then I chuckled, and the chuckle became a laugh. A good laugh. The laughter felt like an expression you'd overheard as a youngster, one that you'd always liked, but had forgotten to use, and now when you did, it came out just as you'd heard it years before. It was like a perfect language. No matter that tomorrow we'd be riding around in Irv's flatbed, the five of us, while his prize Chevy would be parked in the driveway of Jerry Castanzio's house on the hill, another trophy in Jerry's trophy case. I know that doesn't seem funny, but I laughed anyway. I leaned back in the seat as though riding in a limousine, as though I'd hit the big jackpot as though everything I'd ever wished for had been granted. Riding in that back seat without a care anywhere in this world.

Joe

Little things, lately, set the memories off. One day it might be a wind swooping up from the bay, carrying the brackish, festering smell of tidelands over to Irv's ranch. Or it might be the roll and shape of the fog as it spilled over the western hills, the cries the seagulls made blown in from the coast. Other times it might be a pretty young woman walking out of Carithers, a shopping bag in her hands, her beau waiting at the curbside, the door opened on a late-modeled coupe. Irv waved most of these memories off. He knew where they led to—what Johnny Maestretti called Irv's "buck-wild" time in Santa Cruz—days that were all behind Irv now. This was the present, and no time for the impractical, dreamy past. Irv couldn't take it to the bank. It wouldn't pay a bill, or buy groceries at Purity Market. He'd outgrown it, married impulsively, raised three sons, bought a herd of 85 milk cows, and the once-eligible bachelor and man-about-town now worked twelve, sometimes fourteen hours a day stitching his dairy business together. Still, as much as Irv fought off the memories, discounted them, they were like a balm when his spirits drooped, when the cards seemed stacked against him.

What mattered most this particular March wasn't the shape of the fog, or Santa Cruz, or any lingering memories. What mattered at this moment was bringing in a young heifer for breeding. She was in the corner of the dry-stock pasture, and Irv walked toward her with Petey, his cattle dog, a dozen steps in front of him. Arthritis stabbed at Irv's knees, his legs already starting to bow out compensating for the pain. The heifer stopped grazing and stared first at Irv, and then at the dog. Its ears hinged backwards and forwards, its jaw stopped moving. The wet grass brushed against Irv's boots, and made a sound like a skirt rustling. Was it a plaid summer skirt, Irv wondered? *Edith? Or was it Ethel? Something like that. I can see her face like it was in front of me—that wonderful broad smile of hers.*

"You stay with me, Petey." The dog slowed its pace and moved alongside Irv, but when the heifer turned and trotted away, Irv whistled, waved his arm—Petey's signal to cut loose and loop around it.

"Petey!" The dog looked back, and Irv waved his arms toward the road. It scampered off to the right, tracing a circle around the heifer, and pointing it back towards the barn. The dog and the heifer stared at each other, before Petey nipped at the heifer's heels. *Is your father a dentist I asked her? One of my worst lines. 'No, he owns a peach orchard east of Modesto. Could I try the leather pumps on, the ones with the little tassle in front?' I slipped off her old shoe and felt those smooth, wonderful legs, and I had to ask her name. Edith, I'm sure now she said Edith.*

Irv walked off toward the west so that the heifer saw a straight line toward the barns. Petey stayed on the heifer's heels, but then suddenly stopped and stared off toward the road. Irv followed Petey's stare. Something was moving just beyond the fence line, its legs working at a brisk but easy trot. Irv followed it. It was a big, black dog—a spaniel mix, Irv guessed—with long, floppy ears, a tongue lolling out the side of its mouth, its nose an inch from the ground. Another goddamn stray, Irv thought. *Yes, it was Edith. I asked her out that night. We danced to Stan Kenton at the Cocoanut Grove. A wonderful dancer. Like we were gliding along on ball bearings. You know how some women feel good in your arms? How they just feel different from the others? She was like that.* The stray continued up Adobe Road, disappeared past the barns, and out of Irv's sight.

After Irv had corralled the heifer, he walked back into the yard, and there, lying at the top of the driveway was the same black spaniel he'd seen a half hour earlier. It ducked its head, turned its eyes inwards to the tops of their sockets when it saw Irv. Its long tail slapped intermittently in the gravel. Petey walked up to it, sniffed at its ass, then walked away. *Just stay right there. Don't you move now, Gladys. Our waiter's busy, so I'll just sidle up to the bar and order two more drinks there. That was a vodka gimlet, wasn't it?* Irv kept it in his sights, walking backwards into the hay barn, and reached inside the door for his .22. Dorna didn't like him firing guns around the yard, but strays were a problem, especially when they ran in packs. A month earlier they'd gone after a cow and its calf. Irv found the cow in the morning—gashes of hair missing from its face and legs, its ears torn nearly in two, standing over the gutted carcass of its calf. He shot a pair of strays later that week and dumped their bodies in the dry creek bed above the haystacks. Buzzards picked them clean within two days.

Irv stepped inside the barn, grabbed his .22, and quietly slipped out to the corner of the doorway. He peeked out. The stray was still there, its ears cocked, its eyes staring right to where it had seen Irv last. Irv stepped back, pumped the slide-action of the rifle, and then, commando-style, swung back out into the doorway, shouldered the rifle, brought the dog's torso into its sights, and fired. *Click!* He pumped it again and pressed the trigger. Another loud *click.* No shells. *Goddamn it! Would she leave just like that?* The dog slinked away, and disappeared into the orchard. *I'm holding two drinks, sitting at an empty table—minutes ago feeling like the luckiest guy on the coast. Now I'm not so sure.* Irv slammed the rifle back into its corner.

Later that afternoon Irv woke from his nap, and walked out to bring the cows in for milking. Petey loved this time. He barked, nipped at Irv's heels, spun himself in circles, trotting off a hundred yards ahead of Irv, circling above the grazing herd, weaving back and forth, methodically funneling them through an opened gate and down one side of the hay barn. Petey never ran the cows, but set them, one by one into motion, pointing them back toward the barns. The cows—by now docile and indifferent to Petey—walked into the cement corral where they waited to be milked. *See anything you like? We just got some new styles in—smart but very comfortable—something you could wear from work right onto the dance floor. You dance, don't you? Oh, you like the rides, instead? Well, so do I. By the way, my name's Irv. How about joining me later this evening? We could stroll along the Boardwalk. Maybe ride the Giant Dipper.* Music played on the radio. The vacuum pump worked away at the front of the barn. *Funny, but I like the clacking sound the wheels make on the rails—slow, at first, when the cars climb. When they reach the top, the clacking stops. But then the cars head to the bottom, and the clacking speeds up, faster and faster, until it's all one big clatter. So loud, so fast, you think the car's gonna fall apart. It's like a heart beating when you're around someone you like. Do you like me, Madeline?* Irv closed the corral gate, noticed the brindled heifer was bulling, another heifer climbing on its back. When he returned to the milking barn, he saw a movement—something dark, its head jutting above the stump of a gum tree. Its eyes watched Irv.

In the following days, Irv kept his .22 near, even tied a scabbard to the John Deere when he went out to feed the young stock, but there was no sight of the spaniel. *The first time it's a little scary, but after that it's not bad at all. You kinda settle into it, relax more. Don't hold your breath so much, or keep your eyes closed. Here, I'll put my arms around you.* He'd mentioned the dog to Dorna, and how he tried to shoot it, but the rifle was empty. She shook her head. "I don't like you killing dogs. The boys don't like it, either."

"Rather they kill the livestock, instead?"

"Can't you trap them and take them to the pound?"

"Sure, I can do that in all my spare-time—maybe I could find them good homes, too."

"What's it matter if there's one other dog around?" She re-filled Irv's coffee cup.

"It matters—I don't like him."

On a frost-bitten morning, a week later, Irv slipped into his rubber boots, grabbed a flashlight, and walked to the milking barn. He switched on the lights, started the vacuum pump, brought out all the lines and cups, and dropped a scoop of grain into the front of each stanchion. "Waterloo" played on the radio. *I like it down here. Never any frost because you're on the coast, always a little breeze. And if it gets too windy, you just drive over the hills, and park, and look out across the ocean. You ever done that? Just drive up over the hills with the top down on a roadster? You could bring a picnic basket if you'd like.* Once the equipment was set up, Irv walked back out through the corral and hay barn, and out to the field to bring the cows in again. It was still dark. His breath steamed up in front of him. He trained the flashlight ahead and caught Petey's eyes in its glare, but

just beyond Petey's, was another set of eyes. *Am I pushing my luck here? You just tell me if I am, and I'll back off.*
Wherever Petey went, the spaniel stray followed, just yards
away, like its shadow.

It was odd, Irv thought. Petey resented most other
dogs, kept them at bay with an aggressiveness that surprised even Irv. But here, the two were running together,
nipping playfully at each other's backs as though raised
from the same litter. Petey would run up to Irv, and then
disappear again into the morning darkness, while the spaniel always stayed back, its eyes big and wondering, always
moving in the flashlight beam. *That's right—you make
yourself right at home here. I got a blanket if you get too cold.
It's like we've always known each other, isn't it?* When Irv
shook the kibble into Petey's bowl, the spaniel distanced
himself, nervous, yet patient, hopeful, at the same time.
When Petey had eaten his fill, the spaniel ate the remaining
kibble—not bolting it down, either, the way Irv had seen
most strays eat—but slowly helping itself, looking up every
few seconds, before dropping its nose into Petey's bowl
again. They shared the same sleeping mat. It was a rare
time they were ever apart. If the spaniel showed an interest
in one of Petey's bones, the shepherd relinquished it without a snarl, without a growl. *Sometimes I can't see us apart.
You ever think like that? Think about the long haul?*

"A goddamn tramp dog comes in and acts like it owns
the place," Irv told Dorna at dinner. Irv was tired and hungry. Dorna forked a pile of spaghetti onto his plate. He
buttered a piece of sourdough bread. "That's a gaully bastard for you."

"Maybe it's got more brains than you give it credit for,"
she said.

"Brains? They were bred out of it."

"Can we keep him, dad?" Angelo, Irv's youngest, asked.
"Petey likes him. We all like him."

Irv looked from from one son to the other. "One screw-up and he's gone," Irv said. "You hear me?"

The boys called him "Joe" after a hobo that lived under the trestles south of town who was often seen wandering up and down the tracks, a bindle-stiff slung over his shoulder, a crumpled-brimmed hat clinging to the side of his head. The dog took to the name, and when any of them called out *JOE!* he ran to them, lapped at their faces, followed at their heels. But he was restless and energetic, his nose always working, luring his body one way then the other, before racing off again, sometimes disappearing a day or two at a time. The boys pulled at his tail, his gangly ears. Joe didn't seem to mind. He relished the attention, surrendered himself, but remained wary, too, always keeping an eye on Irv's whereabouts, never turning his back entirely to him. Whenever Irv walked by, Joe backpedaled, slunk down. If Irv made the least little motion toward him, Joe would tense, scamper off. As much as the boys wanted him inside the house, Joe never ventured closer than the back porch steps.

One morning when Dorna went out to gather eggs, she'd noticed that something had dug under the chicken coop, and when she walked inside the hen house, three of her Leghorns were dead on the floor. The rest of the hens were up on the collar beams, clucking nervously. Feathers were everywhere. Reluctantly, she told Irv. "What could have done that?" she asked

"What? You think it's a mystery? Irv asked. "I know who done it—he's sittin' under that palm tree right now, guiltier than a sonofabitch."

"But you don't know for certain—it could have been coons." Dorna wrung both hands on her apron.

"Ain't no coons."

"Irv."

"I'll take care of it."

"You don't know for certain," she said.

"That dog's a dark cloud ever since he showed up," Irv said.

Irv walked out into the yard, and glared at Joe, and the dog felt his glare's hardness, slunk down, and pissed in the gravel. His eyes moved slowly up to Irv's, and they locked onto each other's. *We both got a lot in common. We're looking for something, and we'd had to leave our hometowns to find it.* He called Petey and Joe over to his pickup, banged on its side, and shouted, "Up!" Both dogs hopped in the back. Joe stared into the cab at Irv, a surprised look in its eyes. The dogs barked at one another as they left the farm yard. *I bought you these candies from Buckhardt's—I remember you saying how much you liked them when we were on the boardwalk the other evening. No, it's okay. Nothing, it's really nothing. Just something I wanted to do. You know, with the sunlight just now it makes your eyes seem so golden, so warm.*

Irv drove through town and out D Street Extension, to the bottom of Red Hill—maybe nine, ten miles from his ranch. He stopped the pickup. There was a dry creek just below them. The air smelled of pepperwoods. He whistled and both dogs jumped from the back. Then he opened the pickup door, and pulled his .22 rifle out from behind the seat. He motioned Petey into the cab of the truck and shut the door behind him. Irv walked down to the creek. "C'mon, Joe! Come here!" Petey barked and scratched at the truck window. Joe stayed near the pickup and stared at Irv, then up at Petey, and back at Irv. *Just a little further, that's all. Just a couple more feet. That's it. Watch your step. Come on, I ain't going to hurt you. This is where the view is best.* Irv glanced both ways down the road. No cars either way. He raised the rifle to his shoulders. *You ain't never seen it like this, have you? That's what makes all of this so special—just a real special time. I'm going to say this, and I know it might sound foolish—and a terrible line—but I don't know which is warmer—that setting sun or the glow from your eyes.* Irv pointed the rifle at Joe's head, and felt the pressure building around his trigger finger. Joe shifted. The rifle barrel followed Joe's every movement. Irv squeezed and squeezed, waiting for the round to touch off, but each time Joe moved, the trigger finger relaxed, and Joe's big, mournful eyes stared back at Irv. *I've been thinking about this ever since we met. What I was going to do when the time came and we were alone.* He lowered the rifle, and walked back to his truck. He opened the door and Petey licked his face. Irv slid the .22 back behind the seat. "Back Petey! Back!"

"And you stay!" Irv pointed at Joe.

He started up the pickup and turned it around. Joe sat on his haunches and stared.

"You stay!" Irv called out again through the open window.

In his side-view mirror, Irv saw that Joe was now standing, his ears tensed up, his body trembling, those eyes staring back at Irv. The dog grew smaller in Irv's side-view mirror until it finally disappeared. Irv wiped his forehead. Petey barked and whined, and looked behind him through the back window, back to where Joe had been. *Someone told you that? Some one said they'd seen me with another girl? Was it five, six o'clock? Probably Doreen, who works in 'children's clothes.' We're friends, that's all. Nothing wrong with that, is there?* When Irv rounded the turn, he checked his mirror again. Joe was gone.

"Where's the black dog?" Dorna asked Irv later that afternoon. She'd tied a bandana around her dark hair, and rolled the sleeves back on her blouse. "I haven't seen it around."

"I shot it," he said.

Dorna shook her head.

"What are you going to tell the boys?"

"I'll tell them it was a stray. And that it ate chickens. And like most strays they run off. They've seen enough goddamn dogs around here for them to know that."

"Well, you tell them, not me."

Angelo cried the most at the news about Joe. "Why'd he run off?"

"He didn't like it here," Irv said.

"He didn't like it 'cause you were mean to him," Angelo said.

Irv felt lighter, relieved, not having the spaniel around, and wondered why he hadn't done it earlier. *When I saw you there, I thought, this is the kind of girl I'd like to take on the Giant Dipper. How did I know that? It's just a feeling I had, that's all. Don't be scared. C'mon! That clack-clack is like my heart beat—slow at first, and then building up as the cars let go.* The next morning his registered Holstein calved a beautiful little heifer. He walked all the way back to the house just to tell Dorna. "It's a beauty—gonna be big, just like its mother."

Two days later Dorna walked into the milking barn.

"Hey, Irv, what'd you say you did with Joe?"

"I shot him."

"And where'd you shoot him?"

"Out at Red Hill. Between the eyes," Irv said.

Dorna was standing in the breezeway.

"What, you don't believe me?"

"He must have a brother, then."

Irv followed Dorna out into the yard, and there, eating out of Petey's bowl, thinner by several pounds was Joe. He looked up at Irv, and wagged his tail briefly, then returned to Petey's kibble.

"You're a bad shot, Irv."

"Sonofabitch."

"The boys'll be happy," she said.

That night one of Irv's springers breeched a calf, a little bull, that Irv couldn't save.

Irv decided he'd take Joe further away this time—he'd ruled out shooting him. He couldn't bring himself to do it. He was driving to Shellville, out to the tidal flats, twelve miles through Stage Gulch, to buy oat hay. He loaded Petey and Joe into the back of his pickup. Irv loved to drive with the window down, his left arm draped on its sill. He liked to watch the pavement unroll below him. *Sometimes it's just like the Santa Cruz air, with the windows open in the apartment, and the sound of the waves breaking, and the laughter of the girls below, and the sound of the calliope. It's like one continuous carnival. Most days I could hardly wait to get off work, join my friends for a beer, and dancing later. Always the dancing, with so many different partners, I couldn't keep their names straight. On my days off, we'd go to the beach, and I'd see the girls in their swim suits. I love their skin, their lovely skin. And, of course, their beautiful bodies. They were all so friendly, too, as if I knew each of them. Dancing gives you legs like that, doesn't it?* After looking at the hay, he continued down Millerick Road, and out to Wingo, the brackish air filling Irv's lungs. *I work until six tonight. How about a little ride up the coast afterwards?* Irv drove out to the top of a levee and parked. A wind had picked up off the San Pablo Bay. Both dogs jumped from the pickup. Joe ran to the edge of the slough, and stepped into chest-high water. Petey stayed back. *No, I don't tell every girl I meet that same thing. There's just something special about you.* He ordered Petey into the cab once again. Joe circled the truck, staring up at Irv. "You stay! STAY!" and Irv drove off.

Within days, Dorna got a job at the hospital, and a bonus check from the creamery for high butterfat levels arrived in the mail. The John Deere, it turned out, needed a head gasket, and not an overhaul. Junior's Holstein won First Prize in Dairy Division at the county fair. Irv went to Mass on Sunday and found an extra dollar in the pants he wore on Pinochle night, and put it in the collection basket. He tried not to associate these recent turns in his luck with the disappearance of Joe, but it seemed more than co-inci-dental. He felt as though something difficult, bothersome, had finally been left behind, that a path once littered with obstacles was cleared before him.

A week after Irv's visit to Shellville, Dorna was stand-ing again in the breezeway of the milking barn, a look of disbelief in her eyes. "You're not going to believe it, Irv."

She motioned him to follow her. They both stopped at the doorway, and Dorna looked across the yard, and then back at Irv. Dorna smiled. It was Joe—thinner again by a few pounds. He lay on Petey's mat, his head down on the ground, staring back at Irv. His tail slapped the ground.

"The bastard's got a roadmap for a brain," Irv said.

"Never seen anything like it," Dorna said.

The boys welcomed Joe back, showered him with hugs and pats, all of which Joe accepted graciously.

"Irv," Dorna said, "let the dog stay now, okay?"

Dorna found an extra blanket, moth-eaten and riddled with holes, and laid it next to Petey's in the back porch. Joe even got his own bowl for kibble. Irv decided to let the dog be, that maybe on its own, it would just wander off, the same way it had just wandered in. On the days he didn't see it, he'd imagined—sometimes even hoped— that Joe had scented a bitch in heat, and had run off. Dogs had no sense. *No, I saw how you were looking at Rollie, and thought, there goes my chances. But there was something about you, there really was, that I just couldn't walk away from. I knew I'd just have to give it one more chance.* He'd watched how their instincts crazed them, made them fight and mangle each other, and retreat a day later, hobbled, covered with scabs, their tongues swollen and heavy, as disoriented as a bombing victim. *She was someone at work, nothing more. She said, 'Let's go out dancing sometime,' and that's what we did. That's all it was—someone at work that wanted to go out dancing.*

On an afternoon when Junior was late for chores because of Confirmation practice, Irv backed the farm tractor and trailer into the hay barn before starting milking. He shut the motor off, and grabbed a pair of hay hooks and climbed onto the haystack to knock a dozen bales down onto the trailer. As he climbed to the top of the stack, he felt a shortness of breath, a little dizziness—he wasn't a young buck anymore, he knew that—but as the hooks sunk into opposite ends of a hay bale, his chest heaved, a little sliver of pain shot up the left arm. Sweat blistered his forehead. He couldn't swallow. Something lodged in his throat. His breath came in tiny gulps, when it came at all. He straightened up, fought for his balance, and teetered backwards. Barn rafters slipped past him as gauzy as cotton candy. *Hold on tight. You ready? Don't close your eyes! Clack-clack. I love that sound how it goes faster and faster.* He fell backwards. His neck snapped hard at first impact. The shrieks, the cries, and then, whatever sounds he heard were muted, as though moving through water—distant, dream-like sounds. His blood surged, receded, washed through him, carried him like flotsam on a rising tide, before dropping him on the cold sand. A barn floor. *Look at the sea gulls how they're lined along the railing. Buckhardt's? Is that the place you're thinking of?* A dog was barking. Alfalfa scent. Through the barking, voices somewhere. A dog's wet nose jabbing into his eyes and ears. Then nothing. Irv couldn't move.

For two days, the vision was blurred in Irv's right eye. One side of his body felt heavy and slow, detached from the other. Doc Kelly said it was a stroke. Irv recovered quickly, was home within three days. Irv hated hospitals, hated any kind of illness. He asked Dorna to bring his work pants and his cane. He slipped them on and walked out a side door. His cousins, Donnie and Carl, helped Junior with the milking.

"You know how they found you, Irv?" Dorna asked him.

Irv shook his head.

"By Joe barking," she said. "Petey waited by the corner of the barn, the way he always does—but it was Joe that went back in and found you, and ran back and forth between the yard and the hay barn until Junior showed up."

Irv returned to work sooner than Doc Kelly advised. He moved slower now, and there was a slight hitch to his walk, as though the hip socket had shrunk. Junior helped out with the milking. Irv would have to rest on a wooden stool, and watch Junior carry the buckets up to the hopper and dump the milk in. Slowly the strength returned in his right arm. Jack and Angelo did the outside work, all the feeding, the clean-up.

On the days that Joe disappeared, Irv now found himself looking for the spaniel, looking both north and south down Adobe Road, and out across the open fields. *I went by your apartment, you weren't there. I'm a fool, I know. I left a couple of notes tacked to your door. Maybe the wind blew them away.* He'd leave kibble in his bowl. Give an extra whistle when it was milking time. When Irv drove into town, he scanned the passing fields, the roadways, for any little movement—a jack rabbit, a killdeer—hoping now that he'd see Joe's dark form, see that easy, liquid motion, that tireless gait, the head low to the ground, the nose like its own mind, reading each detail rolling out below it. When Irv brought in the cows on those days, it was always with an extra glance over the shoulder. And when Joe did show up, it wasn't anger or disgust that Irv felt, but relief, instead, and a bit of stingy joy.

"The women'll get you," Irv would say. "Learn to live with just one of them."

Around the ranch, Joe shadowed Irv. When Irv stopped, Joe stopped. If Irv approached, Joe backed off. Irv talked to him, softened his voice, tried to convince Joe that it was different now, that Joe had earned his place. There wouldn't be any more one-way pickup rides. No more sighting him down the cross-hairs of his rifle. That had changed. *I'm not like that at all. Okay, I screwed up. I'm sorry. You want to nail me to the cross, go ahead. But I'm different now, you'll see.*

Irv kept kibble in his pocket. He'd toss it to Joe like bread crumbs to a wild bird, and within weeks, Joe moved within arm's reach of Irv, even let him pat the top of his head. Joe slunk low with each pat. He crouched, tense, still nervous, while Irv talked to him in a low, sweet tone. *This one would look great on you—it's your color, your style. Slip into it and walk down to that mirror, you'll see. Don't worry about what it costs.* When Irv was inside the house, Joe was at the bottom of the back porch steps. When Irv was milking, Joe was in the breezeway. When Irv was away, Joe was at the top of the driveway, watching every car and truck that passed. Out in the fields, Joe ran ahead of Petey, turned and ran back to him, circling him, nipping, yapping, covering twice the distance the shepherd ran.

Irv told the story again and again, of how Joe found him after his stroke. He told his cousins. He told it over hands of pinochle to Johnny Maestretti, and Mickey Palucci, and Frenchy Mazza. He told it while waiting for a haircut at Moach's barber shop. He told it to whomever came out to the ranch—Julius Matchol, the cattle dealer, Mike, the feed salesman, Burt, the Colonial breadman. Irv told them how he had the dog clean in his sights the first time he'd come in the yard, and how he'd fired, and how the rifle was empty, and so disgusted with himself he threw the rifle into the corner of the barn. And how twice, he'd hauled Joe away, and twice the dog had found his way back. Irv shook his head, slapped his thighs every time he told that part of the story. *I was worried when I didn't hear from you. Those shoes you tried on earlier? The ones I bought for you. Did you like them? No, it's nothing. And the chocolates from Buckhardt's? The walnut crèmes? I knew they were your favorites.* He didn't understand it. Was it his nose? Was it his memory? Irv didn't know.

Irv would whistle—and Joe would lope over. You could look at the dog, Irv would continue, and see it ain't nothing but a goddamn mongrel—half this, half-that, half something else—a real goddamn mutt—not enough brains to come in out of the rain, but set that sonofabitch in motion and it's a runnin' Jessie. Just going, going, not knowing where, but just going—like it was shot in the ass with a can of peaches! That's all that sonofabitch does is run! Like it was born for it. And wander? Hell's bells—you ask yourself, what in God's name is it looking for? What's out there past its nose that it ain't seen already a dozen times? And always finding its way back—that's what got me. Watch it chase a jack-rabbit, Irv would say. Like a machine. Like an antelope. Like a goddamn running machine with a head and tail attached to it.

Irv had just finished spreading a load of cow manure and was heading back to the pile for another load when he saw the sheriff's car heading south on Adobe Road. *I ain't good at letters and I ain't good at saying it, but if you got your mind made up, there's nothing much I can do.* Petey had trotted alongside the tractor the last couple of loads, but Irv hadn't seen Joe all morning. Irv had dug deep into the manure pile with his front-loader tractor, and the smell was rich, almost overpowering, the manure a perfect consistency, a perfect age for spreading. Irv liked it when things broke right. He positioned the tractor and spreader near the pile, climbed down, and walked toward front-loader. *No, I wasn't going to leave without saying something. I was hoping to find the words—waiting for the right ones to come. And I know you think I'm running away from all of this, but I've made such a mess of things.* When he looked up, Jackie and Angelo, and a sheriff were walking toward him.

"I was talking to your boys about your big black dog." The sheriff had both hands hitched over his gun belt.

"That's Joe," Irv said. "Something happen to Joe? He didn't get run-over, did he?"

"No, it ain't run-over—it's something else." The sheriff wiped his forehead. Irv looked at the sheriff and swallowed hard.

"Don't know exactly, but he's out in the field running around in circles."

"Hell, that's what that dog does, officer," Irv said. "That dog ain't stopped runnin' since it showed up here eight months ago."

"This might be different." The sheriff looked at Irv, then moved up closer to him, and spoke in a lowered voice. "You got a rifle?"

Irv nodded. *I come by to say I'm leaving, going back home. No, I do like it here, and I like you, and everything for the longest time seemed perfect. I don't know who could ask for a better life. But I've been dishonest—not leveling with you. Not leveling with a lot of people.*

"You better come have a look," the sheriff said. "And you decide."

Irv and the patrolman walked over to the edge of the corral, and there, out in the dry stock pasture was Joe. He was running, all right, but not in those big, easy strides that gulped at the ground below him, but this time in tight circles, the front of his body bent around to the back, snapping and baying at an elusive tail, running in a way Irv had never seen Joe run before. Long lines of foamy drool spilled from his mouth, flew back like bunting, streaking his ribcage. Irv could hear Joe's teeth clacking together, could hear the big gasps of Joe's breathing. *No, it's not good-bye, not exactly. I'll come back and visit when everything settles down. They say my job's waiting for me. Nothing has to change at all. No, that's not true—a lot has to change, and I can't explain it.* Angelo started to run toward Joe, and Irv caught him by the arm. "You can't go out there, son," Irv looked into the boy's eyes. "Everyone just stay here with the sheriff."

Irv walked inside the barn, and reached for the .22. He pumped a shell into its chamber and walked back out to the pasture. *Did you want to take one last ride with me? It's a perfect evening with the moon as round and golden as I've ever seen it.*

"No, don't shoot Joe!" Angelo started to cry. "Don't shoot him!"

The sheriff grabbed Angelo by the shoulder.

From thirty yards away, Irv raised the rifle to his shoulder, and followed the black dog down both rifle sights, followed whatever had walked into his life months before, a lifetime before, this perfect combination of motion and freedom and impulse. *I'm going to remember this place, remember all the sunsets, all the dances, how your body felt pressed against mine when the roller coaster climbed and the wheels clacked, and I said that's my heart beating slow right now, but wait, it'll be speeding up clack-clack-clack until it's all one sound. Clack-clack, loud and louder.* And then Irv fired. The bullet struck behind Joe's foreleg, slammed into his ribs with a thud. Joe whimpered, his head corkscrewed between his front legs, his big long body cart-wheeled straight up in the air, the legs still in motion, pawing for some invisible ground, before landing on his back. *Where's my heart right now? I don't know. In my throat? My stomach? Moving all around? I don't know.* Joe sprang back up and resumed the chase. Irv fired again. *I don't know where it's at. Look at the view from up here. Ever seen anything like it? You don't want the ride to ever end, do you? You want it to loop around and around, and maybe stop right at the top and let you see the moon like this, and all the lights below, and maybe steal a kiss. But it does have to stop. You can hear the clack-clack again, slower and slower. Clack. Clack.* Joe's legs collapsed under him, and he went down. The sheriff let go of Angelo, and the boy ran toward the dog. *That's it. The ride's over. Catch your breath and I'll take you home now.*

Papa

"Half an hour, Joseph! Half an hour."

That voice. For nearly fifty years it had cudgeled, policed, drawn boundaries back and forth across Joseph Parettti's world. It had counseled, comforted, at times even saved him from near ruin. But this morning it was as invasive as a dentist's drill, as grating as a splintering bone, a buckling wall. It drove a loaded truck through Joseph Paretti's sacred time, those precious minutes after black coffee had loosened his insides, sent him racing toward the porcelain as if catching a departing bus, *Chronicle Sporting Green* in hand, already slipping the suspenders off his shoulders, fidgeting at the top buttons to his trousers before plunking his bare ass down on the toilet seat. The blessed evacuation followed—a homage to gravity, regularity—when it felt as if all his internal organs had reached orgasm. In the following seconds, Joseph was relaxed and at peace, as if he'd stepped into curative waters. At this moment, anything else that might have occupied Joseph Paretti's mind seemed over-rated, superfluous, a long interlude until the next bowel movement.

He turned to the Horse Racing section, his favorite, studying each individual horse at each individual race at every bay area race track: Bay Meadows, Tanforan, Golden Gate Fields. He knew them all. More contentment followed. He read the horses' names outloud, sounding them like short sonnets, a favorite lyric, a refrain remembered again and again—*Moonrush, Gallant Fox, Twilight Tear, Determine.* Poetry. Pure poetry to Joseph's ears. And their odds of winning? It was called 'handicapping'—the wonderfully simple arithmetic of gain, a Rosetta Stone Joseph had unearthed while smoking his way through successive Chesterfields. Their blue smoke engulfed him like a shroud. He set the paper down and cracked open the bathroom window.

"Joseph! Twenty minutes!" Lena Paretti called again. "Remember what the doctor said—sitting like that makes your piles bleed!"

Joseph Paretti was in the country now. He had driven the forty five miles north from San Francisco in a lumbering Cadillac, its backseat and trunk lined with Macy's shopping bags, all filled with cold cuts—mortadella, bologna, spiced ham, stacks of sliced cheeses, tubes of salame, a half dozen loaves of sour French bread, pasta, cans of tomato sauce, tomato paste, jug wine, Italian peppers, an anvil-sized wedge of Parmesan, five pounds of flour, Lena's ravioli rolling pin, her cutting board, changes of clothes for both Lena and Joseph. Suitcases were an inconvenience, an unnecessary expense.

Their son-in-law, Irv Miller, had been hospitalized recently with a minor stroke, and they were helping Dorna, their daughter, care for the three boys on a dairy ranch Irv had leased several years earlier. Joseph knew nothing about dairy farming only that it was unprofitable—all he needed to know. As much as Joseph wanted to feel at home in the countryside, its expanses of open fields, its unimproved property—all struck him as lost opportunities. The country was filled with raw odors, as well as coarse farmers and large, mostly uncooperative animals that ate constantly, shit, and eventually died. If they didn't run around a track, they didn't interest Joseph Paretti. There were no sidewalks, no corner bars, and save for two weeks during the county fair in Santa Rosa, no horse racing. There were no dense blocks of buildings he could maneuver his funeral hearse between, no union meetings, no glasses of red wine at Capp's Corner after an internment. Instead, there were open fields and flurries of dust and hay chaff that caused Joseph's eyes to constantly water, that gave him sneezing fits so severe he'd re-injured his lower back. On this Sunday morning, Joseph had been conscripted to take his young grandson, Angelo, to Sunday Mass, where Angelo would serve as an altar boy.

He flushed the toilet, buttoned up his pants, and surveyed himself briefly in the mirror. He smoothed a right suspender that had twisted over his sleeveless undershirt. His short, hairless arms, the color of window putty, hung from a set of narrow shoulders, and his neck, the little there was of it, rose in a hump at the nape of his head. Gray slacks, rolled up two turns, hovered over a pair of worn oxfords—what Joseph dubbed his "country shoes." With the wattles below his chin, and a sharp, thin nose almost like a beak, he resembled more an upright turtle that for the moment had discarded its shell, than a semi-retired funeral coach driver two months shy of this seventy-second birthday. "Little Angelo's been ready for ten minutes—why do you always have to disappear?"

"Disappear? I was takin' a crap, for crissakes."

"Ten o'clock Mass—you should go yourself."

"I'm in churches enough."

"Angelo!" Lena called. "Your grandfather's ready!"

Angelo walked into the kitchen. His hair was wetted down, with a sharp part that ran along one side of his head.

A blue bow tie hung crookedly between the points of his shirt collar. Lena walked over and bent to straighten it. "He looks like a little angel, doesn't he, Joseph?"

"No, he looks like a ten year old with his hair all wet."

Lena glared at Joseph. "No stopping along the way, either—"

"Where am I gonna stop?"

"Never mind—I know you."

"Angelo, get in the car. I'll be right out," Joseph said.

Joseph followed his grandson, opened the door to his car, and tossed in yesterday's Chronicle. He adjusted the seat cushion, patted his pocket to check for his cigarettes, and a half dozen labored breaths later, lowered himself behind the steering wheel. Angelo ran his hand along the dashboard, fingering each of the chrome knobs and switches. Joseph started the Cadillac.

"What do you think of it?"

"Real fancy, Papa."

"The choke's automatic now—don't have to bother with the manual one anymore."

It was a dark blue Cadillac Fleetwood, the first new car Joseph had ever owned. Until now he'd driven smaller, less expensive models—Fords briefly and Chevrolets rescued from used car lots and desperate private parties for two hundred dollars and the promise of a paint job. Their torn upholstery Joseph hid with seat covers from Western Auto. If they needed tires, he combed five wrecking yards to find a matching set. And whenever mechanical problems arose, he leaned on his other son-in-law, Gene, to avoid expensive shop bills. In Joseph Paretti's book, everyone owed him something, a future favor he could always draw upon.

"She rides like a dream, Angelo." He slid the shift lever into drive and the Cadillac inched forward. Petey, the dog, escorted them down the driveway. Joseph paused, looked both ways, and looked again before maneuvering onto

Adobe Road. The front of the car rose like the bow of a boat as it reached the pavement. "Sometimes you don't even know you're in a car. You close your eyes and you'd think you're on a sofa in your living room."

Joseph glanced into the rear-view mirror, adjusting it slightly. He wore a hat now, an airy Panama with the brim turned up. "They got a breaking-in period when they're new. They don't want you to drive them over fifty for the first thousand miles."

"How many miles does it have, Papa?"

Joseph looked down at the odometer. "A little over five thousand."

The Fleetwood moved down Adobe Road at forty miles an hour.

"How fast can your car go?"

This one? I don't know—ninety, maybe a hundred."

"What's the fastest you've ever gone?"

"Sixty—sixty five."

"That's all?

"What do you think I am? Some kind of race car driver? I'm not like your older brother."

Joseph Paretti rarely drove over fifty. For nearly half a century he'd led funeral processions for Valenti-Marini Undertakers in the Mission District in San Francisco, and this professional pace had effortlessly, unconsciously, trans-ferred to his regular driving. While others flew by him, or rode his bumper, impatiently sounding their horns, Joseph drove on as though they didn't exist, as though behind him was always a body enroute to the cemetery, as though the roadways were built to accommodate just one vehicle—his own. He ignored drivers' threatening gestures, their vengeful stares. There were at least two lanes to every road, and Joseph, by right, occupied one of them. He didn't drive the posted speed, he drove the *Joseph Paretti Speed*, one designed to take in as much of the passing world as possible without coming to a complete stop, one that allowed for the endless calculations always clicking away in Joseph's mind, that minimized engine and brake wear, and reduced traffic collisions to astonishingly safe levels.

"What time is it now, Papa?"

"You gonna ask me that every five minutes? There, look at the clock. It's right there in the dashboard."

"I just don't wanna be late—it makes Sister Carolina mad."

"Who's Sister Carolina?"

"She's the one that makes the schedule out who's going to serve—and when she gets mad, it's scary—her face turns all red, and it swells up like it's pumped with air."

Joseph glanced at his watch. "It's 9:30. We got plenty of time, don't worry."

"If you miss Mass, Papa, did you know that's a mortal sin?"

"A mortal sin?"

"Yeah, they're worse than a venial sin. If you die with a mortal sin on your soul you go to Hell, but if you die with a venial sin, you go to Purgatory instead."

"Purgatory, huh?"

"Yeah, Purgatory doesn't last as long—it's not forever like Hell is. Sister Martina says it's like a chance at *parole.*" Angelo hesitated. "What's parole, Papa?"

"Parole? Let me see." Joseph had to think this one out. "Why they telling you these things?"

"So when we die, we don't go to Hell."

"You're not going to die for years and years."

"But maybe just in case."

"Parole is like when the bank puts money in your account that you didn't know you had. But you can't draw on it 'til a later date. And it don't earn interest." Joseph seemed satisfied with his definition. "Purgatory," he mumbled to himself.

Hay fields stretched out on both sides of Adobe Road. It was September, and tar weed had spread throughout the oat stubble. Joseph liked the smell of tar weed. It blocked the odor of cow manure, the rotting smell from Royal Tallow that often drifted east. He lowered his window a few inches, stuck his nose up to the opening, and attempted a deep breath. A sneezing fit followed.

"You all right, Papa?'

"Goddamn dust. It's everywhere." He shifted his weight to one side, and pulled a handkerchief from his rear pocket. "This is why I live in the city."

"Dad says you live wherever it's cheapest."

"He says that, huh?"

Angelo nodded his head.

"Well, you listen to your father, 'cause he knows everything. You just ask him."

"We're gonna be late."

"I see what time it is."

Joseph slowed the Cadillac to a crawl as Washington Street approached, then turning the steering wheel, just inches at a time, pointed the car west. Slowly the Cadillac accelerated, and once it had reached its cruising speed of 40 miles per hour, Joseph took one hand off the wheel and pushed in the cigarette lighter. He reached in his shirt pocket, plucked a solitary Chesterfield out, and stuck it between his lips. "There's even a lighter on your side," he motioned to Angelo. "This car's got everything. Hey, Angelo, look at this." Angelo's window lowered. "Electric windows. Electric everything."

"What'd you do with your other cars, Papa?"

"Sold 'em. Traded 'em in. They wanted almost six thousand for this one."

The lighter popped out and Joseph held it up to the end of his cigarette. Two jets of blue smoke curled from his nose. "Six thousand? I said. You're crazy. The guy's name

is Joe Ju. No foolin'. I offered him six thousand, and Joe
Ju says, 'Let me go in and sharpen my pencil and see what
I can do.' You sharpen a couple of them 'cause that's my
final offer. He comes out a few minutes later, and says, "All
right, you got deal—says it just like that—you know how
those Chinamen talk? He wanted more. Everyone wants
more, if they're selling. Less if they're buying. Just the way
it is. They teach you that in school?"

Angelo leaned over and looked at the speedometer.
"Dad says if he dies, he wants you to be driving the hearse."

"Why did he say that?"

"Because if he's going to hell, it'll take you forever to
arrive."

"Like I told you before—your father's got all the answers. Just ask him. Who else would have sold a perfectly
good house in town and bought a herd of milk cows? Huh?
You tell me, Angelo. Who would have done that?"

"I don't know, Papa."

"Nobody, that's who! But you can't tell your father
anything—he's got all the answers."

They were moving west on Washington Street, past an
old two story farm house surrounded with rusting farm
implements. Its windows were broken, and dried stalks of
field mustard grew up across its yard. Joseph slowed. Older
properties, particularly older, *abandoned* properties lured
Joseph. Despite his fears and dislikes of the country, he
still imagined a summer home somewhere on a tidy little
parcel, with a patio in the back, a smooth slab of concrete
he could hose off daily—a place where he could quietly
read the racing sheets, handicap the horses, and spend his
remaining years growing beans and peppers, and stands of
tall corn. These older properties reeked of opportunity,
potential. Numbers danced through his mind as he surveyed the house, the outbuildings. A couple hundred here.
A thousand there. If you had to, what could you turn it

around for? Numbers. Numbers. Hardly a thought passed through his head that didn't contain a number.

"Who owns that?" Joseph pointed to the house.

"I don't know. Never been anyone living there." Angelo pressed his hands together. Joseph saw his lips moving.

"What are you doing?"

"I'm praying, Papa."

"What for?"

"That if I die before Mass, I can still go to heaven. I'm praying for you, too."

"You're not gonna die, and you're not gonna miss Mass."

A pickup truck sped up behind Joseph, closed to within fifteen feet of the Cadillac's rear bumper, then pulled out and passed. Joseph glanced at it briefly in his rear-view mirror, then looked straight ahead. The truck disappeared in front of them.

"Everybody's in a goddamn rush all the time, you know that?" He looked over at Angelo. "Where they all going, that's what I want to know. Sunday morning, too. You'd think they'd take a day off."

"You could drive faster, Papa."

"What, and give into them? Push, push! Hurry, hurry! They want you to be just like them. Pretty soon everyone's racing around. And for what?"

Near McDowell, Joseph spied a truck parked along the boulevard with its tail gate down, loaded with sacks of grapefruit. A sign stood out in back of the truck that read: *Grapefruit, 10 for a dollar*. Joseph slowed to a crawl. A car behind him blasted its horn. Joseph raised his fist.

"You're not going to stop, are you, Papa?"

Joseph reconsidered. "No, maybe on the way back, though."

A block further west Joseph noticed a laundromat. "Good steady income with a laundromat," Joseph announced. "Business interest you, Angelo?"

"I don't know."

"You don't know? You're never too young to be thinking about your future." Joseph flicked the ash off his cigarette. "You wanna milk cows like your father?"

Angelo shrugged his shoulders. "I guess."

"Your father lives in another world, but he don't see it. He signs his life away on a herd of cows because he still thinks it's the war with the government buying up everything, but I told him, 'Irv, the war's over. Now you gotta compete with every other dairy farmer out there.' He didn't want to hear it. And what happens, huh? He works like a fool and gets a stroke."

It was 9:50, and they had just crossed the river downtown, five blocks from church. They waited at the intersection for the light to turn green. Joseph looked over and noticed that Angelo was crying.

"We'll get there, Angelo, don't worry," he tried to reassure him. He reached out and patted the boy's knee.

"No we won't. I should have my cassock and surplice on—

"Your what?"

"The robe that altar boys wear. I should have them on now, and filling the cruets, and checking the hosts and lining up ready to go to the altar."

When the light turned green, Joseph stepped on the accelerator. The big Cadillac lurched forward.

"Your father ain't ever gonna change—I tried to get him interested in property—I told him that's where the money's at—not looking at cows' assholes twice a day."

Angelo stared at the clock. "It's too late, Papa. Father Walsh has already started Mass."

"You still got a couple minutes."

"No, Father Walsh likes to start right on time."

"Okay, so you're a little late."

"You can't be late."

"Who says?"

"*They* say." Angelo motioned toward the church.

"They can start anytime they want. That's the way the world should work."

Joseph's body stiffened. He moved closer to the steering wheel, and accelerated to thirty five, a dangerous, nearly unheard of speed within the city limits for Joseph Paretti. The bells chimed 10 o'clock in the church tower. He turned onto Liberty Street, and a block later, the Cadillac had stopped alongside the rear of the church. Angelo didn't move in his seat.

"Well?" Joseph pushed his hat back and stared at Angelo.

"Father Walsh will be mad."

"You can go to Mass *twice* next Sunday. Tell him that."

"It doesn't do any good."

Angelo rubbed his eyes.

"Well, then, go in. Let them know you're here."

"Papa, it's too late."

"Goddamn it, go in there!"

"I'll just go to confession."

"And what are you gonna tell the priest?"

"I'll tell him that you drove too slow."

"You saw how I drove. Was that too slow?"

"It never takes anyone else that much time."

"That's because I'm not in a rush no more. I gave it up." Joseph pushed the lighter in. "Now, get out of the car, and go in there!"

Just as Angelo pulled the door handle back, the sacristy door opened at the back of the church, and out stepped a priest, dressed in purple vestments, ready to say Mass.

"Who's that?"

"That's Father Walsh."

"See, he's waiting for you. Tell him we had a flat tire."

"That's not true."

"I know it's not true—but tell him something."

Joseph pushed Angelo out of the car. Father Walsh lit a cigarette as Angelo approached him.

"Mister Miller, you're late," the priest said.

"I know, Father."

Joseph watched from the car as Father Walsh stood over Angelo. The boy's head was bent down. Finally, Joseph got out of the car, and walked over to where the priest and his grandson stood.

"Hello, Father, I'm Joseph Paretti, the boy's grandfather." He held out his hand, and Father Walsh shook it. "Angelo's upset because he thinks he got here late—

"He *did* get here late." Father Walsh pulled the sleeve back on his vestment, and glanced at his wrist watch.

"But you haven't gone out to the altar yet, so it's not too late, right?"

"We waited."

"Yeah, okay. I know you waited, and we appreciate that— the boy feels bad—really bad, and I don't like seeing him that way." Joseph looked down at his grandson. "I don't like him feeling bad about every little thing he does."

"There's such a thing as responsibility. As punctuality," Father Walsh said.

"Sure there is. I know that. You know that. And Angelo knows that." Joseph looked back and forth between the priest and his grandson. "He's sorry. I'm sorry."

There was a little pause when no one said anything. Joseph looked at Angelo, and then back at Father Walsh.

"Is the Mass important to you, Mister Paretti?"

"What kind of question is that?"

"If it was important, you'd have been here on time."

"Who says that?"

"It's a matter of priorities."

"Okay, it's the most important thing on earth—does that mean a hundred things couldn't have happened that made us late?"

"I don't want to argue with you, Mister Paretti."

"Papa, please." Angelo wrung his hands together.

"I don't want to argue, either. It's just that I saw you standing over the boy, and he was already feeling bad— so why make him feel worse?" Joseph rocked back on his heels. "If you wanna blame someone—

"I'm not blaming anyone."

"Sure you are. That's what you people do."

"Us people?"

"Yeah, you priests—you pass around blame like it was a bottle of that altar wine you drink. You make everyone feel bad."

"Mister Paretti, please." Father Walsh motioned to Angelo to go inside the sacristy. "Prepare for the Mass," he said, "Go on!" He looked back at Joseph. "I think you have a very distorted view of what we do."

"No, I seen it first-hand."

"Why don't you attend Mass this morning?"

"I go to Mass all the time—it's part of my job. It's like I built up credits."

Father Walsh looked at Joseph, crushed his cigarette under the heel of his shoe. "I have to go."

"Okay, Father."

Father Walsh disappeared inside the rear door of the church. Joseph walked to the corner of Western Avenue, then walked another block east to Purity Market where he bought the *Sunday Chronicle*. He stopped at Schindler's Bakery enroute back to his car and bought a dozen maple bars and a cup of coffee. Back inside his Cadillac, he opened the paper up, slid out the *Sporting Green*, and thumbed back to the horse racing section. He rolled the window down, and lit a Chesterfield. Inside the church, he heard the congregation stand, heard a tiny bell ring, and wondered if there'd be a sermon. With sermons, the Mass was longer.

He thought of little Angelo's pained expression, his concern for arriving late to Mass. Thoughts of Hell and Purgatory returned, something he hadn't thought of for years, as if not thinking about them would make them disappear. In a rare, contrite moment, Joseph folded the *Sporting Green* back together, and placed it alongside him on the front seat before getting out of the Cadillac and entering the church. He walked up a side aisle, past the Stations of the Cross, and found an open pew near the altar and sat down. When Angelo turned at the altar, Joseph waved at his grandson, crossed himself, and muttered a little prayer for forgiveness.

Sally and Stella

I was doing what I usually do most afternoons, evenings—drinking highballs at the Parkside with Floyd and the other regulars: Mitch Moreham, Flo Gleason, Shorty McGrath. Skeeter, the bartender, calls us *The Funnel Gang*. Other times it's the *Genies*. "Just open a bottle," Skeeter says, "and all of you appear." Some of us drink because we have to, others, because we're trying to forget. Mostly I drink to have a good time. It soothes me, shuts out the noise, puts a different spin on a life that's made all kinds of detours. But this one Saturday I want to tell you about, it didn't work out that way.

Floyd and I had been living together nearly six months. It wasn't like we'd planned it. We don't plan nothing except evenings at the Parkside. It's like church to us. A place where we can drink and talk and just be ourselves. I work the mornings as a seamstress for Priscilla Holmes, just off the

Plaza, and after more than four, five hours of sewing, my migraines start acting up. Priscilla knows that, and she's happy to have me half-time. Anyway, after a few months of buying each other drinks, Floyd and me started hitting it off. We'd find ourselves talking to each other more and more, not ignoring the rest of the group, but peeling off from them, just talking between ourselves about things, personal things, about what our lives had been like. After the longer nights of drinking, I'd roll over in bed the next morning, and there'd be Floyd Mooney lying next to me, with no memory of how he got there. Other mornings, I'd wake up at his place. It snuck up on us, the way things developed. We'd known each other a year or so already. This town's a small one—and I knew all about his bouts of bad luck. He knew about mine. We all got them. Until then we both had our separate places. Then Floyd lost his job, got behind on his rent, and I said, 'Hell, Floyd, why don't you just move in with me?' Everything Floyd owned fit in the trunk of his Ford. His divorce had cleaned him out—so it wasn't like there was all this furniture to move, or anything like that. I made some room in the closet, and Floyd hung up the half dozen shirts he owned. We could walk to the Parkside, too.

At first, we seemed like a pretty good fit. We liked our highballs, and Floyd—well, that man, he could make me laugh like no other. He had this way of telling a story—it could be about anything—that just sucked me in. It was no secret I was falling for him and why I hung on every word. It could be the saddest of things, too—a car crash, how his daddy lost his eye—but the way he told it. He was just a natural. Floyd could put a little spin on it, work the story along, and right when you thought you knew how it'd end, he'd twist it up, get that little twinkle in his eye, and say something that just flat-surprised you. Pretty soon he'd have our whole end of the Parkside rocking back, banging their fists on the bar, clapping their hands, wanting to hear more. I loved Floyd when he was like that. I'd think to myself, *we just make all these little stops and detours, but eventually we all end up where we're going. It doesn't have to kill us, and if we're Lucky we enjoy some laughs along the way. It all plays out. It really does.* The problem was Floyd wasn't like that all the time. He had another side to him that he kept hidden. No surprise there. We all got things to hide. Stupid of me to think Floyd was any different, that he'd be just one way—the way I liked him to be.

We pooled our money, and the first thing we did each month was pay the rent on the apartment. Everything 'fair and square.' Then we'd buy groceries—I'm not a great cook, but Floyd was easy enough to please—a couple of lamb chops, mash up a whole bag of russets. Coffee and eggs. We'd run a tab at the Parkside and I'd pay that off each week. I was careful not to let it get too big. What Floyd made on odd-jobs, and the money I brought in doing alterations kept us flush. Not much, but it kept the wolf away from the door, as they say. I rat-holed a little bit away each week, too, in a shoe box at the back of the closet for one of those 'rainy days.' We'd treat ourselves to an occasional over-nighter to Reno on a Lucky 7 Bus Tour. I kept hoping on one of them, Floyd would pop the question, and we'd get hitched Nevada-style. Just walk down to one of those little chapels along Virginia Street. No family around. Just trade vows, he slips a ring on my finger. I never told Floyd about the money—it was like my little secret. I thought, eventually, if it all worked out, we'd buy ourselves a big wedding present. Maybe get a newer car. Then buy Floyd something nice for his birthday.

But little things happened. As soon as Floyd landed a job, well, almost as soon, he'd lose it. I'd meet him at the Parkside certain days, and his face was so long it practically touched his shoes. He had a short trigger, for one, and it was hard for him to take orders. The reasons he gave me for quitting always sounded good, so, at first, I'd take his side, and say, "To hell with him, honey. There's plenty of other work out there. Don't you worry."

The problem was that when Floyd wasn't working, Floyd was bumping the bar tab up, buying rounds when he shouldn't have been buying rounds, talking big, and not being nearly as funny as he was just a couple of months earlier. When Skeeter showed me the bar tabs, I said something to Floyd about it, and he gave me a look I hadn't ever seen from him before, a look he'd kept hidden. A look that scared me.

We were talking less and less, and Floyd was hardly ever home. When I'd meet him at the Parkside he'd ignore me, be off talking to someone else, and I'll tell you, it hurt like hell. I'd try to make conversation, and he'd look past me, hardly hearing a word I said. When I wanted to go home, he'd stay past closing time. I can't work the next day hungover, with no sleep. Then one day I returned from work, fished out the shoe box and, damn, if the wad of bills didn't feel thinner. I undid the rubber band, and counted them out, and sure enough it was twenty dollars lighter. I recounted them, just to make sure. I hoped and prayed my counting was wrong, but it kept coming up short.

Back at the Parkside, I asked Skeeter if Floyd had been paying for the drinks, or running a tab, and Skeeter said Floyd had been buying rounds with cash. "I figured he was back at work," Skeeter said. "But it's none of my business, Sally."

All of this was eating at me something terrible, and, of course, we hardly said five words to each other. We were like strangers. I'd go to bed and Floyd would wander in hours later, when he wandered in at all. This particular Saturday evening, though, I wanted to have it out. I was tired of not knowing, tired of being played for a fool. Tired of being sick from all the worry.

"Floyd," I said, "We gotta talk." He'd just come out of the men's room, and we were both standing in the hallway to the rear of the bar. I didn't want a big scene and I didn't want other folks listening in.

He looks at me and says, "About what?"

"About us."

"Ain't nothin' to talk about."

He starts to walk away, and I grab him by the arm.

"I think you're stealing from me," I told him.

That look boiled up in his face, that same look that froze me weeks earlier. His eyes got small and cold, and his mouth opened with his tongue clenched between his teeth. Before I could even react, he swung, and hit me square, high on the left cheekbone. My head snapped hard. His punch drove me into the wall. The next thing I'm lying on my back, woozy, looking up at the pay phone, and the directory dangling from its chain just above my head. I didn't know where I was, like being woke out of a deep sleep. Then people are shouting, and scuffling, and I hear Floyd yell, "The goddamn bitch called me a thief." Skeeter is down on his knees, holding a wet, terry-cloth towel to the side of my face. The colored neon is swirling on the ceiling. I hear Floyd's voice trailing off the way it had in so many of my dreams. Eventually Skeeter and Mitch Moreham help me to my feet, and walk me over to a booth opposite the bar.

Skeeter brought me a cup of black coffee but all I could do was just stare at it. Roxanne, another of the regulars, sat next to me, stroking my shoulders. "You poor thing. You poor thing," she kept repeating. "You don't deserve none of being treated this way."

When the spinning slowed down, and my head didn't hurt as much, I apologized to everyone for ruining their evening. I said 'good night' and started to leave the bar.

"You sure I can't give you a ride?" Roxanne asked.

"My legs are okay. Besides, the night air might feel good."

"You want me to call the police?" Skeeter asked. "We're all witnesses."

"No, I don't want them involved," I said.

Truth was the police knew me. There'd been some run-in's with them over public drunkenness, but they never wrote me up, never hauled me off. They knew I wasn't a trouble-maker, and that I didn't live far from the Parkside. Sometimes they even gave me a ride home. I'd get a little lecture from them while sitting in the backseat of the patrol car, a warning, and I'd promise not to be out in public drunk again, and they'd let me go.

I arrived back at the apartment, and when I put my key in the lock, the door was already open. I knew Floyd had been there. I walked inside, and at first, everything looked the way it'd looked earlier in the evening. I went to the closet, and Floyd's clothes were gone, and down on the floor was the shoe box where I'd kept the cash. The box was empty. I looked around. My radio was gone, and the jewelry box was upside down. Earrings, necklaces were scattered across the bed. He'd picked through it, and taken my mama's wedding ring, the only thing of value. I sat on the edge of the bed and had a good cry. When I went to rub my eyes, the pain from my left one shot down to my toes. I winced, cried some more, and swore at myself for not moving the shoe box, for just being so stupid, for being the sad, lousy person I'd ended up being.

In the bathroom I glanced at myself in the mirror. I was a sight. My left eye was nearly hidden from the swelling, and all around it the skin purple as a plum, my hair all pushed to one side, the way it looks after just waking up. Mascara had run down both cheeks and dried into two black lines at my chin. I grabbed a face towel and spread it out on the counter by the refrigerator, cracked open a tray of ice, and filled the center of the towel with a mound of ice cubes. I filled a glass with water, shook a handful of aspirin from their bottle, and gulped them down. I took the heaviest blanket from my bed, and wrapped the towel full of ice inside it, and looped the purse handle through my left arm. I closed the apartment door and locked it behind me and prayed the Ford would still be in its garage. I walked to the end of the alley, holding my breath, hoping against all hope that Floyd hadn't taken it. I knew he had the extra key. But there it was, like an old friend, waiting for me in its garage.

I opened the driver-side door, dropped my purse on the floorboard. Then I pushed the blanket across the front seat, and slid in behind the steering wheel. I slammed the car door shut and locked it. It felt safe inside there. The night was quiet. Inside the blanket, I found the ice-pack, and pressed it gently against my left cheek. I winced at first, and moved it away, then pressed it to the cheek again. My left elbow locked itself on the arm rest and held the ice pack in place. My face throbbed, then slowly numbed. Each pulse seemed to wash like acid across my half-hidden eye.

The Ford started right up, and I let it idle while I wondered what to do, where to go. It had a full tank of gas. I'd need it, because world seemed big and unfriendly then, as big and unfriendly as I ever remembered it, and I wanted to just keep driving. No one was spreading out the 'welcome' mat. No one was saying, "Sally, so good to see you. C'mon in." No, all my bridges had been burnt. There were some stretches of bad luck, and this one wasn't any different. They all seem the worst-ever when they first happen, but if you don't die, you grow a skin over what hurt you. It toughens you up, and you think nothing like this can ever hurt you again, but mostly you're wrong.

I backed the Ford out, drove past the plaza, and pointed it south down Broadway. The street lamps seemed to follow me, watching everything like a line of yellow eyes. I wanted to keep driving, right to the edge of the planet, maybe back off the gas a little bit, and then stab it hard when the edge come up and float right out into mid-air like a big metal bird. I wanted to just keep falling and falling—like so many of us do—and never hit ground.

The car moved south like it had a mind of its own. All I had to do was just hang onto the wheel, keep all four tires on the pavement, and it would take me wherever it wanted to—like a big Ouija board you held between your knees and your partner's, and the little arrow moved across the letters and numbers without either of you doing anything, without knowing any of the answers. Nothing. You just asked it a question, and then let it go on its own, not knowing what moved it, not questioning anything.

I talked to the Ford as if it were a friend of mine. "Where are we going? Will we be away long? Do you have a name?" We drove out Broadway, kept driving south out past the A &D Market, following the headlight beams that melted through the darkness. The left side of my face still throbbed. I could feel it growing, swelling, tender as a new boil. When a pair of headlights came up behind me, I snuck a peek at myself in the rear-view mirror. It was shocking. I slowed way down, and let the car pass.

Out at Shellville, Yeo's Café was closed, dark. It was still the middle of the night, no idea what time it was. I switched on the radio, but when it warmed up, it was nothing but static. What did it matter, anyway? What could the radio tell me? That it was dark? That I was alone? That my heart was broken again?

I drove toward the tidelands, down Millerick Road, and out into the hay flats. The sky was clear and filled with stars, and when I rolled the window down, the air was cool, brackish-smelling, the way I always remembered it as a little girl. It felt good blowing against my bruised eye, and I drove with my head halfway out the window. A levee road rose up on the right. I stopped the car, put it

176 THE BODY'S PERFECT

in reverse, backed it to where that road began, and drove fifty yards onto the levee. I shut the motor off and stepped outside. Looking south I could see the few scattered lights of Vallejo along the horizon, but all around me it was flat tidelands floating above a half-darkness, and a dampness blowing in from the bay. My mouth was dry, parched, and I sucked on an ice cube from the towel. Looking up at the night sky, there were no answers. There was nothing. No God, no saving angels, no one reading my palm. Just questions, strings of questions without an answer. Finally, I climbed into the backseat with the towel full of ice and my blanket, propped my purse against an arm rest for a pillow, and closed my eyes. I wanted nothing but to fall asleep, and wake up in the next century, maybe wake up and be an entirely new person, someone with no memory of who she used to be. Then I thought, wouldn't it better if I just didn't wake up at all? That seemed the simplest. I'd been given my chances, and wasted all of them.

I tried to sleep. But as aching and tired as my body felt, the whole earlier scene at the Parkside kept playing and re-playing in my head, like turning channels on the television, and finding every program was the same. Sleep wouldn't come. I counted backwards from 100, counted the pulse rate throbbing still through my eye, but nothing worked. I tried to think of nothing at all, just the darkness behind my eyelids, but colors and patterns danced there. I tried to imagine how good five or six hours of sleep would feel, but my mind wouldn't switch off. It kept returning to Floyd's angry face, and his eyes fixed on me, wide and bright as a cat's, and the neon swirling against the Parkside's ceiling, then all the voices, the shouting and confusion that fol-lowed. And, in the next second, there would be Floyd's face again, but this time the one I wanted to remember—the sweet one, the smile and the glow that surrounded him as he told his stories.

Eventually I fell asleep, and dreamed about my sister Stella, and our dad, two people I'd been trying to drink away since my teens. Dad inherited twenty acres on Adobe Road and raised heifers there. He worked for Wingo Land and Hay Company every haying season for the extra money. In fact, he worked crews on these very tidelands, and while he worked those summer days, Stella and I stayed back at his car, underneath a canvas awning he'd stretched out from its roof, and tied off with two four foot poles. We read *Nancy Drew* mystery stories, we played in Sonoma Creek. We colored in coloring books. We drew pictures and made up stories. We talked about boys, about the ones we wanted to kiss. We drank water from a glass jar that Dad had wrapped in burlap, and ate egg salad sandwiches. Stella picked on me a lot. She was the older sister, and with Momma dead from a blood disease before I could ever remember her, Stella tried to keep me from straying. It was a big job. I was a hard-head, always trying to do things my way. The more Stella threatened me, and the more she pointed out the people I might become, the more I strayed. "You're not my Momma!" I'd shout back at her.

I was in the middle of my worst drinking when Dad died. Bad drinking. His foot got caught up in a hay press, mangled it badly. Infection set in that weakened him, and he never recovered. For several months he just festered and then he was dead. It wasn't Stella that told me, either, but Bud Yenno, a hay broker that tipped a couple at the Parkside. I went to Dad's rosary, but had to leave halfway through it when the shakes started up. A day away from the sauce, sometimes just hours, and I'd get the trembling almost like freezing without your coat on. It took one or two drinks to calm me. The problem was I never stopped at one or two. On the morning of Dad's service, I'd started out for the funeral home in Petaluma, got as far as William's Y before stopping off for a quick beer. That's all it took.

By early afternoon, a welder named Cooper coaxed me out to his truck with a bottle of bourbon. We parked off Stage Gulch, and before I knew it, his whiskers were brushing against my face, and a hand rough as burred steel was inside my brassiere. Later, I went home with him. At least, I woke up at his place, a little tar-papered affair tacked onto the back of his shop. He drove me back to the bar. We hardly said two words. There in the back seat of the Ford were the flowers I'd bought the day before, all wilted and limp. I wrote a card to Stella a few days later, and told her how sorry I was to have missed Dad's service. I told her I was sick, in the grip of something. She never wrote back.

When I woke up, a gray light hung everywhere like smoke. My neck was stiff and aching. The sun still hid behind the Napa hills. There was an awful sour taste in my mouth, and my lips so dry and parched, they could hardly move. I drove back to where I'd passed the hay barns the night before. A wooden tank stood off by itself, with water leaking from a split in its side. I walked under the leak, and let the water drip on my head. At first, it took my breath away, but then I got used to it, and it felt good, felt bracing. The drops landed on the top of my head. Once I looked up, and drops fell right onto my left eye, and I stepped back so quickly I nearly fell over. I wrung the towel out and re-wet it. The sun moved up from behind the hills, and now its light slanted across the flat fields, making long shadows against the levees. I thought of returning to my apartment, but just then the idea of Floyd showing up there scared me. But where else could I go? There were a couple of regulars at the Parkside, that might take me in but it was still so early, they'd all be sleeping still. And even with the regulars, it was a funny kind of relationship we had. If I passed them on the street, and we hadn't been drinking, it was like we were different people, almost like we had to introduce ourselves to each other all over again. We'd fumble for names, struggle to find things to talk about that ordinarily we didn't have to do when holding up a bar stool. Floyd didn't like me mixing with other men, either.

By now I'd driven back up to the highway, and pulled into Yeo's Triangle. The "Open" sign was displayed in the door. I ran a comb through my wet hair. The perm was gone in it, and the ringlets that once thrilled me in Jeannie's Salon hung as limp as baling twine. I put my dark glasses on, and walked inside the restaurant. The first thing to greet me was the smell of brewed coffee. Old man Yeo sat at the end of the counter reading a newspaper. He looked up as I walked in, trying to place my face, to connect it up to someone he might know. I sat down at the opposite end of the counter, and ordered coffee. When he set the mug in front of me, I stared straight ahead.

"Cream?" he asked.

I shook my head no.

Neither of us said anything. Each time he'd turn a page, he looked up at me as if wanting to say something, but then returned to his newspaper. If he asked me any questions, it was only a word or two that came out of my mouth.

I thought about Floyd. We were through, I knew that. No more 'sweet-talking', no more apologies, no more "Sweetheart-I'll-try-to-do-better crap." Anyway, that wasn't Floyd's style. He never apologized because it was never his fault. It was always someone else's. I tell you, I can be such a sucker. Roxanne says it's because I've got such a soft heart. Maybe so, but last night hardened it up. Floyd and me are through. You hit me, and no second chances.

I reached into my purse to pay for the coffee, but my little wad of bills was gone. Maybe I'd spent them all the night before, I couldn't remember. I snapped open my coin purse, found enough nickels and dimes, and left them all on the counter. I got back in the Ford and headed up Stage

Gulch Road toward Petaluma. Just like last night, I let the Ford take me along. I didn't know where we were going. I was buying time, waiting for my head to clear, waiting for it to stop hurting. I remembered the dream last night with Stella in it, and how we were both little girls wearing dresses trimmed in lace, with petticoats underneath that made our skirts stick out like umbrellas. Then we're standing in the creek and the water's torn our dresses away leaving us in only our underwear. I'm shivering, but Stella's enjoying the water, splashing, jumping up and down. I took the dream as a sign to see Stella again, to try to patch up a little of what I'd blown apart. But with one eye swollen shut, and not a cent to my name, it was bad timing, the *worst* timing. The Ford kept moving through the turns in the road as if it knew where to go. Back and forth, back and forth I went whether to see Stella or not.

Just past the Old Adobe, I glanced up and read the creamery sign in front of a dairy that said Irv Miller and Sons. "Irv Miller," I said out loud. The Ford slowed to a crawl. We'd been classmates years earlier, and he knew I had a crush on him so he teased me something awful. I'd daydream in class about him, imagine we were destined for each other, and what we'd name our children, and where we'd live. I'd write "Sally Miller" in the margins of my notebook. When he asked me for a turn at the Roost Club dances, I didn't know a young woman could be this thrilled. Then Irv quit school and the next thing I hear he's selling shoes at the downtown J.C. Penney's. I'd go in there, shopping for shoes, but it was really just to see Irv. I think he knew that. He'd sit on that little stool in front of me, gently slipping shoes on and off my feet. I'd walk back and forth, stopping in front of the mirror, looking at the shoes, but also trying to catch Irv in its reflection, too. His hands always felt so good around my ankles and the backs of my legs. He'd say the nicest things to me. Compliment me on my legs. "You've got some beautiful *gams,* Sally," he once told me.

He even asked me out, and once we drove out to Tomales where they had an outdoor dance floor. A little dance band played there, and you could look up and see the stars, and there was a table off to the side with a punch bowl and a tray filled with sugar cookies. You'd think, if ever time could freeze, this would be the moment to freeze it. I told him that, too, and a little grin formed at the corner of his mouth.

Then one day I slipped into Penney's wanting to see Irv again. I told him I wanted to try a pair of shoes on that I'd seen in the front window but Irv saw through that. He comes out with the shoes, and right away I know something's different. He's all business, like I'm just another customer. It's written all over his face. He's got something to tell me, he says, and the first thing I think is that someone died. He's looking at his shoes, and he's looking out at the street. He's looking everywhere but into my eyes. Then he tells me the news. He's transferring to the store in Santa Cruz. It's a promotion, he says, and he can't pass it up. Just like that, my whole imaginary world with Irv Miller caved in. The house, the kids, the life together, all gone. I congratulate him, ask when he's leaving, and he says they want him to start the following Monday. Something died in me just then, broke all apart and died. I could feel it. "A promotion?" I said, every word forced. "Gee, that's swell, Irv." And then he was gone.

From then on, it seemed like one heart break after another, each one trying to outdo the one before it. Each one promising a new start, all flush with hopes and highballs, before splitting apart. If you wanted to write the story of my life, it'd be a short one—girl meets guy, girl falls for guy, guy leaves girl. A one-pager. The more I'd dream about romance and love, the further it moved away from me. And just when I thought it was my turn—because everyone got a turn, didn't they?—the rug got yanked from underneath me. There were nights I couldn't drink enough to forget about it. Nights when I thought I'd drown—*wished* I'd drown—washed ashore someplace, and be done with all of it.

The Ford inched up Adobe Road, my foot barely on the gas, fighting all the time to hit the brakes and turn back toward Sonoma. At the foot of the long gravel driveway that led up to Dad's place, the sedan stopped. Even though Stella lived there, I still called it 'Dad's place.' Two redwood trees shot straight up behind the house with green shutters. The little farm was tucked into the folds of the hills, its barns and outbuildings barely seen from Adobe Road. Stella never left the property. She married a glazier named Ralph Fratino, and all three lived together—Stella, Ralph and Dad. Stella and Ralph had no kids. Then Ralph had a heart attack—right on the job, dead before they could even get him off the scaffolding. Less than six months later, Dad died, too.

I waited down on Adobe Road for an hour, maybe longer. When cars passed by, I looked the other way, fidgeted in my purse as though looking for something. A dozen times I'd start the car up, and cramp the steering wheel hard left for a U-turn back to Sonoma, and a dozen times I'd change my mind, shut the motor off, and sit and think awhile longer. Where would I go except back to my apartment off the plaza? And right now I had to avoid that place, afraid of meeting Floyd there, afraid of getting suckered once again by those eyes of his, those sweet-sounding excuses, and end up taking him back . *We're done, we're done,* I kept repeating. *Sally Traversi, don't you take him back. Never, never. On your mother's grave, never.* I started the Ford, yanked the wheel to the right, and headed up the gravel road.

The house grew larger, filling up more and more of the Ford's windshield. My heart beat fast, each breath shortened, quick. Nothing stirred, nothing moved. I remembered it was Sunday morning, but Stella had never been a church-goer. Within twenty yards of the house, an old terrier worked his way up onto all fours from the back porch landing, and walked stiff-legged toward my car. I shut the motor off, put on my dark glasses, and opened the car door. The terrier walked up to me.

"Burt? Is that you, Burt?" I asked the dog.

His muzzle was all white, and he had those 'old dog' eyes like a pearl had been dropped into the middle of each one. He wagged his tail, and tried to bark.

When I looked up, Stella was standing at the top of the back porch steps, both hands on her hips. She looked older, grayer, heavier than the last time I'd seen her, years before. How long ago, I couldn't even remember. Her hair was tied up in a bandanna. She had on jeans, and a jean jacket and wore rubber boots.

"Is that Burt?" I asked her.

"That's right," she said.

I stepped away from the Ford, and stood up straight. My whole body ached and felt stiff. Half my face was numb. I reached down slowly to pet Burt.

"What do you want?" she asked me.

"I wanted to come by and say hello."

"Why? You run out of luck again?" Stella glared at me. "Don't think I haven't heard about you."

"I don't want nothing. Just to say hello."

"You drive over here on a Sunday morning to say hello? Not a word from you in years, and this one day you drive over to say hello?"

"That's what I've done."

"You worried about your inheritance, is that it? Afraid I'll die and someone else'll get this place?"

"I hadn't thought about it."

"Bullshit, you haven't thought about it."

"I haven't."

Burt teetered toward the Ford's tires. He lifted a quick leg and peed before moving onto the next one.

"How are you, Stella?"

"Fine. How do I look, huh? Never felt better. Does that answer your question?"

"Stella, can't we be civil to one another?"

"Civil?" Stella repeated the word. "Now that's a word I haven't heard you say before."

I walked toward the steps. Strands of gray hair looped down from inside Stella's bandanna.

"Could we talk, Stella?"

"About what? About what a caring daughter you were? A caring sister? I don't think there's much to talk about there." She put her hands back on her hips, blocking the back steps.

"I'm sorry," I said. "It was tough times."

"Tough times. You tell me about *tough times."*

"It was—"

"Well, it was 'tough times' when Dad was shittin' all over himself the last four months he was alive, and I asked you for help. And what did I get back?"

Stella made a 'zero' with her thumb and fingers.

"Tough times," she waved her hand at me. "I know all about your 'tough times.' And your bar-fly friends. Sorry, sister, but if you're looking for sympathy, you came to the wrong place."

"I'm not looking for sympathy." I couldn't arrive at a good reason, a convincing reason for my visit, not without spilling all the beans. I had to keep talking, though. "You're right—I've run out of luck. Again."

"Well, you ain't staying here—this ain't no board and care."

"That's not why I came."

"So, it looks like everything's been said."

"Nothing's been said," I told her. "Nothing at all."

"What's left to say?" Stella asked. "It's all done with—dead and gone. Kaput. What do they say about 'dead dogs'? Just let 'em lie? That's what I'm doin', sister—lettin' all those dead dogs lie out there."

"There is one thing I'd like before going," I said.

"What's that?"

"How about a cup of coffee? And could I use the bathroom? Then I'll go, and you won't be bothered no more."

Stella thought. "Coffee, and then you're gone?"

"That's right. Then I'm gone."

Stella motioned me inside the house. I grabbed my purse and walked up the stairs, and into the backporch. Everything I saw reminded me of Dad—his old, worn bootjack under the laundry sink. One of his flannel coats still hung on a hook by the back door. I walked into the kitchen, and it was just as I remembered it years ago. How many? I still couldn't remember. Everything smelled the same, too. The Pine Sol, the musty odor, the furniture polish. It was the same table and chairs, the same pictures on the walls—the blacksmith shop and the little boy sitting on a stump watching the blacksmith shoe a horse. The same little braided oval rug you stepped onto from the back porch into the kitchen.

"You know where the bathroom is," Stella said. She filled a percolator with water, and measured out scoops of ground coffee into its metal basket.

I ran the water in the bathroom sink, took my dark glasses off, and stared at the face in the mirror. It looked even worse than it did earlier in the morning. Swelling nearly hid the left eye, the skin even deeper purple than the night before. And the white of my eye wasn't white anymore, but red as a ripe strawberry. I splashed water onto my face, and patted it dry with a towel, then tried to fluff out my hair, but it was flat and matted, stiff as steel wool. I opened my compact and dusted my cheeks with some powder, put a line of lipstick on my bottom lip, and smacked them together. I put the dark glasses back on, switched off the light and walked back into the kitchen. The water was already bubbling up in the percolator.

"Coffee smells so good in the morning, don't it?" I said.

Stella grunted.

"The light hurt your eyes?" Stella asked, "that you gotta wear them glasses?"

"It does," I said.

"Some kind of infection?"

"Sort of."

"Sit down. I made some toast—it's heels. Run out of things. Monday's shopping day."

"That's fine," I said.

Stella stood at the sink. She'd changed out of her rubber boots, and now wore slippers caved so far outwards she walked on the sides of her feet. She'd broadened out at the hips. Her face, too. Her hands were as big and rough as a man's.

"I was sorry to hear about Ralph," I said.

Stella looked up from the sink.

"That's how them things go."

The toast popped up and she grabbed one slice at a time and began buttering them.

"He was a worker, that man. Never complained about nothing." She stopped buttering the toast. "Maybe that's what got him in the end—he was having these pains, and not telling no one. Didn't want anything slowing him down. And when he did mention it, he said it was indigestion."

"I'm sorry."

"He's working at the new Price Motors one day, installing the show room glass, working a bead in on top of the scaffold. Hugh Westman, the general contractor down there, walks by and hears Ralph, and thinks he's choking on his sandwich. Next thing Ralph's on his knees, then falls forward, dead before he even hits the planks. Just like that."

"I sent you a card," I said.

"Oh, I got a lot of cards."

"I been struggling."

"You ain't alone, sister."

Stella brought the plate of toast over to the table and placed it in front of me. She opened the refrigerator and grabbed a jar of orange marmalade. The coffee had stopped perking, and she unplugged the pot and filled my cup and then hers. She sat down on the opposite side of the table and looked at me.

"You gotta take them glasses off. It's like talking to a mannikin in Carither's front window."

When I took them off, Stella leaned back in her chair.

"Lordeee, sister! What kind of infection is that?"

I looked down at the coffee cup.

"It isn't really no infection."

"What is it?"

"It's a bruise."

"A bruise?"

"Floyd done it," I said.

"Who's Floyd?"

"My boyfriend—my *ex*-boyfriend now."

I looked at Stella, and her eyes traveled all around my face.

"You know how to pick 'em."

I didn't want to hear a lecture. "Could I get some ice?"

Stella sucked in her breath, and heaved up from her chair. She went over to the refrigerator, and opened its little freezer door, and brought out a tray of ice cubes. She ran them under the faucet, and broke the cubes loose. She pulled a kitchen towel out of a drawer, and laid the cubes in the center of it. She handed me the towel, and once again I carefully placed it against my cheek bone.

"You ain't had much luck with men, have you?" Stella asked.

I shook my head.

"Just a long train of broken hearts," I said.

Stella sipped at her mug of coffee.

"Never gave a lot of thought to them, myself," Stella said. "Not being much of a looker or anything, had something to do with it. You learn your place early enough."

"Everybody gets a shot," I said.

"Then I run into Mabel Fratino, Ralph's sister, one day at Purity. I knew all about Ralph's first wife dying, and Mabel says I should look Ralph up. I told her I'm not doing that, not with his wife fresh in the grave. It didn't seem right. Then I run into her again, and she asked, 'What if I mention you to Ralph?' and I said, "Why not?" Next thing I know, he drives out here one Sunday, his shirt all starched, smelling of cologne, nicks on his face from shaving too close."

"Is that Irv Miller from town that lives down the road now?" I asked Stella.

"Same one. Been there nearly five years now."

"He's gone from selling shoes to milking cows?"

"There were a couple of other things in between," Stella said. Worked at Western Dairy after marrying a city girl. A pretty thing—dark hair, Italian."

"I had such a crush on him—"

"You had a crush on *all* of 'em."

"Irv was special though."

"Yeah, special."

"Then he moved away, and returned just before the war, and I got all excited that it'd pick up where we left off. But it didn't. It was different. Irv was different. Or maybe Irv was the same, and I just didn't' know who the real Irv was. The next thing I know, he's engaged and I'm left staring at last season's shoes in Penney's front window."

I started crying—just what I didn't want to do. I tried to hold back, but the more I tried, the more the tears came, until I was sobbing, my whole body shaking as if it'd caught a chill. The tears burned, ran into the wet towel, and when I dabbed at my eyes, the pain streaked out my arms and legs. When I started to say something, my voice broke up, and I hid my head in my arms.

"I'm sorry, Stella."

She looked at me and then she looked away quickly, out through the window above the kitchen sink.

"I'm not asking for any charity," I said. "I got a place of my own—"

"What about this Floyd character—he gonna bother you?"

"I don't know."

"You call the cops if he does."

Neither of us talked for several minutes. The percolator breathed on the stove. Stella sipped at her coffee.

"I dreamed about you and Dad last night," I said. "It was haying season, and it was a hot day like it always was down there summers, and we were playing in the creek, splashing water at one another, and laughing. Then you pushed me, and I fell into the deep water. And I remember looking up through the water and seeing the sun, and I was calling out to you, to Dad, to someone, to help me, and the words traveled up to the surface in little bubbles—each word was in its own little bubble—and when the bubble broke the surface, the word escaped into the air. I stayed underwater for a long time, almost like I didn't need to breathe. Almost like I didn't want to ever surface again."

"We fought a lot," Stella said. "You were younger, prettier. I hated that about you."

"And I kept screwing it all up."

"There were these guys that always asked about you—never about me," Stella said. "Daryl Withers and Johnny Pedrazi—guys you didn't give two shakes about, but guys

I would have gone out with at the drop of a hat. But you were off chasing the 'long-shot.' The ones that liked you weren't good enough."

"I couldn't see any of it, Stella. It was like a big haze over me."

"The whole time Dad is sick here, I heard maybe a half dozen 'thank you's' from the man—the whole time. But how many times did he ask about you? Huh?"

"I'm sorry."

"Yeah, sorry."

Anger and hurt, both, stirred up in Stella's face. "I wanted to forget how many times he asked. 'Where's my little Sally?' 'Did you talk to her?' 'Why ain't she been to see me?' And all the time I'm lying for you, and wondering why. I can't tell him the truth about his own daughter, and I don't know why. Maybe because it'll hurt him too much. And the whole time I'm hating you more and more."

"You still hate me?" My hands were shaking now. I wanted a drink.

Stella looked around the kitchen.

"You don't have to," I said, "because I hate myself enough for both of us. I thought I could drink enough to wash away who I was, thought a new person could just appear after the next drink. And sometimes that person did appear, but it wasn't the one I was hoping for."

I looked up at the kitchen clock. It was noon.

"Stella, can I ask you one favor?"

"Yeah?"

"I don't want no money—I still got my job as far as I know—"

"What do you want?"

"Well, two things, really—a tumbler full of bourbon to calm down my shakes." I held out my hand and Stella watched it tremble. "Just one. And a hot bath before I go," I said.

Stella walked over to a kitchen cabinet, and opened its door. She grabbed a bottle of Jim Beam and a glass and set both of them in front of me. She poured the tumbler half full.

"You want ice?"

"No thanks," I said, and poured the whiskey back. It felt warm and smooth going down my throat.

"There's bath towel in the linen closet," Stella said.

I ran hot water into the tub and kept testing it with my toes. Steam filled up the bathroom, and clouded the mirror. I took off all my clothes and lowered myself slowly into the water. I shampooed my hair twice, and when I'd finished, I laid back and closed my eyes. I stayed in the tub until the water cooled, and then I stepped out, and toweled myself off. I slipped back into my clothes, rinsed the tub out, and hung the towel on a bar to dry.

"Thank you, Stella," I said when I was back in the kitchen. "I feel much better."

Stella had rinsed the percolator out, and was drying the two coffee cups.

"I'll be going now."

"Okay," she said.

I grabbed my purse from the chair and walked out into the back porch. Stella followed behind me. I hugged her, but she just remained stiff. Her arms stayed at her side. Out at the car, I said good-bye to Burt, and scratched him at the base of his tail. His legs wobbled.

"Bye, Stella," I said.

She nodded her head.

"Maybe we'll see each other again?"

"Maybe."

"I'll be in better shape then. I'll get things figured out."

Stella nodded her head. "I hope so—for your own sake."

I started the Ford up, and drove back down the driveway and onto Adobe Road. I looked in the rear-view mirror, and saw Stella still standing on the back porch steps. Burt watched the Ford, his ears perked up. The sun peeled through the overcast, and I was on Adobe Road, heading back to Sonoma. Where else could I go? But I didn't feel so bad now. I'd seen Stella, and we'd talked. I'd been wanting to do that for so long, and now I did it. That's all you can do—set yourself one little thing to accomplish and figure out how to do it Sometimes it's better not to even think about it, either, spending days and weeks worrying if you'll do it or not. No, sometimes you just take the leap—even if you end up falling. Leaving Stella's, I knew nothing had changed much and yet, everything had changed. I couldn't explain it, but for some reason I didn't feel as hopeless, as alone as I did just hours earlier. I'd figure things out. My luck would change. When I reached into the purse for my sun glasses, out came a twenty dollar bill. I looked down at it. It was a twenty, all right. My luck had changed already.

Next Dance

A month before his high school graduation, Clarence Mazzoni enlisted in the Marine Corps. Mechanically-inclined, indifferent to studies, infused with a fierce sense of patriotism, college, for Clarence, seemed out of the question. When Marla Maxwell, Clarence's girlfriend since junior high, first heard the news, she broke down, cried for days. It shattered Marla's heart that the only boy she'd ever loved, the boy she would eventually marry and begin a family with, would ever leave her. Through long, passionate evenings, Clarence assured Marla of his undying love, his resolve to return after military service and begin the life they'd dreamed of since first meeting.

But now, with graduation over, and Clarence's reporting date just days away, Marla wanted to plan something, something she and Clarence would always remember during the time they were apart. Clarence, though, wasn't a socializer. He disliked crowds, most gatherings, felt awkward around them, often tongue-tied, so a 'going-away' party seemed out of the question. When asked what he most wanted to do, Clarence's wish was modest: he wanted to spend the evening with his two favorite people—Marla, of course, and Jackie Miller, his buddy since grade school. And with them, Clarence wanted to order a deluxe burger at Lund's Drive-in, and afterwards, in his 1955 Chevy, drive into the Sonoma Mountains, park, and drink Olympia beer. Within hours, Marla had arranged a double date to include herself and Clarence, Jackie Miller and Raelene Robby. Jackie and Raelene seemed like a good pairing.

Just two months earlier, Raelene Robby and Little Frank Borda had broken up in a very loud, very public display during lunch at their high school's Senior Tree. Accusations flew back and forth between them. Nose to nose they peppered each other with a language that would have humbled most truck drivers. At any second, one expected fists to fly. Since then, Raelene was stuck at a bus-stop called Limbo, saddened, certainly, but defiant, and ever optimistic that she and Little Frank were destined for each other.

Marla believed the one thing Ralene most needed now was consoling, and, perhaps, to date other guys. Jackie Miller seemed the perfect candidate. He enjoyed his mother's Italian good-looks, parted his black hair sharply to one side, batted those large hazel eyes, and followed it all with a disarming smile that had seduced a dozen different girls since junior high school. He'd never been able to settle on one; they were all too imperfect for Jackie, lacking in some essential quality. By most accounts, girls found Jackie arrogant, quick-tempered, blustery. Still, Jackie had been a faithful friend to Clarence, and had always treated Marla with a respect that belied his reputation.

The date was set, the same night Little Frank Borda's mother had planned his graduation party in Lakeville. Raelene wasn't invited, and by early evening, Marla, Clarence and

Jackie arrived at Raelene's house in Straubville, where the two girls embraced, and where Raelene promptly joined Jackie Miller in the backseat of Clarence's Chevy. Raelene's bouffant had been teased to new heights, while her summer top plunged to new lows. At Lund's Drive In they wolfed down cheeseburgers and fries, Cokes and chocolate malts, but food was just a preliminary. Stowed away in the trunk of Clarence's '55 Chevy was a half case of Olympia, a fifth of sloe gin and two quarts of mixer. It was the last Saturday in June, a bittersweet time, and they were headed to the quarry.

Marla sat next to Clarence, stroking his left ear, and whispering into the right. She gathered a length of Clarence's curls between her fingers. "These'll all be gone by next week, sweetie."

"You'll be a buzz-head," Raelene added.

Clarence kept one hand over the top of the steering wheel. His shirt sleeves were rolled back behind each bicep. When Marla toyed with his right ear, she traced her fingers across his arm. "Is this where you gonna have the tattoo?" she asked.

"Right there, sweetie," Clarence said. "There's gonna be a big *Marla* written out right there.

In the backseat, Raelene Robby fidgeted constantly. She pressed her generous body into Jackie Miller's. Her thighs spread from under a summer skirt like spilled cream, and her platinum hair, frozen with spray, brushed against Jackie's cheek. With each loop up Lynch Road, Jackie could feel the hard points of Raelene's breasts poke into his ribs, felt her face drawing closer to his until, in a burst of sudden chemistry, their mouths touched. She trembled. She sighed. Her lips tasted like Juicy Fruit and sour Kools when they kissed. "We might as well get to know each other," she said to Jackie. "It's not like we're goin' steady or anything, right?

"Fine with me," Jackie said.

She'd made all the moves, and Jackie, ever dutiful, responded. His lips locked onto hers, his tongue dipping into her mouth, both hands squeezing at her shoulders, exploring Raelene's body with as soft and firm a touch as he could muster. When his hands wandered to her breasts, she pushed them away. "Just wait, Jackie Miller. I'm not *that* easy." If she was in mourning over Little Frank, Jackie saw no trace of it. From Jackie's point of view, they were both along for the ride, and whatever happened, happened. It wasn't the start of something. It wasn't romance. So why ignore each other? It was one evening in June, they'd just graduated from high school, there was a warm body next to his, they were climbing into the hills and Clarence soon would be reporting to boot camp. Things would be different then. Jackie didn't know exactly how—he just sensed it in his bones.

When they arrived at the quarry, a chain was looped through the steel gate.

"Shit, it's locked," Raelene said.

"It's never locked," Clarence said. He put the Chevy into neutral, slipped out from under Marla's arm and walked to the gate. The Chiffon's *One Fine Day* played on the radio. Raelene sang along with the lyrics: "*One fine day you'll look at me and know our love was meant to be. . .*" Seconds later the chain dropped at Clarence's feet.

Clarence motioned Marla forward with his hand. She lifted her legs over the gear shift, and moved behind the steering wheel. The Chevy idled into the quarry. Clarence shut the gate behind them and walked alongside the car until it stopped in a flattened area, the size of a baseball infield. Marla shut the motor off, and in the few, quiet seconds afterwards, Jackie heard the engine ticking. No one spoke. Crickets trilled. The seat springs creaked when Marla got out and joined Clarence. The hillside around them had been scooped out like an amphitheatre, and the rock looked golden in the last bit of slanting evening light. Raelene took Jackie's hand.

"If you think I'm all heartbroken about not being invited to Little Frank's party tonight, well, I'm not," Raelene said. "I know Little Frank. You know, when you're with someone long enough, you can go inside his mind and know all their thoughts? That's how it is with Little Frank and me."

"I always felt you two belonged together," Jackie said, although exactly what combination kept couples together remained elusive to him. He certainly knew those impulses, those urges that stirred between his hips, that drove him to women. But beyond those urgings, that territory remained foreign, forbidding, and certainly no guarantee of something more permanent. Deep intimacy to Jackie remained untested, a sign of weakness, dependency. He didn't like its trappings, the compromise it seemed to require, the baring of the self, the new language one had to learn. For all his arrogance, Jackie remained a close observer. He'd noticed, for example, that even after the most violent arguments between Raelene and Little Frank, within days, Raelene would be back in Little Frank's pickup, sitting so close to him it looked as though just one person occupied the truck's cab. It was puzzling. But why would it be any different this time, Jackie wondered? Raelene and Little Frank were biding their time, working things out in their own way. They were confusing, often hurtful, these matters of the heart, and the reason why Jackie avoided them. He traded on his good looks, instead, his glib tongue, the unfolding drama of his family's ruined finances. He knew just how deep to take his intimacy, and when someone expected more, when someone wanted Jackie Miller to open his heart, Jackie walked away. By default, he'd become a player, cool under pressure, a so-called "lady's man," a title that in his quiet, alone moments, seemed so odd, so misplaced.

"Little Frank's mother's the problem," Raelene broke the silence. "Just because my mom's a cocktail waitress, she thinks we're not good enough."

"They're high rollers," Jackie said.

"Big deal! I'm not Little Frank's left-overs—"

"I know you're not," Jackie said.

"You're sweet, Jackie." She kissed him on the mouth again. "Let's not talk about Little Frank. Or his mother! Let 'em have their stupid party tonight. I don't care! We'll have our own right here!"

Jackie pushed the front seat forward, and he and Raelene stepped out of the coupe. Clarence had popped the trunk open, fished two beers out of the cooler, opened them, and handed one to Jackie, then filled two tumblers with ice, poured sloe gin into each, and topped the girls' drinks off with Seven-up. They stood in a small circle, both doors open on the Chevy, with *Surf City* playing on the radio. The music echoed off the quarry walls.

"A toast to Clarence Mazzoni!" Raelene said, and they all raised their drinks. "May he come back after soldierin' and marry the one, true love of his life, Marla Maxwell."

"Here, here!" they all shouted together.

Jackie slammed most of the beer down in one gulp. He wanted to arrive quickly at that numbing place, where the barriers dropped, the tongue loosened, the fears didn't seem so large. When Marla kissed Clarence on the cheek, Jackie noticed Marla's eyes were filmy with tears. He felt sad for Marla, and how different her life would soon become. If Raelene's and Little Frank's relationship was confusing, turbulent, a succession of outbursts followed by apologies, Clarence's and Marla's was a steady, unwavering one, anchored on bedrock. They rarely argued, they understood and loved each other, and the little disagreements that surfaced were worked out with a minimum of drama and public fanfare.

Marla certainly wouldn't be the only one missing Clarence. Jackie had tried not to think about what it would be like with Clarence gone. Different, he knew that, but exactly how different, only time would tell. Clarence helped fill the empty spaces in Jackie's life. He'd become Jackie's confidante, his one, true friend. With Clarence gone, he'd have to fill those spaces some other way. There was farm work, of course, and the struggle to keep the family dairy afloat. But when Jackie looked ahead, he saw conflicting visions, big spaces to be filled. One option was staying on the family farm, continuing to work it despite the changing milk market, the disappearing small producers. Maybe he'd start a family of his own, and his offspring would follow in his footsteps just as he tried to follow in his father's. That, of course, would mean big changes, and Jackie wasn't exactly sure how those changes would happen. He imagined a shift inside, an alignment of forces that would clear a path for him, point to a future that until then had remained shrouded, indecipherable. The other recourse was to leave this town, this farm, the only life he'd ever known, and step out into the world just as Clarence was about to step out, and try something new. The small town, its gossip, its rivalries, its bickering and jealousies, its subtle class distinctions, all ate at Jackie Miller.

Raelene finished her drink, walked over to Marla and wrapped one arm around Marla's waist. Both of them sang, "*two girls for every boy.*" The music and their voices bounced back from the quarry walls. Raelene was soon singing by herself.

"I'm gonna miss you so much, baby," Jackie heard Marla whisper into Clarence's ear.

"*Two girls for every boy,*" Raelene sang. "Betcha you'd like that, huh, Jackie?"

Jackie raised his can of Olympia. "Two girls! Perfect!"

When Raelene moved next to Marla, Jackie and Clarence slipped away from the girls, walked over to the edge of the quarry, and stared out at the valley below. It was dusk now. The town lights had sprinkled on. Jackie followed the valley south toward Lakeville where the last bit of sun had caught a ribbon of river, and where the valley flattened out into bottomland and tule grass, and where Little Frank's party would be starting anytime at the Grange Hall. If things had been different, he would have asked Letta Azevedo to Little Frank's party, but tonight he and Raelene were the outcasts, the uninvited. It was nothing Jackie himself had done. For all his perceived arrogance around young women, Jackie was, by most accounts, polite, unassuming. He'd been caught in a cross-fire, though, between his family and Little Frank's, a kind of inherited grievance. Their two mothers, in particular, did not like each other. No small part of this was envy. Borda's dairy was like the one you saw on calendars—white-washed buildings, big Holsteins standing in the middle of permanent pastures crisscrossed with white fences, a sprawling house on top of a hill, while Miller's dairy was run-down, a pre-war relic, leased and not owned, its barns weather-beaten, its fences leaning out, half the place, it seemed, held together with baling wire and scabbed lumber. The Bordas drove big new cars and trucks. Evelyn's Cadillac took up two spaces wherever she parked, and the shadow of Big Frank's pickup followed him everywhere from Mario and John's to Golden Eagle Milling. Jackie's mother drove a turtle-back Chevrolet with gutted upholstery, and his father, a flat-bed pickup that belched blue smoke from its tailpipe. The Bordas had "stupid luck," Jackie's mother often said. "They fall into a shit-pile and come out wearing new suits."

"How are you and Raelene doin'?" Clarence asked.

"She's a goer, all right," Jackie said. "We're makin' out, if that's what you mean."

"You gettin' a case of the blue balls?" Clarence laughed, drained off his beer, then bent it in half. "Marla wanted someone to take Raelene's mind off Little Frank and your number came up."

"She's got other crap on her mind."

"So what?"

"She still likes Little Frank."

"Perfect. It ain't no long-haul thing for either of you, right?"

"Yeah, you're right."

"Just hang in there, buddy." Clarence toed at some rocks. He moved closer to Jackie and lowered his voice. "Don't tell Raelene, but I hear Little Frank's been spending time down at Azevedo's."

"Yeah?"

"Who'd you hear that from?"

"I don't know. Somebody. You know how word spreads around this place."

"Yes I do."

"Old man Azevedo's milker got kicked, and Little Frank's been helpin' out down there."

Jackie stared off toward Lakeville. "Good for Little Frank. Maybe he doesn't have his head up his ass, afterall."

"Why don't you get off the fence with Letta?" Clarence asked.

"What are you talking about?"

"C'mon, you know. Don't play dumb."

"You mean about asking her out?"

"Yeah, about askin' her out."

"I'm waiting for her to make the first move."

"And if she doesn't?"

"Then when it's the right time, I'll ask her myself."

"The right time," Clarence repeated. "The right time is sooner than later, old man."

"Sooner, then."

"Bet?"

"About what?"

"When you'll ask her. Five bucks you don't ask her at all," Clarence said.

"Okay, partner." Jackie said, and they shook hands.

It was a long history of missed opportunities between Jackie and Letta. Over the years he'd convinced himself that she wasn't the beauty he imagined himself spending time with. And in some eyes, she wasn't. Stick-thin, with dresses that hung from her bony shoulders, she certainly didn't have that ideal figure that fueled Jackie Miller's fantasies. He imagined someone more voluptuous, like the models in *Argosy*. And unlike so many of the other girls, she remained aloof to Jackie, indifferent to his glances, not unfriendly, but not swayed by him either. He'd found her dark eyes intriguing, full of promise, even daunting, at times, but he concealed his interest in her cleverly, convincing himself she wasn't the one, that she never could be the one. At dances and other mixers, he often saw her standing alone, while her girlfriends were off dancing or coupled up. He'd walk around the hall, collecting himself, calming a racing heart, sometimes even declining to dance with other girls, until he finally mustered the courage to ask her. But when he returned to where he last saw Letta, she'd be gone, disappeared. Still, Jackie often imagined that they would be together, that like Marla and Clarence, once they'd worked out their mutual awkwardness, allayed their common fears, their destinies would align themselves, and they'd walk up to each other and re-introduce themselves as the couple he'd always imagined them to be. It was a matter of time, of being patient.

"I'm getting drunk, Jackie." Raelene had joined them at the quarry's edge. Her mouth pressed against Jackie's ear. "What about you?"

"Getting there, too, Raelene."

"Were you guys talkin' about me?"

Clarence laughed. "All the dirt, Raelene. Everything we could dig up."

"That's not funny," Raelene said. "You be nice to me."

"Why?" Clarence asked.

"Cause I'm a nice person. Even if Evelyn Borda doesn't thinks so. Besides—" Raelene paused here. "She can stick Little Frank's party up her you-know-where."

Jackie smiled at Raelene. Her mascara had started to run. Marla had joined them at the quarry's edge. She and Clarence kissed.

"They're bein' mean," Raelene said.

"Oh, come on, Rae," Marla said. "They're just kiddin,' aren't you guys?"

"Raelene, you're the cat's ass," Clarence said.

"Thanks, asshole."

Jackie's thoughts wandered back to the Lakeville Grange, to where Little Franks' party would be starting any moment. Certainly Letta would be there. He wondered what she might be wearing, what she would look like on this Saturday evening. Would she go by herself? With her family? Odd that he thought about her more lately, and wondered if that time had come, perhaps, when that shift inside might slowly be happening. She wasn't his 'dream girl' by any stretch, but he was learning that dreams—the big ones—were far-off things, and to get there, you had to make stops along the way. Right then, he wished he'd been invited, and that he'd overcome his resistance, said 'to hell' to Evelyn Borda, and asked Letta to go with him. Dream-girl or no dream-girl, that's what he'd wished. Little Frank's party would be the first stop.

"Pretty ain't it?" Raelene wrapped her arms around Jackie's waist. "You never get to see it like this—the way the birds do." They leaned into each other. Jackie felt her warm breath on his neck. "Ever had your heart broke, Jackie?"

"Been disappointed."

"Disappointed? That's milquetoast," she said. "I mean, really had it stepped on? Ground into the floor?"

"Guess I haven't."

"It's bigger than just disappointment. It's like getting all your disappointments piled into one and then havin' a truck drive over 'em." She rattled her empty glass. Clarence had rejoined Marla at the back of the coupe. "You're a funny guy, Jackie. And I don't mean funny like 'laughin' ha-ha' but funny 'odd.' You're still like a little boy."

"Thanks, Raelene."

"No, don't take it the wrong way. I can talk to you," Raelene said. "You're different—certainly different from how the other girls talk about you."

"What do they say?"

"They say you're conceited. Stuck on yourself—that you got your head up your ass."

"Damn! They think that?"

"I don't think that way about you." Raelene seemed to be weighing what she'd just said. She looked past Jackie, her mouth hanging open. "We're gettin' too serious here. I don't want to be sad, goddamn it! Not tonight. Tonight's special, don't you think?"

Jackie nodded.

"It's sad that Clarence is leaving, but tonight let's not be sad, okay?"

"Okay, a deal. No being sad."

"—'cause even though they'll be apart they'll really be together, won't they?"

"That's right—they'll always be together," Jackie said.

"It's that way with me and Little Frank—we're apart, but we're really together. It's like destiny."

"Destiny?" Jackie repeated the word.

"That's what it is."

"You guys'll be back together."

"We will, won't we?"

"You will."

Destiny. The word sounded big, imposing to Jackie. Maybe Little Frank and Raelene were meant for each other, and that Raelene was right—their separation was just a trial period, a time away, before they settled back into each other. Maybe Little Frank and Raelene would defy what Jackie had often noticed, that opposites didn't attract each other, that if you lived in a house on the hill, you ended up with someone else who lived in a house on *another* hill, that if you lived on D Street you didn't end up with someone from the east side.

"You're sweet, Jackie." She kissed him on the mouth, lightly at first, but then intensely, her tongue plunging deep inside Jackie's mouth. When their mouths unlocked, she looked at Jackie, and asked, "Who taught you how to kiss?"

"Why?"

"'Cause you're not doin' it right."

"I'm not?"

"No, you're not." Raelene looked into Jackie's eyes, and already hers were starting to cross. "Your mouth is stiff when it should be looser, and more relaxed, when you want it firmer. Don't fight it!"

"Really?" No one had ever told Jackie this before.

"Yeah, really. When you kiss, you gotta put your whole self into it, like that person you're kissin' is the most special person ever, that it might be the last person in the world you ever kiss like this." She took in a deep breath. "Maybe at first, just pretend, okay? Pretend I'm someone real special," Raelene said. "Pretend I'm Letta Azevedo."

A slight current tickled Jackie when he heard Letta's name.

Soldier Boy by the Shirelles, came on the radio. Raelene screamed, "Marla, it's your song!" The two girls found each other, and started singing, "*oh, my little soldier boy, I'll be true to you.*" They took turns singing verses. "*Wherever you go, my heart will follow."* Their voices echoed back and forth from the quarry walls, and while they sang, Marla and Raelene slow-danced in wide, lazy circles, their feet shuffling along the quarry floor. Clarence fixed two more drinks for the girls, while Jackie found the can opener and started on his next beer. By the end of the song, Raelene and Marla had stopped dancing, and now were just holding each other, sobbing. "It'll be okay, sweetie. It's not like he's going away forever," Raelene's voice sounded muffled against Marla's shoulder.

"Hey, soldier boy!" Jackie shouted. "Front and center!"

"Did you freshen up our drinks there, bartender?" Raelene now held Marla at arm's length. Raelene's speech had slowed, her words slurred.

"Right here on top of the cooler, ma'm," Clarence said.

"And where's my date? Where's Jackie Miller?"

Raelene walked toward Jackie, stumbling slightly. Just steps away from Jackie, the opening trumpets to *Ring of Fire* blasted out of the Chevy's speakers.

"Yes! Yes!" Raelene grabbed Jackie's hand. Both couples were now dancing, Clarence and Marla in a loose embrace, Raelene and Jackie moving toward each other, bumping bodies awkwardly, before Raelene wrapped one arm around Jackie's neck and kissed him again on the mouth. "Like this," she said, pulling briefly away, then pressing her mouth against his again. Her tongue slipped slowly into Jackie's mouth, met his, and the two tongues moved around each other in their own little dance. When their mouths separated, she sang, "*the taste of love is sweet, when hearts like ours meet. Isn't it, Jackie? Isn't it sweet?*"

Jackie smiled. After the song ended, Raelene dropped her arms from around Jackie, stepped back, and raised her glass. "A toast!" She waved the glass in front of her. "First, to Clarence, who went and joined the stupid military."

"It was either that or get drafted!" Marla interrupted.

"I'm serving my county." Clarence saluted.

"To Clarence—get your ass back here as soon as you can!" Raelene paused and looked at each of her friends. "And to Marla, for being the sweetie she's always been. And to Jackie here, who I'm teachin' how to kiss, and finally gettin' to know after how many years? And—" Raelene paused again. "—'cause it's his birthday—to Little Frank—the asshole. No, he's not—really."

"And to you, Raelene!" Marla followed.

"I just wanna dance!" Raelene wrapped both arms around Jackie, and they danced until the song ended. She held Jackie tightly, her warm breath moving down his neck. "You don't like my singin', do you?"

"It's fine, Raelene."

"You don't like it, I can tell."

"Raelene, it's fine."

"I'm sorry I keep mentionin' Little Frank. It just slips out. And I called him an 'asshole' too. Sorry, Jackie."

"It's his birthday—you can call him anything you want."

"You ever been to the carnival, and gone to the Fun House?"

"With all the mirrors?"

"Yeah. I was thinkin' of where the floors moved back and forth, and if you didn't time it right, you'd fall down. One time Frank didn't time it right."

"And what happened?"

"He fell down—right on that big ass of his—and I laughed—'

"What'd Little Frank do?"

"What do you think? He got mad and wanted to leave and I said, 'I'm not leavin' just because you fell on your big, dumb ass. Big deal!' Ain't no one noticed, but it didn't matter to Frank. I said, 'Stop being a goddamn baby' and that's when he blew up. Stomped off, and it took me two hours to find him. Thought I'd have to walk home."

Jackie's hands moved back and forth across Raelene's back, across the bare skin of her shoulders and where the bulge of her bra strap began, his hands moving in rhythm to their dancing. When their faces touched, a warmth mixed with perfume and the heady smell of Raelene's body rushed up from her neckline.

"Little Frank could be a big baby. I blame his mother. She spoiled him." Raelene's face was directly in front of Jackie's, and her eyes opened and closed, looking first into his, then looking past him before closing again. "I'm drunk," Raelene said. "And I wish I hadn't started talkin' about Little Frank. I'm fine 'til I start thinkin' 'bout him." Her mouth pressed against Jackie's ear. "You wish I was Letta Azevedo now?"

"Why do you ask that?" A little tremor spread down Jackie's spine.

"Jackie, I ain't stupid."

"What?"

"Oh, you're good at playin' dumb. I always knew that about you," Raelene said. "You know how I knew?"

"How did you know?"

"'Cause I got extra perceptory sensation. I know things about people they don't even know. Believe me?"

Jackie avoided her eyes.

"I know about lots of folks. I really do." She pulled Jackie's face toward hers and kissed him hard on the mouth again. He tried to make his mouth do whatever hers did, whatever she'd instructed him to do earlier. "You're gettin' better at that, Jackie." She pushed away from him and announced," I gotta pee. Marla, come with me! I gotta pee!"

"How you doin', partner?" Clarence joined Jackie after the girls had disappeared, and handed him another beer.

"Gettin' drunk."

"Just don't close your eyes."

"I'll miss you, Clarence." It was a rare admission for Jackie. "And I hear about this Indo-China thing. Something stirring up over there, and Kennedy thinking about sending more soldiers."

"I'll be back before it gets any bigger."

The two friends bumped beer cans together. "Semper fi." Clarence kicked at the loose rock in front of him. It was dusk now, the sky overhead the color of a ripe plum, but just behind the western hills, it was as orange as molten copper. Minutes later Marla and Raelene returned, still holding onto each other.

"Me and Marla been talkin,'" Raelene said. "We wanna go to Little Frank's party."

"But you weren't invited," Jackie said.

"So?" Raelene said.

"Well—"

"Oh, shut up, Jackie Miller! I know I wasn't invited, but Clarence and Marla were and I'm their guests. We both are!"

Jackie looked at Marla for some kind of help.

"I wanna wish Little Frank a happy birthday. It'll be a blast!" Raelene said.

By now, Raelene was leaning heavily onto Marla. Both their bodies bobbed back and forth. "Fix me another drink, Clarence—please!" Raelene shook her empty tumbler.

Clarence re-filled Raelene's glass with ice, and then added more gin and mixer.

"C'mon Marla, let's look at the view." Raelene pulled Marla toward the edge of the quarry. Jackie stayed behind with Clarence. *Louie Louie* played on the radio, and Raelene shouted, *oh yeah, we gotta go now, yeah yeah, yeah, yeah!*.

"I don't know about Little Frank's party," Jackie said. "Raelene's already hammered, and you're fixing her another drink." Jackie watched Clarence close the lid to the cooler.

"What does it matter?" Clarence asked.

Jackie thought about it. If Raelene and Little Frank were meant to be together, what difference did it make whether it was tonight or next week or next month? Maybe it didn't matter, at all, but just then, Jackie wasn't thinking about Raelene or Little Frank, he was thinking more about himself, and the prospect of showing up uninvited, and confronting Evelyn Borda. He imagined seeing Letta, too, and felt pulled between the two women. Still, he soured to the idea of crashing Little Franks' party.

"I'm not going where I wasn't invited," Jackie said.

"You don't have to," Clarence said.

"What do you mean?"

"Well, you could stay here. We'll come back after the party and pick you up."

"Thanks, buddy."

"What's the worse could happen, anyway? Old lady Borda tells you to leave? No big deal!"

"You gotta cut off Raelene, though."

Jackie thought about it. Clarence was right. The worse that could happen was that Evelyn Borda would ask him to leave. No sweat. He certainly wasn't committing any crime. If Evelyn wanted to make a big scene, then Jackie would slip way, de-fuse the whole thing. But first he'd talk with Letta, maybe even ask her out for a date. He'd stop his beer drinking right now, sober up, swallow some *Sen-sens* for his breath and everything would be fine. Just another stop along the way.

Clarence yelled out to the girls, "Hey, Raelene! Jackie says you're cut-off!"

"What?" Raelene shouted back.

"Jackie says you've had enough."

The two girls turned and walked back to Clarence and Jackie.

"You're getting sloshed, that's all," Jackie noticed how Raelene's movements had slowed. Her head bobbed, her eyes crossed as she tried to focus.

"You like the police or something? Huh?" Raelene asked. "Don't tell me what to do."

"I'm sorry, Raelene."

"I don't like bein' told what to do."

"I was thinking of later."

"Me and Frank got something special, you know?"

"I know you do," Jackie said.

"So don't go tryin' to spoil it."

Jackie lit two cigarettes and passed one to Raelene.

"I'm just looking out for you, Raelene."

"I can't help it if your families don't get along. That ain't my problem—"

"I know it isn't."

"Little Frank and me—well, you know how it is." Raelene's head slumped, her mouth dropped open. "Maybe you *don't* know how it is."

"Hey, you guys, lighten up," Marla said.

"*Oh, yeah, we gotta go now—yeah, yeah, yeah.*" Raelene slurred the lyrics. "Dance with me, Jackie! Don't be mad. I'm sorry. Really, I'm sorry." She stumbled forward into his arms, spilling her drink across his shirt. "Oh, look what I did." She dabbed at his shirt. "What's a birthday party without us, anyway, huh?" Raelene patted the front of Jackie's shirt. "I'll be okay. It'll all be okay. And you're right—I drank too much, but so what?"

"I just don't like crashing parties," Jackie said.

"For crissakes, live a little. Besides, tonight might be your chance."

"My chance?"

"You know what I'm talkin' 'bout."

Jackie felt Raelene's full weight leaning against him. They moved in a slow circle with Jackie's feet sometimes stepping on Raelene's. He kept his eyes opened, staring out into the quarry darkness, listening to the radio playing around them, wondering whether to go to Little Frank's party or not. Evelyn Borda would be there, but so would Letta Azevedo. The weight of one pulled against the weight of the other. Why wait another day to talk with Letta? But weren't there plenty of other days? Days when he could plan out exactly what he wanted to tell her? And why risk a nasty confrontation with Evelyn Borda? But Clarence was right—what's the worse that could happen? She asks him to leave? Barks at him a little? Now he wished he hadn't drunk the beers. He needed his wits, some clear thinking.

"Me and Little Frank—we got history—H-I-T-S-E-R—whatever it is," Raelene whispered.

"Last call! Bar's closin'," Clarence announced. "There's one left with your name on it, Jackie."

"You think too much," Raelene said.

"I know it."

"Always thinkin'. Can't you turn that off for once and just jump in?"

Jackie looked past Raelene's shoulder. Clarence had placed the cooler back in the trunk while Marla gathered up the empty cans and put them in a paper bag. The car radio was turned off. In the growing moonlight, the sudden silence now seemed eerie, even a bit sad and foreboding.

"Two beers left, old man!" Clarence called out. "Let's chug 'em."

Clarence opened both beers, walked over and handed one to Jackie. By now, though, Jackie had reached his limit. He didn't want to admit it, didn't want to tell anyone. He'd never been much of a drinker. He accepted the beer, though, and held it in the same hand that palmed Raelene's back. As they danced together, he felt as if he'd boarded a boat in rough seas. With each surge, his knees buckled, his stomach seemed to twist into a knot.

"Marla, I gotta pee again!" Raelene broke away from Jackie so suddenly, he nearly fell .

"Doin' all right, partner?" Clarence asked.

"Semper fi!"

Clarence laughed. "You look fucked up."

"No shit?"

"Yeah, no shit."

"I ain't going to Little Frank's like this." Jackie brought the can to his lips, and forced the beer down.

Jackie heard the girls laughing one minute, then sobbing the next. It was dark now, and the moon was working its way across the sky. His stomach felt as though a cat had crawled inside it.

"You're not driving, Clarence Mazzoni!" Marla announced as the two girls reappeared.

"Sweetie!"

"No 'sweetie' me. I got the keys," Marla held the keys up in her hand.

Jackie helped Raelene into the backseat, and followed behind her. Marla started up the Chevy while Clarence walked back to the gate and opened it. The headlight beams reflected off the quarry walls, then telescoped out to Clarence waiting at the gate. He held up his middle finger as the Chevy passed him.

Less than a mile from the quarry, and after a series of sharp turns, Jackie rolled down the window, breathed in big gulps of air, trying to settle his stomach. It didn't work. He tasted the rancid beer rising in his throat, felt his stomach convulsing. "Stop the car, Marla!" While the car was still rolling, he pushed the front seat forward and jumped out, staggered twenty yards, bent over and heaved up the cheeseburger, fries, everything he'd drunk the past two hours. He stayed bent over, staring at the ground before him. His knees wobbled, his eyes watered.

"If you feel a hairball comin' up," Clarence shouted back, "swallow it 'cause it's your asshole!"

"Was that nerves?" Raelene asked when Jackie was back inside the car.

"No, that's Jackie not holdin' his beer," Clarence said.

A hundred yards before the Lakeville Grange, Jackie saw the bright red taillights of stopped cars, then lines of cars parked alongside the road, and people walking alongside them. He wished he was home. Further on, a dozen more cars were shoe-horned around Altenbacher's Garage. Marla stopped. The lot in front of the club was filled. Lights rimmed the porch and railings. A new Dodge pickup was parked near the entrance, its doors opened, its hood raised. It had a big bow on its roof, and people were standing around, taking turns slipping behind the wheel. Couples leaned against fenders. Marla found a spot near a stand of eucalyptus, maneuvered the Chevy in and shut its motor off.

"Lots of folks," Jackie muttered. He couldn't see the river, but he could smell it. He could smell the tidelands, too, raw and rotten, and smell the oat hay in long stacks. He looked around, felt a hollowness in his stomach, a metallic taste in his mouth, a feeling he remembered a summer before, staring down at the Russian River thirty feet below and Clarence urging him to jump.

"Think Little Frank'll be glad to see me?" Raelene asked.

"I hope so," Jackie answered.

Everyone was out of the car now. Raelene continued singing lines to all the different songs that had played that evening. Nothing seemed to bother her, Jackie thought. She could swill most of a bottle of sloe gin, have her mascara run in long, dark tears down both cheeks, lambaste Evelyn Borda, tear apart Little Frank one minute, and the next build him back up, and still walk fearlessly into the middle of his birthday party as though she were the guest of honor. Across the road, clusters of people stood around the front porch of the club, holding drinks, talking loudly. From inside, music played—not the music Jackie listened to on the radio, but big band music—Evelyn Borda's kind of music—clarinets, trumpets, a restrained drumbeat. Cigarette smoke drifted out from the doorway.

"Everyone ready?" Clarence asked.

Raelene had opened the car door again, and knelt on the front seat, her mouth just inches away from the rear-view mirror, applying lip stick. In between smacking her lips together, she sang, "*da doo ron ron, da doo ron ron.*"

"I'm not going in," Jackie said.

"C'mon!" Raelene shouted from inside the car. She dabbed at the mascara.

"I wasn't invited. You guys all belong there. Not me."

"It doesn't matter," Raelene said.

"It does."

Marla and Clarence had their arms around each other. Raelene finished applying lipstick, slammed the car door shut, and walked over to Jackie.

"You afraid of Evelyn Borda? Is that it?" Raelene asked.

Jackie avoided Raelene's stare.

"What are you gonna do, stay here the whole time we're inside?" Raelene asked.

"That's right."

"Jackie, Jackie. You're hopeless."

"Just go ahead. Don't worry about me."

"Clarence, can you talk to your friend here?" Raelene asked.

"He don't wanna go in, he don't have to," Clarence said.

"Is it Evelyn Borda?" Raelene stared into Jackie's eyes. "Or is it someone else?"

"It's no one"

"Bullshit!" Raelene said. "Don't play dumb here, Jackie Miller!"

"I can't."

"You can! And if Evelyn Borda doesn't like it, tell her to kiss your rosy-red."

"Let me think about it," Jackie said.

"Good, you think about it—seems you been spendin' a fair amount of your life doin' that."

"Lighten up, Raelene," Marla said. "If he doesn't want to go in, he doesn't have to."

"You guys go ahead," Jackie said.

"Fine. You wanna be a kill-joy, then be one," and Raelene turned away.

Jackie watched the three of them walk toward the club, then pause at the new pickup. Clarence walked around it while Raelene and Marla joined a nearby couple. Jackie leaned against the Chevy's fender, lit a cigarette. Raelene was right. He hated to admit it, but she was right. It was always tomorrow, or the day after, or the day after that, sometime in the future when he'd face-up to what he was slowly realizing as fear—if he'd ever face it all. That's what it was—fear. No other name for it. It nagged at him. It never let him go. He was afraid of so many things, but mostly afraid of moving beyond the familiar, of stepping into new terrain, of asserting himself. The family dairy was failing, and the shame and fear that failing engendered kept him walled in, defined him. It infested the other parts of Jackie's life: the outer part he was forced to occupy with the likes of Evelyn Borda, but it attacked that immense inner part, too, that wide and borderless region, where he seemed condemned to inaction, indecision, to an interminable waiting for things to change, for someone else to assume the initiative. But all the time he waited for this change, he was fearful of it ever arriving. And what did these fears do but push Jackie Miller further out to the margins where he found himself often alone, where the past and an uncertain present conspired against an imagined future. He wondered how it would change, if it would ever change. What great act would it take? Prayer hadn't done it. What grand event would open his life up, move him

from where he'd been stuck for so long? What made someone like Raelene so fearless, so confident? What had she
learned? That she and Little Frank were destined for each
other? That they had "history" together, as she termed it.
That she knew the order of things? Was possessed of some
common knowledge? Is that what gave her the courage
to walk into the middle of Little Frank's party while he,
Jackie Miller, lurked on the outside? Always on the outside,
an observer, watching everyone else, waiting for the day it
would change, but never knowing when that day would
come, both fearful and hopeful at the same time.

Clarence glanced over to Jackie, whistled and waved his
arm. "Hey, Jackie! C'mon!"

Jackie took a couple of steps, and stopped.

"Get your ass over here!"

They each walked to their edge of the road.

"There's enough people in there, old lady Borda ain't
gonna see you. C'mon! Besides, I ain't gonna be around
here much longer." Clarence motioned again with his arm.

"I can't, Clarence. Not right now."

"I'll get you a drink."

"No! That's the last thing I need."

Jackie stared at the Grange entrance. A wide hallway
ran straight back to the kitchen, and midway down the
hallway, another doorway opened into the main salon. It
was crowded and noisy. Jackie had been here before for
birthdays and anniversaries. He knew the big room with
the stage at its south end, its high ceiling and hardwood
floor. On its west side, another pair of doors opened onto
a deck that overlooked the Petaluma River, the same river
he'd seen a couple of hours earlier from the quarry.

"C'mon, Jackie. The old lady's ass-deep with people
around her," Clarence said.

Jackie hesitated. "I'll go around the other side."

"Suit yourself."

Around the south end of the salon, Jackie climbed another set of stairs onto the deck. It was crowded with people as well, all holding drinks in their hands. At the edge
of the deck, Jackie stopped, mostly unnoticed, and looked
through the first in a row of opened windows. Streamers
looped from the ceiling, and a large poster written on butch-
er paper read, "*Congratulations Little Frank.*" Waitresses
were busy clearing dinner plates from tables lining each
side of the salon, and refilling the guests' coffee cups. The
Ralph Rawson Orchestra played, but for now, no one danced.
Jackie recognized Letta Azevedo's family—mother, father,
even her grandparents, seated at one table. A chair beside the
grandmother was empty. At the other end of the table sat Big
Frank Borda in a starched cowboy shirt and bolo tie, his hand
wrapped around a highball glass, talking to Len Hartman.
Jackie looked around the salon until he saw her—her hair
tied back this evening with a pink ribbon trailing almost to
her neck. Letta was standing with a group of friends, mostly
classmates, talking and laughing, as radiant and animated as
Jackie had ever seen her. When the music stopped, Evelyn
Borda, squeezed into a satin dress, looking like an aged prom
queen, walked quickly to the front of the band. A long table
had been set up now at the foot of the stage, and while Evelyn
Borda tapped the microphone, two waitresses carefully set
Little Frank's birthday cake down below her.

"Everyone, could I get your attention—all you folks outside. Please!" Evelyn's voice boomed through the loudspeak-
er. She backed away from the microphone. Guests from the
outside deck jostled into the main room. *Shssssssss* spread,
and the talking and laughing soon quieted.

"Tonight's Little Frank's night, and the party is a kinda
three-in-one affair," Evelyn announced. "Two of 'em's a
surprise, and one ain't."

With the room crowded as it was, Jackie slipped inside
the door, and moved along the wall until he found Raelene,

Clarence and Marla gathered in a corner. Raelene took his hand and smiled nervously.

"It's Little Frank's 18th, but that ain't the surprise. So maybe we could all sing him 'Happy Birthday' first," Evelyn Borda said. A waitress lit the candles on the cake, and a group of Little Frank's friends pushed him toward the front of the room. Little Frank's face was flushed red. His big, fleshy neck spilled over the collar of his shirt.

"Make a wish, son!" Evelyn urged.

The guests sang 'Happy Birthday,' and when they finished, Little Frank bent over his cake and blew the candles out. Everyone applauded. By now, Raelene had moved in front of Jackie.

"The first of the two surprises tonight is something happened we weren't sure would." Evelyn Borda paused here for effect. Her eyes, nearly lost behind her big, full cheeks, flittered around the room. "What happened was that Little Frank *graduated!*" The crowd laughed. Evelyn stepped back from the microphone and clapped her hands. "He saw it through—I know it was tough—and we're proud you did, son."

Little Frank raised his arm, and smiled.

"Maybe the next announcement, we should let Little Frank make himself—what do you say, Little Frank?"

Little Frank turned and faced the guests. The room had quieted. His fingers twisted into his front pockets, his eyes fastened on the toes of his cowboy boots. He swayed back and forth, looked from one wall to the other, as though the words he was about to say were written there. He held his hand out, nodded his head toward the group where Letta stood. She walked toward him. In those few seconds, in the time it took Letta's hand to reach Little Frank's, the room grew tomb-like, as though it had slipped off its foundation, slid into the river, and now floated toward the bay, toward the future. Jackie had waited too long. The realization was like a small burst of damning light. The inevitable, that imagined 'destiny' wasn't to be. It was a fabrication, a dream as flimsy as the colored streamers looping from wall to wall. Everyone around him, the room, all the things beyond, dissolved in those few seconds that Letta Azevedo's hand touched Little Frank Borda's. Seconds, minutes, a crumbling civilization later, Jackie reached out for Raelene, wrapped both arms around her waist as though she were about to fall from a steep cliff. She trembled.

"Boy, a lot of stuff's been happenin' lately," Little Frank began. "I don't even know where to begin."

"What's been happenin' Little Frank?" a voice called out.

The guests laughed.

The trembling grew within Raelene's body. Jackie felt it convulse. He pulled Raelene closer to him. Marla grabbed her arms.

"Well, as my mom said, I graduated." Letta Azevedo stood next to Little Frank, looked at him, smiled, then looked to where her family sat, and smiled back at them. "And I turned eighteen. A couple of times I never thought I'd do that." More laughter circled the room.

Little Frank waited. Sweat had beaded on his forehead. "And—" Little Frank paused here until the fateful words rushed out. "And I asked Letta Azevedo to marry me!"

The entire room held its breath, then exploded into applause, as though the room itself had surged up from the river, like a breeching whale, and now opened its doors wide with a sound growing louder and louder, as though a locomotive was roaring through its middle. Letta and Little Frank looked at each other, and then he pulled a ring from his hip pocket and twisted it onto her waiting finger. Jackie felt Raelene's breathing mounting in short, hard blasts. He tightened his grip on her waist, and felt her pull away. He grabbed her even tighter, but it wasn't enough. She lunged forward into the middle of the room.

"You *BASTARD!*" she screamed over the applause. "You lyin' bastard!"

The room deadened. Little Frank's mouth dropped to his belt buckle.

"You said it would always be me and you. You promised! You said that!" Her words broke up as she stared at Little Frank.

"Somebody get her outta here!" a voice sounded from the crowd.

Jackie stepped toward her and grabbed her hand. She swatted it away. "No! Leave me alone!"

"Who brought her?" another guest asked.

Jackie walked out and grabbed her arm, but once again she pushed it away.

"Leave me alone!"

Jackie reached out to her. "Raelene, please—

"Shut up!"

She twisted away from Jackie's grip. Clarence joined him, and they both grabbed her, pulling her toward the doorway. She resisted, fought back.

"Let me go, goddamn it!"

Out on the deck, Clarence and Jackie still held onto her. Her body convulsed with each breath.

"He's a liar, a goddamn liar!" she shouted back through the open doorway.

"Raelene—it's okay," Jackie said.

"Screw you, Jackie Miller!"

"We gotta get her outta here, Clarence."

"No! I'm not goin' nowhere! I need to talk to Little Frank!"

"You're not talking to anyone," Jackie said. "Not now!"

Marla had joined them, and began stroking Raelene's back. "Hey, sweetie. Oooh, you okay?"

Raelene cried, choking whenever she tried to talk. The two boys pushed Raelene into a chair.

"We can't stay here, Raelene," Jackie said.

"He promised—"

"Folks break their promises," Jackie said.

Marla had moved in front of Raelene, and wrapped both arms around her. Clarence and Jackie stood by, looked at each other, and then at the girls. The salon doors swung open, the noise and smoke rushed out, followed by Evelyn Borda. She marched straight toward Jackie, her face quivering, alive and agitated. She stood directly in front of him, their noses just inches apart.

"You're a goddamn sore loser, Jackie Miller! Just like the rest of your family," Evelyn Borda shouted. "You can't have it your way, so you want to spoil it for everyone else."

"That's not how it was." Jackie stepped back. Evelyn's breath smelled sour.

"Don't tell me how it was." Evelyn's eyes had narrowed. "I ain't blind. And I ain't stupid. And you, Raelene Robby—you're pathetic—just like your bar-hoppin' mother!"

"Screw you, bitch!" Raelene sobbed. "Screw you and everybody else in your family!"

"How long did it take to plan all this out, huh?" Evelyn shifted away from Raelene and glared back at Jackie.

"I didn't plan any of it out—I didn't even want to come here."

"My ass, you didn't."

"That's the truth."

"The truth? That's a good one." Evelyn spit on the deck. "You wouldn't know it if it came up and bit you on the ass."

"Let's go, Clarence, Marla." Jackie motioned toward Raelene, and grabbed her arm once again. Clarence grabbed the other. "Raelene, c'mon, let's go."

Raelene wouldn't move.

"Please, Raelene—there's nothing here for us."

"That's right," Evelyn said. "Nothing! Never was."

Clarence and Jackie each put an arm around Raelene and walked her down the stairs. Jackie glanced once behind him, and Evelyn Borda still stood at the edge of the deck. "Pretenders! Nothin' but goddamn pretenders. If they can't have it themselves, then nobody can have it. Spoil it all. That's it. Spoil everything!" Evelyn's voice trailed off as Jackie rounded the corner of the hall.

"What a fuckin' mess!" Clarence said.

Raelene still sobbed, and Marla walked in front of her, dabbing Raelene's eyes with a napkin. "It's okay, sweetheart, it's okay," Marla said. They crossed the road, and Marla walked ahead and unlocked the car. Raelene still sobbed. A car's passing headlights shone on the group. Raelene's face was swollen, her eyes hardly more than watery slits buried behind her cheeks. She stared back at the grange hall, saying nothing. Jackie lit a cigarette and passed it to her. A neon beer sign glowed from Altenbacher's shop window. The band started to play "*My Blue Heaven*" and through the music, Evelyn Borda's voice trumpeted, "Everybody dance! C'mon, everybody! This is Little Frank's night!"

Raelene finally sat down in the front seat, her legs sticking out the side of the Chevy. Marla knelt in front of her, stroking Raelene's face, and talking in a low, reassuring voice. "You ready to leave, Raelene?" Marla asked. Raelene shook her head, took a long drag off her cigarette.

Jackie and Clarence leaned against the Chevy's trunk, smoking cigarettes, looking across at the grange hall.

"Maybe it's not such a bad thing to be leaving this place," Jackie said. "I almost wish I was leaving with you, going someplace different, someplace I've never been before."

"Letta and Little Frank." Clarence shook his head. "What were the odds of predictin' that one?" Clarence turned back toward the girls. "You guys doin' all right?"

"A few more minutes," Marla said.

The song ended from across the road, and a new one started up. People were leaving the hall now, walking back to their cars. Jackie's eyes followed several of the couples. In the doorway he saw Letta, accepting congratulations, saying good bye to guests. Then she was by herself. She looked out to Altenbacher's, climbed down the stairs, and walked toward the garage, finally crossing the road, and stopping in front of Clarence and Jackie.

"I was looking for the party crashers," she said.

Jackie stared at her.

"Well, you found 'em," Clarence said. "We're a bad bunch."

"How's Raelene?" Letta asked.

"Marla's with her," Clarence said.

"I'm sorry about what happened," Jackie said. "It wasn't what we planned—honest."

"Jackie's right," Clarence said. "He was against us comin' here—we just didn't see any of this happenin'—the engagement, Raelene reactin' the way she did. Everything."

"Well, it took me by surprise, too," Letta said.

Jackie and Letta stared at each other. She was as beautiful as he'd ever seen her, like a long-dormant bud that had suddenly broke into a lovely blossom. Neither of them spoke.

"I should get back," Letta said.

"I'll walk you across the road," Jackie offered.

Letta tucked her hand inside Jackie's arm.

"Congratulations, Letta." Jackie said when they were alone. They stood at the shoulder of the road, waiting for a car to pass. "I never saw you and Little Frank as a couple, but now that I do—"

"It sorta came out of nowhere. Little Frank was helping out when Mario got hurt, and we started talking more and more—then, before I knew it he hinted at something more serious—"

"And it's what you wanted?"

"I told him 'yes,'" Letta said. "No one had ever talked to me like that before. All the other girls had boyfriends, were going steady—and then there was me—a wallflower. It seemed like nothing would ever happen. And then he asked me."

"What if someone else had?"

"Like who?"

"I don't know—"

"Like you, Jackie?"

"Yeah, what if I'd asked you?"

"I can't look inside other people's minds. I don't know what they're thinking—I didn't know what you were thinking. I wanted you to talk to me so many different times."

"I was afraid—"

"Me, too. How I wanted to just walk up to you and say 'hello' and just start talking and never stop."

"I'm such an idiot."

"No, you're not. You're like me. You're like so many people out there."

"I was going to build up the courage, too, and ask you out tomorrow, even tonight. I told Clarence just hours ago about my plans."

Letta touched Jackie on the arm. They hadn't crossed the road yet.

"This is all water under the bridge. I'm sorry, Letta. I wish the two of you a lot of luck, I really do." Jackie looked at Letta. "You have no idea how hard it was for me to say that because—"

"Because why, Jackie?"

"Because I thought I'd be saying something different, but I didn't know just when."

There were no cars either way, and the two of them crossed toward the hall.

"This is as far as I go," Jackie said.

They embraced briefly and he kissed her on the cheek. Her skin felt soft, supple. Her hand slipped out of his and she walked away, toward a very different life than Jackie had imagined just hours earlier, but a life as it had always been, without him, without her. Little Frank was standing at the top of the stairs, staring across to where Jackie stood. Little Frank looked serious, concerned, but as Letta approached him, his big round face relaxed, and he smiled. Jackie couldn't tell but he thought Letta must be smiling, too, smiling at the funny way things turned out. And Evelyn Borda? She was smiling more than anyone. She was smiling because she'd been right all along, smiling because, yes, it was Little Frank's night.

Opening Day

When my cousin, Emil, fell off a ladder and broke his ankle, an extra spot opened up for deer camp. Club members drew names out of a hat, and though I never had much luck with drawings, or gambling, or taking chances of any kind, I won the spot. My two oldest boys, Junior and Jackie, both wanted it, but there was never any doubt who I'd give it to. The timing seemed just about perfect. My youngest son, Angelo, had just returned from Vietnam, and it was like God himself had looked down and made drawing that ticket happen. The boy always loved hunting. When everyone else was throwing baseballs, chasing girls, Angelo was off by himself with just his 20 gauge, bringing back bags of quail or doves. And when he was just twelve, he bagged his first deer out at Red Hill, a little forked-horn whose antlers I hung my coat on in the back porch. In the army he got a *Sharpshooter's* medal, and I thought to myself, if there was more soldiers that could shoot like Angelo, that war over there wouldn't last two months. He was a natural hunter, that boy, with a keen eye, and good tracking sense. And patience. Something I never had.

I meant to surprise him, and put the winning ticket under his dinner plate one evening. At first he didn't want come out of his room, said he wasn't hungry, until Dorna knocked on his door. "Angelo, I fixed your favorite—meat loaf with carrots and potatoes on the side. You come out now and eat with us." She looked at me. "I don't like him spending so much time alone. It's not good for him."

Finally his door opened, and he walked over to the table and sat down. Dorna made him put his cigarette out. He stared at the plate of food in front of him, and didn't say anything. The boy's always been quiet, kept to himself. He's different from my other two. Those two are natural talkers, *promoters*. They could sell you your own shirt. But not Angelo. Sometimes you can't get two words out of him. Dorna thinks it's because his two older brothers crowded him out, hogged all the talking. I don't know what to think. I used to call him the *philosopher* because his eyes got that far-off look to them, and you could almost hear the cogs inside his head turning around.

It drives me crazy, though. I want to know what's on people's minds, and when I don't, it leaves me to guessing. It leaves Dorna guessing too, and she always imagines the worst. She wants me to talk to him, but that father/son stuff leaves me a little shakey. We want our kids to be a certain way— like most parents do—and when they're not, well, it throws a monkey wrench into things. That's why I thought deer camp would be good for Angelo. He'd be out in his element, not cooped-up around here, pounded with questions.

"Are you going to see Kelly? She's been asking about you." Dorna pushed the salad bowl toward Angelo. Kelly and Angelo were boyfriend/girlfriend before he got drafted. Two opposites, really. She was a perky little red-head, a cheer-leader at high school, all energy, and chattering constantly, and crazy about Angelo. They seemed so different—but what can you say about who ends up together? People thought Dorna and me a stretch—a country boy and a city girl—but here we are, nearly thirty years later, still together.

"I saw her," he said.

"And?" Dorna waited. "How is she?"

"She's fine," he said. "Gettin' ready to return to college."

"Does she have a boyfriend?"

"I didn't ask her."

Dorna and me just looked at one another. I cut another slice of meatloaf and slid it onto my plate.

"So, Angie, you have plans? Decided what you want to do?" Dorna kept at him.

"No, nothing yet."

"Nick said there's an opening at the creamery, if you want it," I said.

"I'll find a job, don't worry."

"We're not worried, son," Dorna said. "And you're welcome to stay here as long as you'd like. This is your home, too."

"If you're interested in the creamery job, just say so," I said.

"Okay, Dad."

"Junior got a job in the DA's office in Alameda County," Dorna said. "He and Pam are so excited. He worked hard, that boy—putting himself through law school the way he did. Who'd have thought he'd end up an attorney?"

"Well," Angelo said, "he always liked to argue. And he always liked to be right."

Dorna and I were proud of Junior, proud of *all* our boys. After we auctioned off the cows, everyone was sent scrambling, trying to figure out what to do next.

Western Dairy hired me back, but I always felt bad about giving up the cows, the whole dairy business. I felt like I'd let the boys down, that I couldn't pass along something to them the way other fathers did. Way down inside, I failed them. It's an awful feeling. Dorna says it wasn't meant to be. That we just couldn't work hard enough, that things were stacked against us. "Jinxed," she said. We were jinxed.

"You like the meat loaf?" Dorna asked.

"Yeah, it's fine."

"Then why aren't you eating it?"

"Not hungry, I guess."

Angelo got up from the table, walked to the refrigerator and returned with a can of beer.

"Is that all you're going to have for dinner? A couple of beers?" Dorna asked.

"I'm not that hungry," he said.

"I got my tags yesterday." I wanted to change the subject. Angelo didn't like all the questions. "Bud Milner's got yours down at his store. He says they're on him this year. Just go by and pick them up."

"Yes, sir. I can do that."

"It should be a good season," I said. "And, Angelo, you don't have to call me 'sir.'"

"Habit, I guess. Sorry."

Dorna and I talked during the rest of dinner, and tried to include Angelo in the conversation, but the best we could get were just one and two word answers, before he excused himself from the table. He walked out the front door. Dorna asked him where he was going, and he said, "For a walk." Clifton Bartlett, our neighbor, says he sees Angelo walking all the time in our neighborhood, stopping at Kenilworth Park to smoke a cigarette, or sitting in the shade of the Sunset Line and Twine building, always by himself, always smoking a cigarette. Johnny Mastretti's seen him as far south as the railroad trestle, three or four miles from town, walking along, transistor radio stuck to his ear. There's some nights when he doesn't come home at all, others when we hear him talking to himself in his room. Next thing we hear is the back door closing, and he's gone, sometimes for hours, sometimes all day. We never know.

"The war changed him," Dorna said.

"Maybe," I said. "He'll come around, though. It'll just take a little time."

I never served in the army. Years ago, before Pearl Harbor, Frenchy Bazo touched off his 30-ought-6 right along side my head. It was a joke Frenchy was playing on me. He was hell for jokes. We'd both been drinking up at deer camp. Right after Frenchy fired his rifle, though, I knew something was wrong. No sound at all from my left ear except a real high-pitched whine, and a feeling like a cork had been stuck inside there. My balance was thrown off, too. When I told Frenchy, he laughed it off, said the same thing happened to him once, and a week or so later, everything was back to normal. Some of my hearing did come back, but not all of it, and when the army called me for a physical, they found my left ear drum had been punctured. "Unfit for service," they wrote on my papers. It was my own fault, not Frenchy's. We were just two guys who drank too much that evening.

A week before leaving for deer camp, I started gathering all my gear together. Dorna hung our sleeping bags out on the clothes line, and I oiled my boots, cleaned my rife, laid out the pants and shirts I'd be taking with me. I traded days-off with Ellsworth at the creamery so there was plenty of time to get things ready. That was one thing I didn't miss about milking cows—you could never leave the place. You were married to it. If you wanted to hunt, say, you'd have to find somebody you could trust to work on the ranch, and not ball things up. My cousin, Carl, spelled me when I had my stroke, but I wouldn't let anybody else near. Sure, there's lots of times I wish I was back on the ranch, but when deer season comes around, that's not one of them. I've settled back into working for wages, rejoined the union, and Dorna and me now rent a little two bedroom house a few blocks off Lakeville Highway. We're building a little nest-egg back up. We're not getting rich, but we aren't going broke either like before. On my days off, I putter around the garden, and during summer afternoons, Dorna and me put a couple of lawn chairs out in the driveway shade where it's coolest, open a couple cans of cold beer, and listen to the Giants on the radio. I pay into a pension, the boys are on their own. Angelo'll find his legs soon. I'm not worried the way his mother is.

The day before leaving, I was loading the pickup. "You got your stuff together?" I asked Angelo.

"Yes, sir."

"You gonna take the 30/30, right?"

"Yes, sir."

"Did you clean it like I asked?"

"No, not yet."

"When you gonna do that?"

He looked at me, and said, "Right now," and disappeared inside the house. When he returned, he pulled the 30/30 carbine out of its case, worked the action opened, then held the rifle up, barrel-end to his eye. He rammed a swabbed cleaning rod down its barrel and twisted it until it peeked out at the rifle's chamber. He worked the lever back and forth, and squirted drops of oil into its action. He worked without saying a word, worked like he could clean a rife in his sleep. I watched how fast his hands moved around the rifle. When he was finished, he handed the rifle to me, "There you go. A clean weapon."

"The war's over, son."

"It's not over, Dad."

"It's over for you, though, ain't it?"

"Not yet," he said. "It's thousands of miles away, but it doesn't feel like it's over for me."

"It's over if you let it be over."

"Yeah, that's what I've got to do. That's what they tell me at the VA's—let it be over."

"I never fought in one," I said, "so maybe I'm talking out my ass. Let's just enjoy ourselves, have a good time, okay?"

"Sure, we can do that."

"I didn't start the war, Angelo."

"No, but someone did."

"You wanna let those commie bastards run wild, is that it?" I could feel my blood rising, but I didn't want to argue. Angelo won't stand in your face the way Junior does. No, it's different with Angelo. He takes it all in, might say a couple of words back, shake his head, then he walks away. It's not like he's given up, or even agrees with you, but he reaches this certain point when he's heard enough, and wants to be alone. He takes things in deep. He broods, sometimes walks around like he's carrying this heavy weight. Dorna thinks it's because he left the church, that he'd given up on God. I don't know. I've learned to back off with him, to not push things because I'm afraid of losing him. I seen it in others. I don't want him to disappear. I want the boy to settle back in, to forget about the war and what happened over there. I want him to be normal, to grab onto something like you would a life preserver. I thought deer camp would be a start.

There's nobody that loves camp more than I do. It's the one thing I look forward to every year. I can be with my friends, away from work here. Even the few days away from Dorna does both of us good. She's happy to see me go, to get me out of the house. I feel like a little kid at camp. I love the smells, the pepperwoods, especially, and the campfire in the morning with Bib brewing coffee, and how the air seems so clean and clear up there. I like how the smell of the campfire soaks into your clothes, too, and the feeling of being far away from everything with just your friends, and how for a few days you've got no cares, no worries. You eat, sleep, drink and hunt, and when you're not, you talk about hunting. You sit around the campfire at night, sometimes drinking until you pass out, sometimes just falling asleep right there on one of the stumps.

There's more goddamn stories and jokes passed around that your stomach hurts from all the laughing. Everyone's got his favorite, and every year the stories get repeated. We all take our turns telling them. I'll always be the guy in the shitter when my cousins, Carl and Teddy, pulled it over with their horses, and dragged it halfway down the hill. I'm trying to pull my pants up the whole time, and push the outhouse door open, but every time I do, the door slams shut, and the outhouse takes a couple more turns downhill. By the time it comes to a rest, and I climb out of it, my pants are down at my ankles, and the whole camp's on their backs, feet kicking in the air, laughing themselves silly.

We packed the truck up the night before leaving. Angelo helped—a good sign. I wanted him to be as excited as I was, for everyone to get along, and when they don't it bothers me. I'd made a list and checked everything off at least two or three times. I finally went to bed but hardly slept at all from the excitement, and switched the alarm off a half hour early. Dorna got up with me and made coffee and toast, and later, after we roused Angelo, she scrambled up a half dozen eggs. We ate, ran through our checklist before we piled into the pickup and headed north up 101 to Hopland.

"Excited, Angelo?" I asked him.

"Yeah, back in the woods," he said.

"I sure am."

It was 6:30 AM when we reached the highway. There was hardly any traffic, just a few lumber trucks driving south. Angelo smoked cigarettes, one after another, a habit he'd picked up in the service. The quiet between us seemed awkward at times, and I filled it with talk about work, about camp, about who'd be there. I wanted to ask him about the war—it was in the news so much—and how he felt about it, but thought, let him bring it up. Don't push him. At Dry Creek Road, we stopped at an ice-vending machine next to the Tip-Top Cafe and bought four big blocks of ice and put them in our coolers. We fit in cans of beer, cheese, eggs, anything that needed to stay cool, around the ice.

"I want you to feel safe." The words came out sudden, like they'd been written out in front of me, rising up out of the darkness.

"Safe?" he said.

"Yeah, safe. When you're quiet, all inside yourself the way you get, your mother feels like you're slipping away, like you don't want to be with us. It scares her."

"That's not it," he said.

"You know how your mother is—she worries about everything."

We passed by Geyserville. The sun was at the tip of Geyser Peak, outlining the whole shape of the mountain as though drawn with a fine pen. I rolled down the window, and could feel the heat building the further north we drove.

"If you ever want to talk about what happened over there, I'll listen."

"If I told you, it'd blow your mind." Angelo's voice got deeper, his words slowed to a crawl. "You wouldn't understand. None of it made sense. Besides, I don't think you want to hear what we done."

"If you ever want to talk about it—that's all I'm saying."

"I wasn't the hero you think I was."

"It took guts to do what you did."

"What all of us did was try to stay alive—simple as that."

"You can tell me anything you want."

"Then you'd tell Mom what I told you, and she couldn't deal with it."

"What if I don't tell her?"

"Dad, you're lousy about keeping secrets."

"I won't tell her."

"She'll ask. She'll keep asking and then you'll tell her."

"And you don't want that?"

"To tell you the truth, I *would* want that," he said. "I'd like to be able to say exactly what's on my mind, to tell you exactly what I did over there and what I was feeling, but I don't think you—Mom, in particular, could handle it. I mean, what have all of us done since we were little kids, but sugarcoat the shit in our lives so you two won't freak out.

"I won't tell her anything."

"Deal?"

"A deal," I said, and he reached over and shook my hand.

"I'm going to talk as I see it. No bullshit. And, if you don't want to hear it, you just say so, and I'll shut up. But I won't say shit just because it's what you want to hear." He took a drag off his cigarette. "I put my ass on the line for two years, so that gives me some kind of right, don't you think?"

I nodded my head.

The sun was above the eastern hills by now.

"Could you pour me some more coffee from the thermos, Angelo?"

I passed the thermos cup to Angelo. He filled it, and passed it back to me.

"Cy Bingham's bringing one of his boys up to camp with him this year, the younger one, Johnny, the football star at high school, remember?" I said.

"Yeah, I remember him."

"The kid don't know his ass from a hole in the ground about deer hunting, but he wants to try it. He'll be a good brush-beater."

"Johnny was the star football player, all right." Angelo said.

"You never know who'll show up, and who won't. Every year it's different."

I had to piss, so we pulled over above Cloverdale. You could hear the Russian River flowing below us, booming against the canyon walls.

"Breathe in that air, son, ain't it wonderful?"

"It's cooled some from the river."

We stood there, listening to the sounds of the water. It was daylight now, the heat building by the moment. I peeled off my jacket.

"Did you ever kill anyone over there?" I asked.

"No." Angelo stared off at the canyon walls. The river seemed to grow louder. "They transferred me out of infantry."

"Why'd they do that?"

"Problems I had."

"Problems?"

"Yeah, problems. I ended up working in a hospital."

"You didn't see any action then?"

"At first—that was the problem."

The river boomed up from the canyon. Angelo was quiet. Several minutes passed. He lit another cigarette, or what I thought was a cigarette.

"What's that you're smoking?" I asked.

"Pot—you know, marijuana. A habit I brought back from 'Nam." He held it out to me. "You want some?" I shook my head.

"Hell no!"

"Why not? Afraid you'll go out and overthrow your country?"

"Never mind."

`Why you have to smoke that crap?"

"Because it calms me—it takes the edge off."

"It's bad for you, son."

"Dad, I don't want to get in a pissin'contest over what's bad for me and what isn't, okay? You say it's bad for me— all right, it's bad for me. So was the fuckin' war."

"Just don't smoke it around your mother, okay? And not around the guys at camp. They won't like it."

"See, this is what I mean about being who we are—and why that's so hard to do around you and Mom. You want us to be a certain way—

"I don't want you fucking up."

"Everybody fucks up."

"What is it you want, son?"

"I want to be left alone. And not hammered with questions all the time."

"You don't want to talk about the war?"

"No, I don't. Not right now."

Angelo lit a cigarette from the one he'd been smoking. We walked back to the pickup. "Dad, I'm grabbin' a beer."

"Help yourself," I said.

"You want one?"

"Too early for me."

Back on the highway, we didn't talk. I turned on the radio to drown out the silence but it was just static, and I switched it back off. Both of us stared out into the early morning light, fidgeting in our seats. I thought about camp, and what it would be like this year, and I thought about this war going on, too, and how it'd divided everybody. I used to think there were clear answers to these things, a clear place to stand—about war, and who we were fighting, and what the aim was—but lately I'm not so sure. I imagined Angelo, and thousands of kids just like him, dropped into a country they knew nothing about, given a rifle, and asked to hunt down another man. His letters home never said much about what he did, or what he wanted to do once he returned. I wondered, too, what I'd do if I was in his place, the kind of person I'd be once the shit started, those same thoughts that cropped up when guys I knew shipped out, and I stayed behind.

We reached Hopland and turned east on 175. The sun was already bright and warm, glaring right into our eyes. I dropped the sun visor down. We drove through vineyards and a couple of remaining prune orchards. Just as the highway route started to climb into the hills, we veered off on Old Toll Road. The road here turned to gravel, filled with chuck holes, so I slowed the pickup, shifted to a lower gear before the road narrowed above the last bottomland. We drove right through the middle of a farm yard, the house on one side of the road, the barns on the other, beef cattle grazing out in the pasture. We climbed and climbed, until we reached a little spur road off to our right with a metal gate. I stopped the truck and handed Angelo the key to the lock. You could feel the heat now like a furnace, like it had never left from the day before and the day before that one. It mixed with the smell of pepperwoods and oaks, until it seemed as thick as syrup. Not a breeze anywhere. Everything still, but with heat waves shimmering off everything. Good for deer hunting. I watched Angelo as he worked the lock, slung the chain back and walked the gate open. His hair was growing out again. He was lean and muscled like myself thirty years earlier. I tried to remember what that was like: trouble in Europe, then Pearl Harbor, me working on my brother-in-law's ranch, a girl in town, girls everywhere. I was a young buck. The world burning up while I danced to big bands all over the county.

Nothing eating at me the way it did with Angelo, but he'd tell you it was different. A different time, a different war that he got dragged into.

When Angelo was back in the truck, I said, "Goddamn it, I'm glad you're home!" And I punched him on the arm. "I mean that. I thought about you a lot over there. And you know your mother did, too. Worry, worry, that woman. I knew you'd be takin' care of yourself, kickin' ass."

"Kickin' ass," he repeated to himself.

"Yeah, kickin' ass!" I looked over at Angelo. "Let's eat some of that chicken your mother fried up last night. I know it's early, but what the hell? This is deer camp, right?"

"That's right," he said. "It's deer camp. Let's drink a beer." He jumped out of the pickup, and returned with two Olympias from the cooler. We opened them in the cab of the pickup. He sat forward in the seat, and smoked a cigarette.

"They can't arrest us up here, can they?" he asked.

I handed him the container, he crushed the butt into the ashtray, and picked out a chicken leg. Maybe it's different with other fathers and their sons, but Angelo and me never talked that much. I guessed ever. When I say 'talk' I mean about what's going on inside us. That's something I'm just not very good at. The words get tangled up, and nothing comes out the way it's meant to. I think we understood each other, though, and that can replace a lot of words. And what Angelo says about his mother is true. For as much as she's seen and been through with her own family, you can't hit her with the hard truth. It needs to be softened. If it's not, she falls apart.

I put the truck back in gear and we crawled along a road with coyote brush and scotch broom growing right up to its edge. Dust billowed behind us. We ate chicken and winged bones out the window. One time a yellowjacket flew in and landed on the piece Angelo was eating. "Kill the bastard!" I said, but Angelo just stared at it, watching it gorge itself on the meat. I hit the piece of chicken with the back of my hand, and chicken parts flew everywhere.

"He would've flown away," Angelo said. He picked the pieces up from the floorboard and chucked them out the window.

"Didn't want you getting stung, that's all."

We drove on. The pickup bucked and shuddered over parts of the road wash-boarded from last winter's rain. Dust tumbled in through the open windows and covered every-thing—seats , dashboard. It got in your ears, your eyes and your hair. You could slap your jeans and clouds of it would poof out. Dust was part of camp. After a couple of days, it made everybody look twenty years older than they were. Dust was on all the oaks and brush along the gravel road. I learned years ago, before buying the camper shell, to tarp everything with canvas for the ride up. There's heat here, too—dry, baking heat different from back home. Just ask Bobbie McClondon from out at Point Reyes. He's used to fog and it being cool. The first day up here he got heat stroke so bad his face and neck turned the color of a cooked crab. He put a scare in all of us, but we packed him with ice, like a goddamn fish, and he was fine. There's yellowjackets, too, some years worse than others. Don't really know why. And snakes. Rattlers. Can't forget about the snakes. Everybody at camp's got a snake story or two to tell. Guys kill them and put them in each others' bunks all the time. You ain't been fully initiated until you head to bed with half a heat on, and slide over on a goddamn snake. The guys end up busting a gut laughing. It never gets old.

Camp was less than two miles away, at the mouth of the canyon. The road here rolled up and down with the terrain, through oak and madrone, manzanita and coy-ote brush until you reached McDowell Creek, a beautiful stream flowing year-round. Big oaks hung over the water, and it was cool here, even in the hottest part of the day. We'd built one wooden shack years earlier, fifty yards above the highest run-off, and lined two of its inside walls with bunks. Off an exterior wall, a lean-to roof stretched out with a porcelain sink set in a crude drainboard. There was no running water. You just fetched it from the creek in buckets. In the center of camp was the firepit, built up with big rocks, and open on one side where you fed it chunks of oak. My cousin Art, a welder, had fabricated a grill that hung between two supporting arms that you could crank up and down, or just remove entirely. All around the campfire were oak rounds that worked as chairs. There was a corral beyond the camp, as well, when we used to bring horses up here.

"I'm getting excited. What about you?"

"Mellow, Dad. Real mellow."

"You still like getting out like this?"

"Yeah, like I said, 'mellow'."

"You're gonna be all right, aren't you, son?"

Angelo looked over but his eyes slid past me. They were glassy now.

"What's it like smokin' that stuff?"

"It takes the sharp edges off," he said. "Slows everything down."

"Why you want to do that?"

He looked at me and grinned.

"I told the guys about you coming to camp, and they're all excited to see you. They've been asking about you."

"Just don't tell them I'm a goddamn war hero, okay?"

The road crested at the last hill before it dropped down towards the water. You couldn't see the creek yet, but if you were quiet enough, you could hear its water tumbling over the rocks, and you could feel the air gradually cooling. The grass was still green here in the shade, but out on the hillsides and in the hot sun, it was bone-dry and crackled against your boots when you walked through it.

"We're almost there, Angelo."

Clarence Cummings had painted the last gate post red so he'd know he was almost to camp. He'd painted it 25 years ago, and the paint was faded now.

"Leave the gate open," I told Angelo. "There's others behind us."

The range cattle been taken out a month before because ranchers were afraid they'd get shot. Guys get jumpy—particularly the new ones. They've been known to kill a steer or two. Most of the year, deer feed on grass right along with the cattle, but come summer, the deer move up to the higher reaches, like they got a sixth sense that season's opening on them. There's lots of cover up in the canyon, too, and they like that. They'll feed early mornings, early evening, then hunker down during the day and chew on their cuds. They cut little trails to the water, too, some you never notice.

The last gentle knoll cropped up in front of us before it dropped to the camp site. From here you could see the tops of the three big oaks surrounding camp. Guys hang their deer from the lower limbs of these same oaks, usually at night when it's coolest. Once down at the creek, the land flattens into a long narrow meadow that runs right alongside the water. The creek flows over parts of this meadow until the rains let up in April, and by June the bunch grass is thick as carpet in some places. We park our trucks out here, and hoof it the remaining distance to camp, about fifty yards. It was noon on this Friday morning when we finally arrived.

Bib waved to us from the kitchen lean-to. He was always first here, the *"chief cook and bottle-washer"* as he liked to say. Bib and me go way back. Years earlier, he introduced me to Dorna at a dance in Boyes Springs. I walked over to him and we shook hands.

"You remember Angelo?"

"Sure do." Bib wore his Nulaid cap. He was short, and Camels had hollowed his voice. "Welcome home. Welcome to camp."

"Thank you, sir," and they shook hands.

"Place looks about the same," I said.

"We ain't done much," Bib nodded toward the bunk-house. "We added some shelves above the drainboard, and stiffened up the door after someone tried kickin' it in. But that's about it."

Angelo lit a cigarette.

"Should be plenty of room in the shack," Bib said. "Bill Alva sleeps in his camper. Roy Caspers pitches a tent. And Cy pulls a little pop-up trailer behind his pickup. I don't blame 'em. With all the fartin' and snorin' the bunkhouse can get pretty noisy."

"Sounds good to me," I said.

"There's a wheelbarrow here, if you want to haul your stuff back," Bib said.

Angelo wheeled it back to the truck, and I followed behind him.

"Bib's been with Nulaid fifteen years already—Union job, pension." I raised the camper door and loaded a cooler into the wheelbarrow. "Same as the creamery. Something to think about, son."

"Oh, there's plenty to think about. Don't you worry."

"I ain't worried," I said. Angelo's not lazy. None of my boys are. They might bounce around, try different things, but when they find something, it's nose-to-the-grindstone. I'd like to think they learned that from me. More than any-thing, though, I wanted them to follow in my footsteps, wanted to give them a place to start, one of the reasons I bought the dairy cows in the first place. Good, honest work. No punching a time-clock, you're the boss, but it wasn't meant to be. I felt bad about it, but Dorna told me there's no shame in working hard, even if it goes belly-up.

It's only if you didn't work hard, she said. Still, I feel like I'd failed Dorna and the boys, but she's got a way of making me see another side to things. Now, my work day ends after eight hours, and if it doesn't, it's time and a half. No staying up with sick cows, no sweating what the milk market's going to do. It's a guaranteed paycheck twice a month, a couple of weeks vacation. Retirement ahead of me. Best of all, we don't owe my in-laws any money.

Bill Alva's pickup pulled into camp just as we'd finished loading our gear into the wheelbarrow. Bill parked his truck alongside mine, and got out, rubbing his knee. "Damn thing's been actin' up on me," he said.

"That's 'cause you're gettin' old," I said.

"This Angelo?" Bill looked over at Angelo. "He's all grown up now, isn't he?" They shook hands. Bill owns his own hay truck, and two years earlier bagged one of the biggest bucks ever taken from here—a beautiful three-pointer. "Welcome back."

"Thank you, sir."

Just minutes later, Cy and Johnny Bingham pulled into camp. Roy Caspers sat between them. They towed their jeep behind them. Right behind Cy and Johnny were Ed and Todd Cadazzo. Clouds of dust hung above the road, and trailed after each pickup. We waved to each other, shouted out and shook hands, like it was a high school reunion, and in ways it was. We joked about how old we'd gotten, and whether we could still get up and down the hills. Our laughter boomed through camp. There's so many different times during camp that I like, but this might be one of my favorites, when the guys, some of them you haven't seen in months, sometimes since the last camp, start arriving. Angelo said hello to Johnny Bingham, then wheeled our gear back to the bunkhouse and lugged it inside. When he unloaded the wheelbarrow, he brought it back to our truck.

"Anything else?" he asked

"I think that's it for now," I said. Angelo walked back
to the center of camp. He pulled a beer from the cooler,
walked over and sat on a stump.

"How's he doin'?" Bill asked in a low voice.

"It's a change for him, being back," I said.

"Good to be up here, ain't it?" Bill said.

"Nothing like it."

And there wasn't. It's the *feel* of this place. The heat
and the dryness, the sounds the crickets make at night.
The coyotes yelping and knowing there's deer out there,
and whether you can outsmart them or not. It's the hills
around camp and further upstream, how the canyon nar-
rows until some places it's like looking up at sheer walls.
So different from the flatlands where we live. There's trails
cut into the canyon sides, but just as many trails that disappear, covered by rock slides where it's just like walking on
marbles. It's easy to lose your footing in these places. It's
happened to me more than once. One time I slid a hundred yards, tore the ass right out of my jeans. Frenchy had
a good laugh over that one.

You won't find a flat spot anywhere until you're out
of the canyon, and even then, it's not flat but rolling. It's
mostly oak around here, and brush. On the north flanks,
where it's cooler, pines grow. I can't hunt the sides anymore because of my knees. Now, I mostly sit point, and let
the young guys run them to me. Anywhere you go around
here, it's a climb. You can't forget about the poison oak, either, and I already mentioned the snakes. We used to trailer
horses up here, but too many of them weren't sure-footed
enough. Frenchy pulled a good one on me. This was before
the war. He hauled up a half-dozen horses in his cattle truck.
Half of them looked like mustangs. He gave me this grey
one, and said it was a good trail horse. It was wild-eyed and
spooked easy, and I should have known better. It took me

ten minutes just to get a saddle on it. Frenchy said, don't worry, they grew up in country like this. Hell, the first rifle shot, that goddamn horse took off, the bit stuck in its teeth. I couldn't stop it. It went right down an embankment, stopped short of the creek so fast, I flew right over its head and landed in waist-deep water. The horse looked at me, and I looked back at it—and maybe it got lonely, because the next thing, it leaped into the water and landed right next to me. Frenchy and the guys still laugh about that one.

"Someone want to bring firewood in?" Bib asked. "It's all bucked up."

"Angelo," I said. "You want to help Bib?"

He loaded a big armful and walked back to the fire pit.

"You can just stack them against the barrel there," Bib said. We kept a 55 gallon drum filled with water near the pit. After Angelo finished carrying firewood, he went in and laid down on his bunk. Through the open door I could see his arm dangling over the side of one of the bunks. Frenchy arrived a short time later with his son, Justin.

By 3 PM, everyone had arrived in camp, and by 5 we were all sitting in a circle, drinking cans of beer, stripped down to our t-shirts. It was hot, even in the shade. Angelo had woken from his nap and joined us. Frenchy took his cap off and wiped his forehead, and you could see the line where the sun burned his skin—his face the color of leather, the top of his head as raw as a peeled potato. You could look around the circle and see the sunburned arms and necks of the men and where their shirts had hidden the sun.

Bib had already marinated a pile of steaks for dinner and wrapped a dozen big spuds in tin foil, and lined them on the grill. He stuffed newspaper under the kindling and lit it. Flames shot up, then lowered as the paper and kindling burnt down. Within fifteen minutes, Bid had a good cooking fire going. The men moved their oak rounds back from the fire.

We talked about how the group would break up for tomorrow's hunt. Us older guys who didn't like bucking brush, usually sat *point* or *stands* while the young guys, the *drivers,* we'd call them, drove the deer out ahead of them. Three of us would ride with Cy in his jeep back to the Old Toll Road, and head further up the canyon, and find our points. I liked a spot at the top of a little draw that funneled down to the water. When the deer started moving, especially after shots were fired, they scampered up this crease, heading for the thicker cover above. My stand overlooked an opening, a tiny meadow between the top of the draw and where the coyote brush and manzanita started. There were two good points here that looked right down on this opening, and where the hunters could see each other. I'd take one point, and Angelo the other. The guys below would go upstream, hopping rocks, and fan out, working their way up the canyon sides, driving deer up to the ridges.

"What do you want to do?" I asked Angelo.

"It doesn't matter," he said. "If you want me to beat brush, I'll beat brush."

"You might want to stay with your old man," Bill Alva said. "Maybe just the first day out, until you get the lay of what it's like up here."

"Sure," Angelo said.

"More beers anyone?" Bib asked. He reached into an ice chest and pulled out a half dozen cans of beer. The men passed them around, followed by the can opener. "Them spuds gotta bake now."

"How about something a little harder?" Ed Cadazzo said. He walked over to the bunkhouse and returned with a bottle of bourbon.

"Now we're talkin'," Frenchy said.

They passed the bottle around, each man taking a pull until it had gone full circle.

"Miller, I was gonna bring up one of my horses for you—"

"Yeah, you shit, too," I said.

The men laughed.

"You finished with the army?" Todd Cadazzo leaned toward Angelo.

"Finished," Angelo said. "Two years."

"No re-uppin'?"

"Nope, two years was enough."

Bib returned with an armful of metal coffee cups. He passed them around. "We need to toast this young man, here," he said. The bourbon circled the fire pit again, and each man poured himself a couple of strong shots. "To Angelo!" and we all raised our cups up.

We sat in a big circle, finishing off our steaks, drinking beer, stomping the empty cans flat with our boots. You could look around and see the guys leaning into the fire, forearms resting on their laps, their eyes heavy and blood-shot, watching the sparks spit and pop from the embers, their mouths hanging open. Frenchy poured brandy into his coffee, and offered the bottle to Angelo. He tilted the bottle into his cup, and passed it to Todd sitting next to him. The bottle worked its way around the circle.

"I joined the reserve," Todd said to Angelo.

Angelo nodded his head.

"I'm ready to go if they call me up," Todd said.

Angelo lit a cigarette from the end of a burning branch he'd stuck.

"Any advice if I end up goin' over there?" Todd asked.

Angelo never answered a question right away. He had to think about it first. "Yeah—don't' get killed," he said.

The men laughed.

Angelo stood and walked off to the edge of camp.

"Irv, you got a good son there," Frenchy said.

"I'm proud of him all right," I said.

Cy Bingham had bought a new rifle, a 243 caliber, and wanted to show it to the rest of us. He came back from his pickup, and pulled it out of its case. It was a beauty—a Remington, bolt action. He passed it around the circle.

"The larger caliber was tearin' too much of these small deer up," Cy said. Besides, you're not shootin' anything more than a hundred yards away."

"If you didn't shoot 'em in the ass, that wouldn't happen," Frenchy said.

Cy laughed.

Angelo returned and sat down. His eyes were even redder now, and glazed. He avoided my stare.

"What was it like over there?" Johnny Bingham asked after Angelo had sat down, and opened another beer.

Angelo looked into the fire. Its embers popped, and sizzled. For the first time all afternoon the men stopped talking. Angelo just stared into the fire like the words might be found somewhere in the flames. Seconds passed before he said anything. "Fucked up," he finally said.

Ed Cadazzo walked over and retrieved another beer from the cooler. "If you ask me, we should put all our troops back on ships, get 'em far enough away, then drop the big one on those commie bastards. Just like we did with the Japs."

"You kill anyone?" I heard Johnny ask Angelo.

Angelo lit another cigarette. "No," he said.

"You guys had enough to eat for tonight?" Bib finished the last of the dishes, and hung the towel on a line he ran from the bunkhouse to a nearby oak.

"Good, Bib. We're all good, arent' we?" Bill said.

"What else you got?" Cy asked.

"How about Baked Alaskan?" You'll find that on the dessert menu." Bib took the kerosene lantern off its hook and walked back to campfire. "I'm turnin' in," he said. "This has been a long goddamn day, but it's good to see all you bastards again."

"Thanks, Bib." Bill raised his tin cup. "I'm headin' back to the camper, myself."

"Just make sure that fire's down before you turn off the lights." Bib disappeared inside the bunkhouse.

Angelo and me were the last at the campfire. "You going to bed, son?"

"Pretty soon," he said.

I like to walk out beyond camp at night, far enough away where you don't hear any voices, and let the quiet surround me. You'll hear owls screech, and critters moving in the dark, things you don't ever hear living in town. Sounds run out across the canyon, too, and come back so clear. You've never seen so many stars, either, and how bright they are. And the moon? There's nights I could read a newspaper by its light.

I thought about what Angelo had said earlier in the morning about why he smoked pot, and how it slowed things down for him. I wondered what things he wanted slowed-down, and if it was moments like this one right here that he was aiming for. I didn't know. When I returned from my short walk, the men were gone, and it was just Angelo sitting by himself at the campfire.

"You going to bed, son?"

"Pretty soon."

In the bunkhouse, I rolled out my sleeping bag. Bib rustled in the bunk above me. Just before crawling inside it, I peeked out the door. Angelo was still out by the fire, staring into the last of the coals. The flames had all died down. It was mostly still and peaceful, and I fell asleep.

The next morning everyone was up and dressed, drinking coffee by 4 AM. We hunt early in the morning while it's still cool, and the deer are moving. Bib lit the Coleman stove to heat water and fry up eggs for sandwiches, rather than build a fire. We moved around camp, quietly. Those of us riding in Ed's jeep slipped our rifles into the scabbards he'd fitted on the jeep's sides. We filled our canteens with water, our thermoses with coffee, checked our ammo, packed sandwiches into our rucksacks. Guys moan a lot this time of morning, especially if they drank too much the night before. Angelo moved around quietly. We each took a flashlight, and I gave him our binoculars.

By the light of a lantern, we scratched out in the dirt again how we'd split up, and work the north side, from the creek bottom to the ridge top. Everyone talked in low voices. For that first morning, Angelo and me would ride further up the canyon on Old Toll Road with Ed and Bib, then walk to our points and wait. Todd, Roy Caspers, Cy, Johnny and Frenchy would go up-creek to where the canyon forked, then start moving up the canyon sides to the ridge above. A lot of the terrain around here was rough-sledding—steep in places, with tangles of manzanita, and in the higher reaches where tree cover thinned, the brush spread out thick as stubble. There were faint trails you could pick up that made the going easier. I'd hunted here enough to know the little clearings and the outcroppings above them that made for ideal points. There was no magic formula, though, for deer hunting. What worked one year, may not work the next.

Angelo and me had hunted together before—ducks, pheasant, doves and quail. He was a good partner, quiet, patient, with a natural feel about things. I liked to think he learned this from me, but it seemed more an ability he'd grown into, that hunting suited his aloneness, his love of the outdoors. He read how the land laid, if there was a breeze, how the weather was that day. He could track, too—read hoofprints, tufts of hair stuck in the brambles, the way people read the newspaper. And the boy had energy. He could walk and walk, something I can't do too much of any more with my knees hurting the way they do. The extra weight I'm packing around doesn't help either.

Ed stopped his jeep at the familiar road-cut, and we climbed out. Angelo slipped his rucksack on, and we both pulled our rifles from their scabbards. I waved off Ed, turned on my flashlight and picked up the trail that would take us to our points, a twenty minute walk away. Angelo stayed behind me several steps, following in the beam my flashlight made. It was still dark, but you could feel daylight sneaking up below the horizon. Everything around us started taking shape—the trees and brush, the rock formations, the outlines of the canyon.

I stopped every few minutes. "You doing okay?" I whispered.

Angelo would nod his head.

The deer up here aren't big. They dress out at maybe a hundred, a hundred twenty pounds. But they're very quick, though, and agile, and much harder to shoot than the bigger white-tails. They can slip past you sometimes without you even seeing them. You doze off, they're gone. They've got great senses of smell, too, so it's important to be as down-wind from them as possible. And, they pick up on any kind of movement, as well, so when sitting point, you're still, and against some kind of backdrop where you blend in. It might just be a split-second, at most, when you've got a shot. Any longer, they disappear in the cover or race off. They're a naturally nervous animal anyway, and when that first shot's touched-off, they're scared and moving fast, very fast.

"Your head woozy from last night?" I whispered.

"A little bit."

Minutes later we arrived at the first point. I motioned to Angelo. "There's a little shelf up there," I whispered, "It looks right down into this opening. I'll be past you, maybe forty yards away."

I left him and walked to the further point. I leaned my rifle against the rocks behind me, fished out the thermos from my rucksack, and poured a cup of coffee. Daylight was coming fast. I felt good, felt like there was no other place I'd rather be than right here, sitting point, my son just yards away, both of us in our element. It was just a matter of waiting now, of being patient, and quiet, of letting it all come to us. Light grew by the minute until everything had taken shape around me. I could look across now and see Angelo, sitting still as a statue, a rifle across his lap. The heat was building, too. I peeled off my jacket, my eyes and ears cocked. I was ready.

It was quiet. I sat there and wondered what the morning hunt would bring. I didn't care whether I bagged one or not, but I hoped Angelo would. It'd be a good *welcome-home* for the boy, a first step toward putting that war behind him. I looked over toward Angelo and nodded my head. He nodded back.

Minutes later the first shots rang out. They cracked against the canyon walls, and rippled back to us, sounding like firecrackers. If there were any deer below, they'd be running now. This is when my heart speeds up, feels like it's pumping right behind my eyeballs. The rifle's across my lap, its safety off. I'm fingering the trigger, eyes scanning everything below me for any kind of movement. Every sense of mine on alert. I'm ready. It's like I've crawled into the skin of another animal. I'm hungry, I'm eager, and, in a funny way, scared, too. If you stayed this way too long, your nerves would burn up.

The canyon quieted before another shot rang out. My eyes followed along the opening. I heard it before I saw it. A doe. It bounded quickly into the opening and then stopped, her ears flapping back and forth like a gate swinging in the wind, looking one way then the other, like it was waiting for something. And she was. Just behind her a forked-horn buck appeared. I raised the rifle slowly to my shoulder, finger pressing on the trigger, but I wasn't going to fire. This was Angelo's. I looked over at him, motioning not with my head, but with my eyes, whispering, "Take him! Take him!"

I stayed low on the point and turned my eyes again to Angelo. He'd shouldered his rifle now, and he had a clear shot. Any second he'd fire. I waited. But nothing.

Another doe ran out of the trees below and stopped with the two in the clearing. Their bodies shook. I motioned with my head, but still Angelo didn't fire. "Take it, goddamn it!" I whispered. I followed the buck through my rifle sights, aimed right behind its front shoulders. I waited. Still no shot. He must have seen it. "Angelo, squeeze it off, for crissakes! Now!" I could take him anytime but this one was his. I waited. The buck looked quickly from side to side, then leaned back in its haunches ready to spring off. "Now!" I yelled to Angelo. "NOW!" But he didn't fire. The buck turned its ass toward me, and before it slipped into the brush, I touched a round off. It hit him but it wasn't a clean shot. His back legs collapsed, he went down on his ass but got back up again. The two does, panicky, leaped headlong into the brush, stumbled to their knees, before disappearing. The buck went down on its ass but somehow sprung up again and into the brush.

"Let's get him!" .

Angelo didn't move.

"Come on!"

There was blood on the ground and a trail that led into the thicket. Not really a trail so much, but an opening not much wider than a deer's body where the brush had been pushed away. I put my arms up in front of me and used the rifle to fight my way through. Blood painted the branches. Ten feet in front of me I found the buck lying on top of the brush, all four feet off the ground, still alive, its whole body heaving. Its head was twisted back, tongue hanging out the side of its mouth. "Angelo!" I called out.

No answer.

I fired a finishing shot into the buck, poked it with the rifle barrel to make sure it was dead, then grabbed its hind legs and dragged it back into the opening. Angelo still sat at point, head in hands, his rifle on the ground by his feet.

"We got him!" I said. "He ain't big, but we can hang a tag on him."

He didn't look up. Both hands covered his head.

"Angelo?"

Still, he wouldn't look up. "Why didn't you take him?" I asked.

I climbed up to his point, and set my rifle down, and touched the top of his cap. He looked up. Tears filled his eyes. He was sobbing. I didn't know what to do but stroke the top of his head. "I'm sorry, son, I know it wasn't a clean kill. I'm sorry it wasn't."

He looked up at me and shook his head. "I can't do this anymore," he said. "It's all been taken out of me."

"I'm sorry," I said.

"I can't do this—I can't."

I dropped the buck at my feet.

My boy was broken. Sent out to fix something, he came back broken. I didn't know how or why—or even when it started, or if I was a part of it. What did he see and do while he was away? What had I done but pray he'd come back alive? I didn't know what else to do. And I still don't. Was it because I'd done nothing? I didn't know. Only that my boy was sitting in front of me crying about something big and hurting. Something our words couldn't surround. Something I didn't understand. I just looked at him, and said, "It's all right, son. It's all right." And then I reached out and touched him on his shoulder.

After the War

i

I was working on the east side of town—Bucky Lambert and me and the rest of the framing crew—sometimes standing up an entire two-story home in one day, when the accident happened. It was my own fault. It had been the *straight-and-narrow* for 189 days, not touching a drop, going to meetings, giving myself over to a higher power, working long hours, and feeling as though the worst was behind me.

We'd begun our shift at 6 that morning and knocked off for lunch five hours later, just after we'd finished nailing the sheer walls off, and before the crane operator had lowered three bundles of roof trusses onto the top plate. Bucky and I drove down to the 7/11 on Washington Street, and bought burritos and sodas, but just as we were heading back to the car, Bucky ducks back inside and comes out holding a paper bag under his arm. I knew the shape well. He opens the bag inside the car and it's a sixer of tall ones. Bucky cracked his first before we even left the parking lot. "Goddamn it, Bucky, why'd you go and buy those?" "Why?" he asks. "Because I was thirsty—you don't have to drink none." Bucky doesn't know what an impulsive guy I am, doesn't know the voices outside my window—those sweet, seductive little Sirens. He doesn't know how I'll slip away at the smallest of pretexts. He's a family guy, a little crazy, but he doesn't know much about me. He never went to war. Any way, the whole idea of those icy beers grew so big that finally I said, "Screw it," and asked him to crack me one. Before we got back to the job site we'd slammed down three each, and topped it off by twisting a joint of home-grown and smoking it down to the nubs. I stepped out of the car, and into the heat, gliding on a cushion of air.

We put our tool belts on. The bundles of roof trusses now sat on the top plate. Our job was to walk each truss to its spot on the plate, square it up to layout, plumb it, nail it off, then return to the bundle, grab another truss and re-peat the process. The whole time I like the way I feel—no guilt ripping at me as it had in the past—just being quietly within my own mind and body.

I kept looking east toward the farm I'd grown up on—standing on the second-story plate you had a clear view of it across the remaining hay fields. The gum grove, the tank house and hay barn jutting up, the two palm trees like a pair of distant toadstools—all of it stood out in fine de-tail, like a scrimshaw drawing. Every month the houses we framed crawled closer to the old farm, and as it grew larg-er, more distinct, I wondered if we kept building like this if the farm and all the ones around it might someday be gobbled up, driven over by bulldozers and disappear forev-er. Anyway, I was stoned, lost in thought, remembering a hundred different things about growing up on that ranch, and what had happened to me since leaving it. The alcohol and dope had found a welcoming home inside me again, mixing with the heat and the smell of tarweed that rose up from the mowed fields like a rank perfume, and I felt sad and good at the same time, like I was ten years old again, wandering the fields, exploring Tony Paula's creek with my brothers, but realizing, too, those times were long behind me. My mind drifted, I lost my bearings. Maybe I was trying to walk back to that farm, trying to walk to someplace in the past, when I stepped out past the plate, and in a nano-second of surprise, disbelief, felt nothing under my boot, and fell like a rock sixteen feet to the ground below. I didn't land on my head, although sometimes I wish I had, but hit hard enough to dislocate my hip, break my right wrist, my collar bone, and crack a couple of ribs.

I spent two days in the hospital where doctors re-set my hip, wrapped my right wrist in a cast, and then slung the rest of my arm up because of the broken collar bone. Doc Murray said I was lucky the spleen wasn't crushed. I could tell he wanted to say more, but he didn't. I returned home to my folk's place, feeling a mixture of pity and anger toward myself. For six months I'd gone to the meetings, asked some "Higher Power" for help, and in two seconds it all tumbled down. Every night falling asleep with the radio on, exhausted from work, being a regular "Johnny Lunchbox," hoping the more I do this, the faster I'll adjust, the faster I'll fit in, and those things that didn't square up would meet like a nicely-mitered corner cut. Sure, the whole world was exploding around me—cities on fire, people out in the streets, the war dragging on—but I'd done my hitch, seen some of the worst of it, and now it was time to move on, to build for the future. And then what happens? One little miscue, one little shot at being high, one mis-step, and I'm back to square one, laid-up, not a direction to move in that didn't hurt somewhere. *Higher power*, my ass. Right then I was Humpty-fuckin'-Dumpty, great fall and all.

My folks were disappointed when they heard about the accident—my mother, as always, concerned, frightened, blaming herself for my shortcomings. And Dad? Well, he was plain disgusted and wanted me out of the house. He'd gone back to work for Western Dairy after selling off the cows and pulled a few strings to get me a job there as an apprentice pasteurizer just three months after my discharge. I never liked the job. It was graveyard shift, which was okay because after nearly two years in 'Nam, my sleep was shot anyway, but in those three months between returning home and returning to work, I grew to wandering about all times of the day and night, stuffing a quart or two of Rainier Ale into my knapsack and passing an entire day at the trestles south of town. I was looking for something, but I didn't know what. I'd sit on a bank of the river, watch it swell with an incoming tide and shrink back as it was sucked south toward the bay. There were other folks down there, too—hippies, burn-outs, long-time alkies, piss artists of every stripe. Guys played guitar and sang Bob Dylan songs about cannonballs ringing out, and this one fellow, Gus, introduced me to Thoreau and Gandhi and non-violence.

"I don't know much about that," I told him.

"You're the only one here that's seen the beast," he said. "And now we have to tame it." While we talked, girls wearing long skirts danced in circles.

But work at Western Dairy changed all that. I'd start my shift after being high all day, and there were a lots of details to remember about the job, and all these different steps and procedures that had to be done at just the right time, and in just the right amount. Miss one step, leave a valve open, or forget to replace one, and the whole system flashed *TILT* like a pinball game. After a while I resented it.

My dad's attitude toward working there, of course, was very different. We'd lost our shirt in the dairy business, and he was glad to have his union job back. It was hourly rate multiplied by numbers of hours worked, time and a half for over-time, a pension waiting out there in twenty five years, two weeks off annually for deer camp, or plopping your ass by a lake, casting a line out, holding your catch by its gills, posing for the photo, then showing the photo to the guys back at work where they stick it on the bulletin board above the time clock. But for me, none of those job perks mattered. It was soul bartering. A big clock ticking all the time inside your head. The present time was something I tried to block out, which was near-impossible. The only time that mattered was the future, five minutes from now, when it was time to clock out, time to shed the uniform and head to the trestles.

I started missing work, calling in sick. Mostly, I was hung-over, my head cottony from all the dope I was smoking, the lack of sleep. Then one morning after finishing my shift, Nick, the plant manager, called me into his office, and said he had to let me go—the absences, the inattention toward the work—he said I didn't seem ready for the job. My dad had pleaded with him to give me another chance, but I'd run my string out. I didn't blame Nick. Again, it was my own doing. Nick suggested I contact the VA's office, and try some counseling, whatever it would take to right the ship, and that there'd be a spot left open for me when things got sorted out . At the VA, they encouraged me to enroll in classes at the junior college, using the GI Bill, and for a couple of weeks I read about ancient civilizations, tried to write five-hundred word essays. After class one day, a pretty brunette asked me what the war was like. I answered, "Fucked up." Maybe it was the way I said it, my expression—who knows? She never asked me again. A week later I stopped going to classes.

It was time again to fend for myself. My dad couldn't hide his disgust anymore and tossed me out of the house. Chez Yamamoto, a friend of the family's, offered me a little trailer to live in at the back of his property in Penngrove in exchange for cleaning out chicken houses and working in his vegetable garden. The trailer was at the end of a long gravel road north of town and miles away from the trestles. I hunkered down, and that tiny trailer became my sanctuary. I cut back on the Mexican pot and listened to music, read Hesse's *Siddhartha,* and worked in Chez' garden for hours at a time when I wasn't moving chicken shit around. I imagined I was some kind of monk, saving my little piece of the world, my remaining sanity, by not bothering anyone, by withdrawing, by trellising string beans, and tossing tomato worms to Chez' chickens, by pulling the tall jimson weed that grew everywhere. I could step out the front door, look east toward the Sonoma Mountains, and see nothing but rolling hayfields, chicken houses, dairy farms. I liked living there—it was quiet, and people left me alone. Mom stopped by each week with a pot of stew, and kept me informed of family doings. She said my time living in Chez' trailer was something I had to pass through, some phase, until I landed on my feet again. She said the whole world was off its rocker and that she was lighting votive candles for me whenever she was near Saint Vincent's. The breaks and sprains healed rapidly, and the crutches were tossed aside in less than a week. Before long I was walking the two miles into Penngrove, picking up my mail at the post office there, and spending an occasional quiet afternoon at Kelly's, sipping a draft beer, listening to the juke box, sometimes shooting a game of 8-ball. The rest of the world was out there somewhere. I read about it in the newspapers.

Then my two brothers, Junior and Jackie, showed up at my trailer one Sunday afternoon—it was Labor Day

weekend, and they'd driven over to invite me to a family bar-
becue at Mom and Dad's. I knew about the event, but opted
not to go. There was still bad blood between dad and myself, and the safest response was to keep my distance. A year
and a half had passed since I'd last seen Junior. He stepped
out of the sedan he was driving, looking heavier than I remembered, wearing slacks and dusty oxfords, any remnants
of dairy ranching long behind him. He was now an Assistant
DA in Alameda County, and by all the usual standards, had
done well—a scholarship to USF, graduating near the top of
his class in law school, clerking in the city attorney's office,
working his way up the ladder—a natural prosecutor. Junior
had adapted. Selling off the cows hadn't turned his world
upside down the way it'd done with mine. He found a direction, and he followed it. I envied him—envied his success,
his focus, the confidence in his beliefs. Our history together
had always been a long, complicated one—like most families—and all the clawing ours did to stay afloat eventually
drew out the differences between us. As I moved into my
teens, we drifted further and further apart, what I valued
and what he valued clashing constantly with each other. We
couldn't talk to each other without an argument erupting.
Jackie had joined the Army Reserves after finishing high
school and began an electrician's apprenticeship at Mare
Island Naval Shipyard in Vallejo. He still wore his hair with
that sharp part to one side, still flashed those Italian good
looks, and his clothes, always in the latest style. He'd re-
connected with a former classmate, Jill Davidson, and after
two months of dating, they announced their engagement,
and were married by Christmas. They'd bought a home
on the east side of town—not far from where my accident
happened—and Jill was four months pregnant.

We shook hands, and I invited them to sit at a table in
the little patio. I stepped inside the trailer and returned with
three beers. I opened them and slid one toward Junior, one

toward Jackie. We raised them together. "To the working man," I said.

"I heard you were banged-up." Junior ran his finger around the rim of his beer can, studying the table top as he spoke. Junior knew Frank Ferraro, the framing contractor I'd been working for when I fell, and it was this connection that landed me the job. I told Junior I'd gotten a little careless, fell off the wagon and the roof. He weighed my words.

"So, what now?" he asked.

"I'm on the mend. After that, I don't know. What do they say? 'One day at a time.'"

"You going back to framing?" Jackie asked.

"I don't know. Right now everything's healing. I'm shoveling chicken shit and working in Chez' garden."

Junior looked at my can of beer. "You're drinking again?"

"I am, but not like before—a couple of beers a day, just so I don't think about it as much. The thinking got as bad as the drinking," I told him. "I'm making peace with it."

"Seems like it's best just to leave it alone," Junior said.

"I hope you didn't drive out here just to tell me that."

"No—I wanted to check in, see how you were doing— maybe talk you to coming to the barbeque today. Mom told me about your fall. She's upset—"

"She's always upset—it's what keeps her going—you'd think she'd get tired carrying around the weight of the world, believing she's the cause of our every fuck-up."

"She's not going to change." Junior slid his chair back.

"It'd mean a lot to her if you stopped by their house today," Jackie said. "Everyone'll be there. And Jill'd like to see you. She always liked you."

"So, things are okay?" Junior asked.

"I'd say so—better than a few weeks ago when everything inside me hurt."

Junior studied the fuchsias hanging in a pot just above him. "I can't even remember the last time I saw you."

"I can—it was at Mom and Dad's," I said. "The dinner she cooked just after I returned from 'Nam." I watched Junior as leaned back in his chair, compiling details. He had a way of observing things, always quietly analyzing the situation to himself.

"You like it out here?" Jackie's question contained an undertone of disbelief, maybe even wonderment, that someone could actually enjoy living in a cramped trailer like this. He'd become suburbanized, and, like Junior, had adapted and done well. I was the remaining hold-out.

"I do—it's my sanctuary, a place where I can be mellow. No distractions. I like working in Chez' garden—I'd never gardened before. It's calming—reminds me of all the Vietnamese we'd see bent over, working the rice fields. All hell going off around them, but they'd just work away as if there was no war at all. Weird."

A period followed when none of us spoke. You could hear the thrum of insects in the early afternoon air, and the low din of Chez's chickens clucking in unison from the nearby barns.

"Is Dad still pissed at me?"

"He has a hard time understanding you—thinks the service fucked you up, and the dope made you lazy, that it killed your spirit," Junior said.

"Well, something fucked me up—he's right about that. As to being lazy? I don't know about that one. There's just fewer and fewer things I wanted to do. Dad and I are different—you both know that. He'a a mule, a work horse. Point to a job, and he does it. Few questions asked. 'Just be grateful you're working,' he says. He wanted me to be like him, to work like that, not ask questions, and I couldn't. Everything in lock-step. Say 'yes' to the man. But it all shut down inside me."

"He's set in his ways—that's for sure," Junior said. "Thinks if everyone was like him, it'd be a better world."

"Don't most folks think like that?" I said.

Junior and I looked at each other, and then he looked away.

"And then with the dope and drinking—that's when he finally lost it—thinks you did it just to spite him," Junior said.

"I did it as a way to run for cover when everything was blowing up around me. It wasn't about him or anyone else— and I don't think it was to spite anyone—unless it was myself. It was a fox-hole when all the shit was raining down." I paused. "Both Mom and Dad saw everything we did as as either to their credit, or—in my case—to their blame, don't you think? Almost like we couldn't think for ourselves, decide for ourselves without them involved in some way."

Jackie nodded his head.

Junior hadn't served in the military. At his pre-induction physical he was disqualified for having flat feet. But when the war heated up, he supported it, though, that much I knew, and as it dragged on, he supported it even more. It was a common-enough attitude around here—the domino theory—the commies were out to get us, and we had to get them first. There were some voices against it—mostly around the colleges. Everybody chose sides. I doubted everything, but I doubted the war most of all. Still, I didn't have it in me to head to Canada, and my conscience was too muddled for a CO deferment, so I went in, figuring to make the best of a bad deal.

Jackie kept his opinions, his position on things to himself. But Junior was different. He was never timid about expressing his views, and the night of that dinner at our folk's place, he broadcast them freely, and with authority. He said he was proud of me, of my service. I listened as he went on about how the dominoes would fall, and how Vietnam was the bulwark to check communism's spread. He'd obviously thought it all out. He's a convincing speaker, no doubt about it. I just listened, wishing I was someplace else—like at the trestles, watching the river disappear. I was no hero. I was the one who'd been to that war he was talking about, knew it first-hand, felt my doubts about it grow with each week of duty, felt the revulsion, the disgust festering within me at all the death and destruction. There was nothing noble about it. We did what we could to stay alive, to keep each other alive—that was always our motive, our reasoning for doing what we did.

Finally, though, I reached a point where something broke inside me—spirit, maybe, my soul taken—I don't know—but it happened on patrol one day. Everyone in our platoon was on edge. Jittery, nerves shot. Some guys totally stoned-out on Thai-sticks just to survive. Half the time we never knew who we were fighting, if we were fighting anyone. It was endless marching, patrols, search-and-destroy. Often guys just poured lead at anything that appeared threatening. There'd be a movement in the bush, and guys opened up on it, and when there was no more movement they closed in to see what they'd shot. Half the time it was a water buffalo, or some farm animal, and its owner never far away, holding his hand out, wanting some kind of compensation.

We were doing re-con early one morning and came across this young fellow—maybe fifteen or sixteen—carrying a sack over his shoulder just outside this village, and the sergeant barked an order at him—an order he didn't understand. This scared look flashed across his face and he started to run away. The sergeant yelled out again, but the boy kept running. Then someone—I don't know who, but someone behind me—iced him. The shot lifted him off his feet, as though he were jerked upwards by some invisible cable, before falling flat on his face. The bag split open when it hit the ground. It was filled with rice. Minutes after the shot, a woman runs toward him—turns out it's the boy's mother—and she's holding him in her arms, stroking the hair back from his forehead, sobbing, talking to him in Vietnamese, but the boy's dead. After that, everything emptied inside of me, everything except a growing hate and contempt for what we were doing over there. I requested a transfer out of combat duty, told my commanding officer I'd starve myself before aiming a rifle at another person. They re-assigned me to a field hospital.

Junior's a guy that likes to draw contrasts, and must have foreseen the collision course I was on after being drafted. To my brother, I'd always been a dreamer, an idealist—someone stuck in an imagined past where we still plowed fields behind teams of horses, lived with no electricity, no conveniences, no God to believe in but the God of Nature, where progress was scorned, all institutions questioned. Everything just simple, and small. Everything manual, done by hand, with very few moving parts. Imagining everyone a good, decent person, looking out for the next guy.

And what about the rest of the world, he'd ask? What about the world the way it *really* is? What about evil? What about Russia? China? Do you think they're going to stand still, stay locked up in the past? You want to be a communist, is that it? You want to lose everything our ancestors fought and worked for?

"So, what do we do if we don't work, Angelo?"

"I'm not against work—it's what work's become that bothers me."

"What's it become that's so bothersome to you? So unacceptable?"

"Much of it is dull and mindless," I said.

"Jackie, is your work 'dull and mindless?'" Junior asked.

"It repeats a lot, but that's okay," Jackie said. "We're all about safety, following established procedures."

"What kind of work isn't, in your opinion, Angelo? Farm work? Is that ideal work?" Junior was shifting to court-room mode. "We need to be productive, and being productive involves routine, repetition, technology."

"Work has to have a connection with us—some kind of deep connection, something immediate and meaningful," I said.

"And if we feel that connection, that's good work?"

"I think so."

"You didn't feel that at Western Dairy?

"No, I didn't."

"What about the framing work?"

"It felt good that I could build something, that I had a skill. But it was repetitive work, and the houses were ticky-tacky. We always had to work fast, like some giant clock was ticking all the time. Finish one, move to the next. And then to see the houses spreading across the open fields, and the bulldozers ripping into even more land. It always bothered me. I couldn't make the separation any more between my craft and the impact of what I was doing."

"That's growth."

"I don't care what it is, it still bothered me."

"You're from another century, Angelo."

"Maybe so."

"Anyway, I didn't come up here just to argue politics. We're different, and I respect that." He reached into his shirt pocket and pulled out a folded newspaper clipping. He carefully unfolded it, and pushed it across the table. I picked it up and read it. It was a funeral notice: *Chester Washington Winslow Witherspoon, gone to his Maker on August 28th, 1970. Survived by his wife Della Maxine. Brothers: Dupree, Charles, Chandler; Sisters: Minerva, Hatley, Magnolia. Children: Chester II, Jackson, Floretta, Victor, Magnolia and Benton. Born in Tupelo, Missisippi. Age 70.* The rest of the notice listed the surviving wife, Della Maxine, brothers and sisters, parents, both deceased, and a half dozen children. Services to be held at the Ebenezer Baptist Church, 86th

Avenue, Oakland, California on Tuesday, September 5th.

"Chester Washington Winslow Witherspoon?" I repeated the name several times to myself.

"It's Willie," he said. "Willie the wire-man."

"Willie wasn't even his real name?" I said.

"Apparently not. Probably a name Dad gave him, and it stuck. I think he called every black man, 'Willie'."

"How'd you know it was Willie, then?"

"He had a couple run-ins with the law, and one day I was in the courtroom for an arraignment, I look over and see this black man, and we both stare at each other a long time. Something about him looked familiar, but I couldn't place it. And he's looking at me the same way, I can tell. Then he comes up to me afterwards, and asks, 'You Junior?' Soon as he mentioned my name, I knew who he was."

"What was he in court for?"

"Assault."

"I'd forgotten about Willie," Jackie said. "I remember riding down to Jenkins' place with you and Dad and seeing all the sheriffs' cars, and the ambulance, but most of that has just slipped away from me. I remember he drove an old beat-up truck."

I re-read the notice several times. Sixteen years had passed since I last saw Willie being driven away in a sheriff's car after shooting Buster Jenkins, but, unlike Jackie, I'd never forgotten about him. They booked Willie into the Petaluma jail, and he was released shortly afterwards. His truck was towed back to our ranch. It stayed there for three weeks, and each day I expected to see Willie, and to talk with him again as we'd always talked, maybe even go out and hunt rabbits again, but each day the truck remained there, spider webs looping across its side mirrors, its tires starting to lose air, but no sign of Willie. Then one afternoon I returned from school, and Willie's truck was gone. I ran up to the space it had occupied, as though this space would offer up clues to the truck's disappearance. I ran back to the milking barn and asked Dad where the truck had gone, and he said Willie had come up that morning with another man, replaced the damaged radiator, got his truck running, and drove off. Before he left he said to say good-bye to "Mistah Red."

"After I'd seen Willie in the courtroom that day, I requested his file from the Jenkins' incident, but the details around that incident were very sketchy," Junior said. "The initial charge was 'assault with a deadly weapon,' but then had been reduced to "self-defense." Each of the charges crossed-out, then hand-written over to a lesser charge. Dad may have had something to do with that. He and Judge Webb were old school buddies."

"And Willie never came up here again, did he?"

"I asked him about that, and he said he sold that load of metal, and put the truck up for sale. 'Pickin's was no good, no more,' is what he said." Junior finished his beer.

"And what happened with the assault case against him in Oakland?" I asked.

"Eventually, the charge was dropped when all the details finally surfaced."

"He wasn't a violent guy," I said. "He just wanted to be treated like everyone else but the cards were stacked against him. You know how it was—how it still is, in a lot of cases." I looked over at Junior. "He always felt you didn't like him."

"He did?"

"That's right. When Dad hired him to dig the ditch—remember that? And you got all pissed-off because Dad paid Willie the fifteen bucks that you wanted to make so you could put it toward buying your jeep? Willie felt bad about that—even offered to give the fifteen bucks back."

"I remember him digging the ditch, all right."

"And when he was skinning the rabbits in the tank house, and you walked in. Remember that? The rabbits had boils all over their backs, and you gave Willie that look like 'who'd ever eat a goddamn rabbit like that?' Willie talked about that stuff. He told me a lot."

"How old was I? Fourteen? Fifteen? What'd I know then?"

"And then his shooting Buster Jenkins—like it was all Willie's fault."

Junior pushed himself away from the table.

"I didn't know what you knew, but you know what I've wondered since?" I asked.

"What's that?"

"If you thought Willie was just another nigger?"

Junior's face dropped. He turned his beer can in circles. "I didn't like him. I thought he was a slow-talkin' sort of confidence-man, playing off the fact he was black, playing off of Dad's guilt, too. But, again, how old was I? We all make mistakes."

He looked me right in the eye to emphasize that last point. "I've come around a bit since then, Angelo—how else could I do what I do now in good conscience? I have to look beyond skin color. It's taken a while."

"It was something I've always wondered about," I said.

"Seems like another world ago, doesn't it?" Junior said. "The ranch out there, everybody working themselves crazy. Willie coming along. I wanted it to be a success—for my sake, sure, because I'd made big plans to be a business-man—but more for Dad's sake, because it's what he really wanted to do, what he'd bundled his hopes around."

"Well, you're a success now, aren't you?" I asked.

Junior shifted in his chair. An awkward expression spread across his face.

"And, I guess you can say that Dad's a success, too—he's finally putting a couple of dollars away. He was always so proud to show me his paycheck stubs. He wanted the same for me."

"There was nobody that worked harder," Jackie said.

"Nobody," I said.

"I'd read books, go to other dairies that were modernizing—trying to get Dad to make some changes, to try to survive, but he wasn't hearing it. He couldn't see what was happening—or didn't *want* to see it, and, I guess in hindsight, there wasn't much he could do—you two are a lot alike in that way." Junior looked into my eyes. "We didn't have the money to get bigger, to buy up other contracts. We just treaded water, hoping something would change. Well, it did, but it wasn't the change Dad was expecting."

"Another beer?"

"No, thanks, I'm good. Pamela's back at Mom and Dad's with the kids, and I told her I wouldn't be gone too long."

"Jackie? How about you?"

"I'm good, Angelo. There's a cooler full of beer back at Mom and Dad's—you are going to come over, aren't you? You don't have to stay long."

"Let me think about it, okay?" I stood up from the table. "Can I show you the garden?"

We walked over to Chez' plot, nearly an acre of summer vegetables that Chez and his family marketed along with their eggs. We shouldered our way through tall stands of corn, our shoes sinking into the soft soil. Beyond the corn were dozens of tomato vines, all heavy with tomatoes. Junior stopped where the beefsteaks grew, many of them the size of grapefruit.

"You two want some?" I asked.

"Sure. We can take them to the barbeque." Jackie said.

I returned with two small cardboard boxes, and the three of us began filling them.

"Take the softest ones if you want to eat any today," I said.

"What about right now?" Junior bit into one, and its juice splattered across his shirt.

I looked over at Junior. "I'm thinking I might go to Willie's service."

"Really?"

"Yeah. He'd always talked about Della, and how everything he did was to please her. And what a good cook she was—I felt as though I'd already met her."

"It's in a rough part of town," he said. "Off Heggenberger."

"I'll take my chances."

Junior stood up, stretched, gave my place a final survey. "I can see why you like this place."

"A little bit of peace here." I said.

"That's not always easy to find." Junior opened the trunk of his car, and he and Jackie placed the boxes of tomatoes inside. "See you at Mom and Dad's?"

"Okay," I said.

We all three shook hands.

ii

The family sat in lawn chairs in a wide circle in Mom and Dad's backyard. Under the patio arbor a table was set with a gingham table cloth. A big bowl of potato salad covered with plastic wrap was in the center of the table along with a green salad, a bowl of pasta, condiments and a stack of plates. Nana and Papa had driven up from the city. Jackie and Junior were both at the grill, turning the chicken and flipping burgers. Their wives and Mom all sat together in one part of the circle. Dad was throwing a big rubber ball to his grandchildren. Mom stood up, excited to see me. "Oh, Angelo, I'm so glad you came!"

I'd brought a shopping bag filled with freshly picked corn. Maybe it was a peace offering, I don't know. I wanted everything to be mellow.

Dad glanced over at me and nodded. I nodded back.

I hugged each of my sisters-in-law, and my mom and

grandmother. Papa sat with a can of beer, the brim on his summer fedora, like the cuffs on his trousers, all turned up.

"It's the stranger!" Nana announced. "You got skinny!"

"He looks fine," Papa said. "Like a young Kirk Douglas."

Each one asked me about the accident, if I'd recovered, and what my plans were. I told them what I'd told Junior and Jackie—that I was lucky, that my body had healed quickly. As to future plans? I said I liked the place I'd arrived at, that the route had been a long and twisted one, but that right now it felt like the place to be. The gardening and the physical work suited me fine. I was trying to forget about the war. Trying to re-build.

"Maybe you'll find a girl," Nana said.

"Maybe."

"You going back to Western Dairy?" Papa asked.

Dad looked over when he heard Papa's question.

"Not anytime soon," I said.

Mom had boiled the corn in a large kettle on the kitchen stove and brought the corn out stacked on a long platter. When the burgers and chicken were done, everyone moved their chairs around the table and began serving themselves.

"So, Dad, I forgot to tell you, but Willie, the old black wire guy died." Junior took the obituary notice out and handed it to Dad.

Dad read the notice. His face changed expression. "Willie—quite a character, that fellow. I liked him more than the others except he'd get something on his mind, something that bothered him, and there was no peace with that man."

"Like being treated like shit, you mean?" I looked at Dad and he looked back at me. "Told he can't do something because he's not the right color?"

"I sided with him on that one," Dad said. "If it was me, I'd a shot that Buster right between the eyes—

"Irv!" Mom said.

"He sure liked them jackrabbits." Dad laughed.

"Angelo says he's going to Willie's funeral," Jackie said.

Mom looked at me. "Why?"

"Because I want to," I said.

"Where's the funeral?" Mom asked.

"Oakland," Junior said.

"Jig-town," Papa chimed in.

"Joseph!" His wife glared at him.

"And when is it?" Mom asked.

"Tomorrow. I'm driving down tomorrow," I said.

The barbeque was a relaxed affair—no one spouting off. The war was touched on, but largely avoided. Politics were kept to a minimum. Conversations centered on immediate affairs—Jill's pregnancy, their new home. Junior's career, Pamela's job in the bank. We ate watermelon afterwards, and I talked to Dad about his work and if he was going back to deer camp again next year. "Every year they'll have me," he said. "Every year I can still get up and down to where I need to get."

"That's good," I said. "You always liked it up there."

This was my family. We'd all arrived here, mostly intact. What had been splintered apart, might stay apart, but some of it had been glued back together, as well. Time, forgetfulness did some of that. Each of us was different, but maybe wanting the same thing—a peaceful place to grill a burger, to grow an ear of corn—to be able to sit around and be civil to one another.

"There's going to be traffic heading back home," Junior announced, "so we'll be heading out now."

After saying our good-byes, I walked with Junior out to their car.

"Take care of yourself." Junior and I shook hands. "He may not have shown it, but Dad was glad to see you."

"That's good," I said. "He's always been a hard guy to read."

Junior looked up from his car window. "The church is down off the east end of Heggenberger, south of downtown. Mother's Cookie's out there, and the Langendorf bakery. When you smell them, you'll know you're getting close. It's a good smell. A rough part of town that always smells good."

"I'll remember that."

iii

Junior was right. South of Oakland, the sweet smell of baking bread hung in the warm morning air. Off Heggenberger, I drove past the orange and brown Mother's Cookie plant, and into neighborhoods of apartment buildings and crowded bungalows, industrial shops and tiny groceries, all crammed together into tiny lots. Occasionally, a school yard or church provided a brief open space. Cars were shoe-horned into driveways, sometimes spilling into what had once been lawns, and interspersed with these cluttered, grassless yards, an occasional tropical garden emerged with lush banana plants and climbing bougainvillea nearly concealing a shaded cottage. There were fences and barred windows, razor-wire and barking dogs, and men working underneath cars. Small clusters of locals sat on dairy crates, passing a paper-bagged bottle between them.

A faded Cadillac hearse was parked in front of the Ebenezer Baptist Church, a building so white and brilliant in the sun that it hurt my eyes as I walked toward it. It was 11 o'clock in the morning, cloudless and sweltering. A full-figured black woman wearing a floral print dress greeted me at the church's entrance. "You here for the Witherspoon service?" she asked.

"I am."

"Well, welcome, welcome."

Inside the narrow church, it was cool, and organ music played softly. Twenty, maybe thirty people sat on each side of the aisle. All the men wore suits, and all the women wore dresses. The younger sported afros in different sizes. The older women wore tiny hats placed precariously on full wigs, while the older men's hair was shiny and brilled back. I sat near the back of the church. The women fanned themselves with the service bulletin, some with choir hymnals. The music ended and the minister appeared behind a pulpit. He looked over the congregation, and then back at me. "Join us up here, brother," he said.

I looked around.

"Yes, you—join us," he repeated.

The entire congregation turned to watch as I walked up the aisle. After I sat, he commenced with a brief prayer. Everyone bowed their heads. After the prayer, a silence followed as the minister gathered his words.

"I knew Chester," he said. "He was my friend—a good man, a family man—a hard-workin', kind-hearted man." He looked to the front row. "Dellah, we share your grief at Chester's passin'." I'd hear the name 'Chester' and have to remind myself that it was Willie, as though they were talking about someone else, and Willie hadn't really died but was off gathering scrap metal somewhere. "But quiet as Chester was, in him was stirrin' a strong sense of right and wrong. Now, he didn't go around paradin' it—no, sir. But it come out. Those of you know the times I'm talkin' 'bout. He didn't go 'round lookin' for trouble—I know no one who'd avoid it as much as Chester, but when it looked him in the eye, Chester knew what to do. Chester acted." The congregation all answered together with each of the minister's pronouncements.

I never cared for sermons but as the minister talked, I was moved by his simple words, felt a tightness in my throat and chest, and when I blinked, tears had escaped, and tracked down my cheek bones. Different pictures, memories, of Willie would flash before me—Willie swinging a pick, or gouging out boils from a rabbit's back— and the minister's words would trail off in a low thrumming, like a motor idling, and for seconds, perhaps minutes I'd be walking alongside Willie packing a burlap sack full of dead rabbits. Then the congregation's voices would interrupt me, and I'd shift back to the present, and the minister's words would return again. When he stopped talking, he invited a young woman to the pulpit. She began singing, "His Eye is on the Sparrow." Each time I thought the hymn would end, she'd repeat the final chorus, her voice swelling, growing in volume, ringing off the church ceiling, out through its open doors, filling all the space around us. Members sang and chanted along with her, shouting out agreement, raising their arms and waving them together. At the hymn's end, the minister walked back to the pulpit. "We invite all of you to Fellowship Hall, to partake in a meal. Food can be very comforting in time like these. So, please join us."

I'd identified Della. Even on this warm morning, she wore a long, white coat, white heels, and a tiny white hat with a bit of netting that reached down to the middle of her forehead. She had a broad, kindly-looking face, her teeth as white as the church's exterior. The different congregation members formed a line in front of her, and she embraced each one. She glanced over at me. Her expression was, at first, quizzical, then she smiled and returned to accepting condolences. I stood in line. When we were finally face to face, she asked, "Should I know you?"

"I'm Angelo Miller."

She looked puzzled. "Angelo Miller? Don't know no Angelo Miller."

"Your husband used to call me 'Mister Red."

"Mister Red?"

"That's right."

Her eyes looked upwards. Nothing seemed to be registering.

"He'd drive up to our ranch in Petaluma in his truck and—"

"Lawd sakes! You that Mistah Red?" Della's face broke into a wide grin. "Chestah talk 'bout you like you was his own. That's years ago."

"Fifteen or sixteen—I was just a little guy then."

"That man love it up there—more 'an anything. Always talkin' 'bout it everytime he come back. 'Della, he says, I gotta bring you up there so you can see for yo'self. He always talkin' 'bout raisin' hogs, and how the air up there's so clean. And how yo' daddy had names for all his cows. It just tickled that man." Her voice dropped. "Then come that trouble, and it take the heart out of him."

"Willie got a bum deal."

"Willie?"

"We always knew your husband as 'Willie.' Didn't know it was Chester until my brother showed me the funeral notice just a few days ago." I told her about Junior, and how the two of them had met in a courtroom one day.

"You gonna eat lunch with us? They got fried chicken and mashed potatoes. Sweet potato pie, too."

"I'd be glad to."

We entered Fellowship Hall together. It was lined with long tables, with a kitchen in the rear of the room. The women were shuttling plates filled with food to waiting friends and family members. Della introduced me to each of her children, and she'd tell them who I was. "Yo' daddy shot the rabbits with this one here," she said. "Remember them rabbits?"

Della's daughters turned up their noses. "He made us eat 'em," the oldest daughter said. "I don't want to eat no rabbit, I told him—they too cute. Ain't ever eat one since."

I shook hands with each of them, and with the boys, particularly, it was like shaking hands with a young Willie, the same inquisitive eyes, the broad smile and high cheekbones.

I finished lunch and said my goodbyes. Della walked with me to the sidewalk where we embraced. "Bless you, child," she said. "Chester always say you was lucky, like you was on a kingdom up there, and you was the prince. How that fahm doin'?"

"We don't have it anymore," I said.

"That sad?"

"Yeah, that's sad."

"You find something else, then."

I nodded my head, and smiled back at her. "I'm trying."

I turned and started to walk away, then turned back again. "I liked your husband—he was a good man."

"Oh, I knowed that."

"A great heart."

"A little boy's heart."

She was right.

It was early afternoon, and hot. On the way back to my car I saw Willie again and again, wiping his forehead, laughing at the China-men in their funny hats, wishing he could move the ditch he was digging closer to the shade. Maybe hoping for rabbits without the boils, or a new truck, or a plot of land with hogs and a freezer-full of sausages.

Additional copies of this book may be ordered
directly from the author. Contact Christopher
Riebli at: chris@bluehotelmusic.com

Or order *The Body's Perfect: A Novel in Stories*
online at: www.createspace.com/3903933 and
other online retailers.